CHEATED BY DEATH

HTTP://WWW.LLBARTLETT.COM/INDEX.PHP/JEFF-RESNICK-BOOKS-2/

L.L. BARTLETT

Polaris Press

DESCRIPTION

Jeff Resnick faces a new dilemma: someone is stalking his sister-in-law, Brenda, who fears that violence from pro-life supporters will escalate near the women's clinic where she works. Or could the vandalism, threatening phone calls, and letters against her have come from her abusive ex-husband? Meanwhile, Jeff grapples with meeting his estranged father and the sister he never knew existed. What does Patty Resnick have to gain with Brenda out of the way?

COPYRIGHT

CHEATED BY DEATH
A Jeff Resnick Mystery
by L.L. Bartlett

THE JEFF RESNICK MYSTERIES

Murder on the Mind
    Dead In Red
    (When The Spirit Moves You)
    Room At The Inn
    Cheated By Death
    (Bah! Humbug)
    Bound By Suggestion
    Dark Waters
    Spooked
    Crybaby
    Eyewitness
    Shattered Spirits

NOVELLAS
    Evolution: Jeff Resnick's Backstory
    A Jeff Resnick Six Pack

ACKNOWLEDGMENTS

The manuscript for CHEATED BY DEATH has been read by many past and present critique partners over the years. My thanks to all of them. However, several of them stand out in my mind. They are:

Leslie Budwitz
Kate Doran
Doranna Durgin
Gwen Nelson

My thanks also go to Sharon Wildwind who was generous with her medical expertise, while Colleen Keuhne and Shelly Franz helped with proofreading and file formatting.

For more information on the Jeff Resnick Mysteries, please visit my website:

LLBartlett.com

PROLOGUE

It was not an easy death.

But it wasn't a satisfying death, either. Witnessing it didn't cancel out the emptiness. That never went away no matter how many pills, how much whiskey or empty sex. It was always there, eating at the soul like acid through wood.

The old man's eyes stared vacantly at the gray sky, his mouth hung open, as though to scream. But the hollow wail had never come. Knees blown away, then gut shot—his empty belly had been drained of life.

Revenge wasn't powerful enough a word to convey the emotion behind it. The Bible said an eye for an eye, and the old man had finally paid. Maybe he'd even welcomed it. He'd lived with his sin for more than two decades.

Payment in full.

Almost.

Scuffed boots kicked the lifeless corpse. Each death brought closure nearer. The killings gave life purpose. One person remained. One life left to snuff out . . . one last person to blame.

And it didn't matter how many others were sacrificed to accomplish it.

1

———

My long-dead father came back to life on a mild afternoon in early November. He'd never been dead it turned out, but I didn't know that at the time. It's funny how one incident can snowball and change your life forever.

Take me. Eight months ago, I was mugged; had my arm broken and my skull fractured. That's when things changed. The way I see things changed. Feelings come to me, and sometimes fragments of information. Stuff that makes me interested in other stuff.

Stuff that gets me into trouble.

And then there are times when I'm still blindsided by life.

On that balmy November afternoon two weeks before Thanksgiving, I was playing one-on-one basketball with my half brother, Dr. Richard Alpert. He's twelve years older than me, and rich as sin, but he still cheats at one-on-one. He'd just tripped me—definitely against the Marquis of Queensbury rules, should they ever be applied to basketball—and I ended up face down on the dusty driveway, panting for breath. He helped me up.

"That's enough for me," I said.

"Come on, Jeff. You're not hurt."

I brushed off my sweatpants. "Maybe I should go to a decent quack and find out."

"Sticks and stones," he countered, dribbling the ball.

"You've got a height advantage."

Richard looked down at me. "What's six inches?"

"And forty pounds on me."

"So eat more," he said, making a sweet lay-up shot.

I captured the ball and dodged him. "But I'm an orphan."

He skirted round me. "*I'm* the orphan. Your father's still alive."

I stopped dead, thinking I'd heard wrong. He snatched the ball, sent it arcing for another two points—and missed.

My fatigue vanished as adrenalin coursed through me. "What did you say?"

The amusement left his face. "Your father's alive."

My eyes narrowed. "He's dead. He died when I was a kid."

"Who told you that?"

I didn't know. All I knew was that the bastard left us and never looked back, and that he was dead.

That I *believed* he was dead.

Richard bounced the ball, caught it, and hitched it under his arm. "I saw him at the clinic yesterday. He's a patient." Richard doesn't need to work, but he volunteers his time a couple days a week at the low-income clinic associated with the University at Buffalo's School of Medicine located at one of the local hospitals.

"What's wrong with him?"

"Emphysema. He's in pretty bad shape. On oxygen twenty-four hours a day."

The ground rolled beneath me. I got a flash of something—too quick to register—more an impression. Of death.

And hadn't Richard broken some kind of privacy laws by mentioning it?

"Why tell me now? I don't care about him."

"That's what I figured you'd say."

"I don't!" I said, the statement negated by the emotion behind it.

"Then why are you so upset?"

"For thirty-two years I thought the guy was dead. Finding out he isn't threw me, that's all. Come on, let's go for another game."

He shrugged, bounced the ball, faked a throw, Nikes squeaking on the drive as he pivoted then threw for real. Rim shot.

I grabbed it. "Is he dying?"

"I thought you didn't care?"

"I don't." The ball hit the backboard, missed the hoop.

"Yeah, he's dying." His back to me, Richard dribbled, turned, went for a long shot. Two points.

I captured the ball. "Did he know who you were?"

"I said my name a couple of times, but I don't think it registered."

I bounced the ball, threw it. It danced around the rim. Missed.

Richard seized it.

"Are you sure it was him?" I asked.

"Chester Resnick. Do you want me to get his address?"

"What for?"

"I know you'll want to send flowers after he's gone." He tossed the ball at me, and hit me in the chest.

"Screw you. I wouldn't waste my time—let alone money."

I bounced the ball a few times, went to throw and he blocked me, and took back the ball. I wiped the sweat from my eyes. "When will you see him again?"

"I'll find out his next appointment and make sure I see him instead of one of the other doctors."

"Don't bother. He left us. Never got in touch with me. Why the *hell* would I want to see him?" I took a deep breath. "Look, I'm sorry. I guess this got to me more than I'd like."

Richard dribbled, dribbled, dribbled. For such an old guy, he kept maneuvering out of my reach. I made a grab for the ball, but he was too quick.

"Gimme the damn ball," I growled.

Dribble, dribble. "If you decide you do want to meet him, don't wait too long." He took a shot. It soared through the hoop and net. Perfect.

I snatched the ball, and started getting one of those feelings —the ones I know better than to ignore—about my father. Richard ducked quick, took it from me again. I hadn't even known the old man was alive, and now I knew with certainty he'd soon be dead. One of my skull-pounding headaches, a remnant of the mugging that had nearly killed me, stirred.

"Don't worry, Jeff. Nothing says you have to see him or talk to him, let alone make your peace with him."

Slam dunk.

I picked up the ball and started for my apartment over the garage. "I've got to get ready for work."

"Think about it," he called after me.

"Sure," I grumbled. "Later."

Much later.

THAT NIGHT I tended bar at a local tavern where I work part-time. The Whole Nine Yards was nothing fancy, just a neighborhood sports bar with one large-screen TV and a middle-class clientele. I was grateful for a slow night, because thoughts of my father kept me preoccupied. After screwing up my fourth drink order, my boss, Tom Link, asked if I was trying to drive him into bankruptcy. I apologized, but he laughed, gave me a thumbs-up, and headed down the bar to talk to one of his cronies.

I was drawing beers for two guys watching the Sabres pregame show on the tube when Maggie Brennan, my lady of five months, walked in. The bar wasn't on her usual route home from work. She looked professional in her business suit, her shoulder-length auburn hair wind-tossed and sexy.

"Hey, baby," I said, using my best Bogie slur. "Can I buy you a drink?"

She slid smoothly onto a bar stool. "I think I could be coaxed into it."

"Cosmopolitan?" I offered.

"How about a glass of cabernet?"

"Coming right up." I poured the wine and put out a fresh bowl of pretzels. "What brings you here?" As if I didn't know.

"A little bird called and said you might need a friendly face to talk to."

"This *little* bird wouldn't happen to be six-two and sporting a mustache, would he?"

"He might." Her expression softened. "Richard told me about your dad."

"He's not my dad," I snapped, instantly regretting it. "Sorry, babe, but he was there for my conception—and not much else."

"I know about how he left your mom and you."

"Yeah, so the hell with him."

She raised her glass in salute. "The hell with him."

"Right. Why would I want to meet him, let alone get to know him?"

"He's not worth your time."

I frowned at her too-casual attitude.

"I'm just agreeing with you," she said, and took another sip of wine. "Yeah, why would you want to know the man who gave you life? You don't need to find out what went wrong with his marriage to your mother. But what if he'd wanted to be more to you? What if leaving was a mistake he always regretted?"

"And what if it wasn't? What if he is just some piece of shit who isn't worth my time?"

"And what if he isn't and you never prove it to yourself before he dies? Will *you* be able to live with that?"

I glared at her, yet some part of me was thinking exactly the same thing.

"Jeff?" Tom caught my eye, thumbed toward the hockey fans.

I poured another round and rang up the sale. I took my time washing the glasses, thinking over what Maggie had said.

A couple of guys came in and ordered mixed drinks. "I'd better go," she told me and collected her purse, then leaned across the bar to give me a kiss. "You don't have to make a decision tonight. Just think about the pros and cons of meeting him."

I rested my fingers on top of her hand. Because of this psychic crap I'm cursed with, she was one of the few people I felt comfortable touching. "Okay."

"I'll be home if you want to talk later," she said, and headed out the door.

Despite my efforts to keep busy, the rest of the evening dragged, leaving me plenty of time to consider all she'd said.

I kept catching sight of myself in the mirror behind the bar. Did I look like the old man? How much of my character reflected his? That sobering thought haunted me in the form of relentless self-examination, reigniting thirty-two years of submerged anger.

"Don't wait too long," Richard had said.

I'd already waited thirty-two years.

Far too long.

I DIDN'T SLEEP well that night, obsessed with vague, unpleasant dreams. Images of a dead, faceless, white-haired man, and an overpowering feeling of dread haunted my sleep. I didn't need a shrink to help me figure out the significance of that subconscious message.

I chose the phone book as reading material to go with my morning coffee. Only two Resnicks were listed—I was one of them. The other was C. Resnick. I didn't call. That might indicate I gave a shit about a man I barely remembered.

I wasn't scheduled to work that evening and spent the day staring out the window or pacing the confines of my apartment. Finally I hiked down the road to the community golf course and shot a roll of black-and-white film. The temperature had reverted to autumn norms, and the gray sky made the landscape look as bleak as I felt. I returned to my darkroom and developed the negatives, but didn't bother with more than making a contact sheet. Photography's a hobby that sometimes lands me money. That day it merely kept me occupied.

Twilight came and I grew tired of my own company. Almost five months before, I'd moved into the apartment above the garage —or the carriage house, as Richard's grandmother used to call it. The big house, where Richard and his wife, Brenda, lived, was across the driveway. Located in Amherst, at the edge of Buffalo, New York, it was less than an estate—but not by much. The neighborhood screamed old money, although I think Richard was the last remaining descendent of that wealth.

Using my key, I let myself in. Richard's kitchen was cavernous and gloomy compared to my snug digs. I hit the light switch, grabbed a chair at the table, and thumbed through the local section of that morning's edition of *The Buffalo News* to kill time.

The Police Blotter was full of the usual: DUI, assaults, robbery, rape. The State round-up on the side column caught my eye. A shooting somewhere in the Southern Tier. A one paragraph story told where, when, and how, but not who, pending notification of next of kin. Poor bastard. Just another deer season fatality. Right?

Maybe not.

I stared at the paragraph until the words began to blur. Something about the assemblage of facts bothered me, but I didn't have time to think about it as Richard's Lincoln Town Car pulled up the drive. I tossed the paper aside. The door handle rattled, and a few moments later a tired, depressed-looking Richard came through the butler's pantry and entered the kitchen.

I looked over my shoulder. "Tough day?"

"Yeah."

"Where's Brenda going?" I asked, as the car backed down the driveway again.

"To pick up a pizza. You want to stay?"

"I'll think about it."

He dumped his coat on the back of a kitchen chair and headed straight for the scotch bottle in a cabinet above the sink. He plunked ice into an old-fashioned glass and filled it.

"What happened?"

He took a deep swallow. "I had to tell a woman that her three-year-old daughter's brain tumor was malignant and inoperable. We discussed radiation and chemotherapy, but that sweet little girl is going to die."

My gut tightened.

"Then not ten minutes later, an older woman came in. Her son's pit bull attacked her a week ago. She didn't think her health insurance would cover an emergency room visit, so she made an appointment and waited. Between the infection and nerve damage, she'll probably lose the use of her hand." He took a shuddering breath, and then another long pull of the scotch.

I listened to Richard vent for another ten minutes. He was always too hard on himself when he couldn't help his patients. We rarely talked about his own situation. Five months before, he'd tended to a shooting victim. He hadn't been wearing latex gloves. Five tests for HIV had been negative. He had one more to go before we could all breathe easier. After hearing about his day, I couldn't ask if he'd remembered to dig up information on my father. Especially since I supposedly didn't care.

Brenda came in at last, carrying a pizza box. "Oh, good, I was hoping you'd be here. There's no way the two of us can eat all this." She gave me a quick peck on the cheek, deposited the pizza on the counter and went off to hang up her coat.

Richard and Brenda are a study in contrasts. He's tall, she's petite; he's into computers, she's into antiques; he's white, she's black. She would've made one helluva Boy Scout: loyal, trustworthy and sometimes she's got the gift of second sight. Not like me, but she's a kindred spirit. Most important, she's family.

When she came back, she took plates out of the cupboard while I gathered a knife, spatula and napkins, and Richard poured a caffeine-free Coke for her and got me a beer. We sat at the table, each taking a slice of pizza.

"Did you tell him?" Brenda asked, and took a big bite.

"I completely forgot," Richard said. "I saw your father today."

Every muscle in my body tensed. "And?"

"When I told him who I was, he cried. Apparently he has a lot of regrets."

Was I one of them?

"He didn't know you were back in Buffalo," Richard continued.

"How'd he know I ever left?"

Richard shrugged. "He knew you were in the Army, and that you'd lived in New York. He even knew your wife was murdered. He seemed to know more about your past than I do."

I wasn't sure how to react to that—anger came close. "Then why didn't he ever contact me? Why—?"

"I don't know. But he wants you to call him." Richard reached into his pocket and withdrew a slip of paper.

Spidery handwriting noted my father's name, address and phone number.

"He said he goes to bed around nine-thirty, so if it isn't convenient tonight you can call him after eight tomorrow morning."

I didn't know *if* I wanted to call him, let alone when.

I stuffed the paper in my pocket and turned my attention to the pizza on my plate. Too many things crowded my brain. Too many conflicting emotions threatened to choke me.

Richard and Brenda ate in awkward silence for a minute or two. I sipped my beer and tried not to think. Finally, Richard broke the quiet. "Peterson is out for the next six weeks. They asked me to cover for him."

Brenda looked up. "Oh, hell."

"Who's Peterson?" I asked.

"One of the clinic doctors. He broke his leg rollerblading with his son over the weekend." He looked at Brenda. "I'm going to need some serious time off by Christmas. How about a trip?"

"The Quebec Winter Carnival is in January," she said.

He nodded. "Maybe."

Despite talk of vacation plans, the tension seemed to grow. I pretended not to notice.

"Jeffy," Brenda said casually. "Can you drive me to the clinic tomorrow?"

I swallowed. "Sure. Is the car acting up?"

She shook her head. "I'd just feel better if I didn't park it in the lot for a while. There's been some trouble."

Richard looked up. "Oh?"

"The protesters," she said offhandedly, and got up to refill her glass, but even across the room I could feel her anxiety rise.

"I thought things were better," Richard said. He turned his attention to me. "Eat."

"I thought so, too," she said, "but they're hanging in there. Today they started chanting like monks. It's unnerving," she said, not facing him.

The two of them had started out volunteering together at the hospital's clinic, but since mid-summer Brenda had worked several days a week at a women's health center where the occasional abortion was performed. That didn't set well with some of the area's religious zealots. For Brenda to even mention it meant she was concerned.

Though there hadn't been a major incident in Buffalo in the years since Dr. Barnett Slepian was murdered, Amherst still seemed to be the focus of the pro-life movement in this part of the state.

"We've talked about this before. It's time you quit," Richard said.

"What I do is important."

He let out a long breath, and I wished I wasn't sitting in the middle of a discussion I'd heard too many times.

"Yes, it is," Richard agreed. "But you don't need the money, or the aggravation—especially now."

She looked away. "It's only until they find someone to replace me."

"Do you promise?" he asked.

"Yes."

They both looked at me expectantly. "Sure, I'll take you to work. You'll be safe with me."

"Thanks," Brenda said, sat down again, and took another slice of pizza. I wasn't even half way through my first piece. "Eat up," she said, "it's getting cold." The food could never get as cold as the frost generated by that conversation.

I thought about the slip of paper in my pocket and felt colder still.

2

———

Brenda and I are more in sync than either of us care to admit. Even without touching her, I could sense her radiating an assortment of emotions: trepidation, anxiety, and dread. I wasn't sure what it meant.

"Are you okay?" I asked.

She glanced at me then looked away. "Sure. Just a little nervous."

"You didn't tell us everything yesterday, did you?"

Her voice was small. "No."

I waited, and she exhaled loudly. "Somebody egged my windshield last week. I had to pay extra at the carwash to get it off."

"Was it only your car?"

She shook her head. "Other cars in the lot got it, too."

"And?"

"And a couple of days later it was lipstick, only that was on the doors and across the trunk."

"What was the message?"

"*Death monger*, among others."

"Is that it?" I asked, knowing it wasn't.

Her mouth tightened. "I think somebody followed me home the other night."

Brenda wasn't the paranoid type. My fingers gripped the wheel. "What kind of car?"

"I don't know, but it was blue."

"Have you seen it again?"

"No, but I reported it to the heath center's security. They said to be careful. That's why you're driving me to work. Did you call your father?" she asked, changing the subject.

"No."

"Are you going to?"

"I don't know."

"Richard thinks you should. So does Maggie."

"How about you?"

She shrugged. "You have to do what you have to do." I braked for slowing traffic and she looked at me with wry amusement. "Do I detect a little hostility here?"

"After thirty-two years of indifference from him . . . yeah, I'd say I feel hostile."

Those thoughts evaporated as we approached the Williamsville Women's Health Center, and I could see why Brenda was nervous. Ten or more men and women marched up and down in front of the parking lot across the street—more than the requisite fifteen feet from the drab, one-story brick building, just as the law demanded. The first amendment allowed them to "sidewalk counsel" anyone who passed by. Each carried a placard: *No More Slaughtered Babies*; *Pro-Choice = Death For Babies*; *Baby Butcher Shop*. Other signs bore grisly color photos of bloodied, mangled fetuses.

I pulled my car into an empty space along the curb and watched as a Toyota Prius approached the lot. The protesters broke formation only long enough to let it in. The driver got out of her car, briskly crossed the picket line, ignoring the protesters' haranguing voices. She hurried up the concrete steps and yanked open the plate glass door and escaped inside.

"Why hasn't this been on the news?" I asked Brenda.

She glanced at the crowd. "Because they've been at it for weeks. But it's still upsetting."

"Why didn't you say something about this sooner?"

"I didn't want Richard to worry. He's . . . ." She caught herself, seemed to think better of telling me. "He's got a lot on his mind right now."

I let her words sink in. Something besides his next blood test? "Anything I should know about?"

"No. Not right now." She pawed in her purse for her office keys. "He keeps trying to talk me into quitting. And I can't. Not yet."

She'd sidestepped my question. Okay. Richard had had a couple of bad days at the clinic. What else could be bothering him?

I eyed the protesters' angry faces and got a flash of something: Panicked protesters and clinic security, running footsteps, a bloodied hand.

"I gotta agree with Rich on this one. It doesn't look—or feel —safe to me. And if you want to give the poor guy a break—"

"You're a man. You can't possibly understand. Women deserve control over their own bodies, their destinies, without being dictated to by a bunch of—"

"Hey, you don't have to convince *me*," I said, jerking a thumb at myself.

She looked back at the crowd. "We don't even do that many abortions. We're a *women's* health center—for all aspects of *women's* health."

"That still doesn't tell me why you feel you have to be here."

She stared at the dashboard. "Women used to die from back alley abortions."

"Tell me something I don't already know," I said, losing patience.

The glare she turned on me could've blistered paint. "My Aunt Vonnie died from massive infection after her football playing, big-man-on-campus boyfriend took her to some jerk with a rusty coat hanger."

The venom in her voice made me wince. "When was this?"

"A year before Roe vs. Wade. She was almost sixteen." Brenda looked away, but I saw her lower lip tremble. "I wasn't even born. I only know about her because her sisters loved her and kept her alive with their words—their memories. But she's dead—and it's only her family who cared."

"I'm sorry, Brenda."

"Yeah, me, too. For all the Vonnies—past, and future, if these damned protesters get their way." She reached for the door handle. "I have to go."

I touched her shoulder. "I'll pick you up at four." She nodded gratefully. "Want me to walk you to the door?" I added.

She shook her head. "I won't let them intimidate me. See you tonight." She got out the car and hurried past the crowd of protesters, never making eye contact, ignoring the jeers and taunts. I waited until she made it safely inside the building.

She wouldn't admit it, but she was already intimidated.

I studied the odd assortment of people marching up and down the sidewalk, wanting to memorize each face, and realizing the futility. But I could photograph them. I'd use black and white, grainy film. Catch them in the act of grimacing, sneezing, anything embarrassing. How childish of me.

One three-point-turn later, I was on my way back home to get my Nikon. Maybe none of these protesters were violent, but plenty of their counterparts in other cities were. The idea both sickened and fascinated me.

Arriving home, I took the steps to my loft apartment two at a time. I changed into a dark, hooded sweatshirt to insure anonymity, grabbed my camera, film, the zoom lens, and started back for the health center.

I parked a couple of blocks away and hoofed it, staying across the street and keeping well away from the protesters. No way did I want their wrath turned on me. Then I snapped away for nearly half an hour.

Later, I fed a sheet of photographic paper into the enlarger grid, exposed it, then plopped it into the developer. Agitating the tray, I watched under the orange glow of the safelight as the image appeared: a skinny woman with stringy hair—her mouth wide open, exposing crooked teeth, her lips curled in an epithet. Not exactly a poster child for the right-to-life movement.

Print after print was the same. There was a story there and I hadn't captured it. But I did have half a brick of film. I'd have to go back and try again. This time I'd take photos of the women entering the clinic, too. And maybe I could make a few bucks from this little exercise. I knew just where to go to do it, too.

THE NEXT DAY, I called the newsroom at *The Buffalo News*. Sam Nielsen, my former schoolmate, told me to meet him at the paper's lobby at precisely noon. Naturally, he was twenty minutes late.

Sam and I go way back—if you count being taunted by Mr. Campus for being a basketball-playing geek back in high school as going way back. Anyway, we buried the hatchet earlier in the year when I gave him an exclusive interview after I'd beaten up a killer in church. And he'd helped me on another case since then, but that's another story . . . .

Sam was now one of the best reporters on staff and I had no qualms about pressing him for a favor.

"Hey, Resnick!" he called, entering the lobby from an outside door.

He held a Styrofoam cup of coffee in one hand and a Burger King bag in the other. Though still tall and lanky, he'd lost his dark, wavy hair. His now-balding pate shone under the newsroom's fluorescent lights.

"Damn," I said. "If I'd known, you could've brought me a bacon cheeseburger."

"Get your own," he said without rancor. He got me a visitor's pass and I followed him up to his office, where he yanked out the chair and sat down at his desk. He waved a hand at the visitor's chair in front of his desk. "To what do I owe the pleasure?"

"I want to show you some photos."

He looked unimpressed. "Not a bunch of kids at the beach or any of that crap, I hope."

"Give me some credit." I opened my portfolio case and withdrew the photos, tossed them at him, just missing his burger and fries. I scrutinized his face as he shuffled through the ten or so prints and decided he'd probably be a pretty good poker player.

"Not bad, but what's with the black-and-white shots? When are you going to enter the twenty-first century and buy a digital camera?"

"Give me a break. Most of my stuff is black-and-white art shots. If you buy enough of these prints, I might be able to afford a digital camera."

He shook his head. "What else have you got?"

"I brought other samples, but these are the ones that count. I want you to do a story on the pro-life protesters at the Williamsville Women's Health Center."

He spread the prints out across the litter covering his desk. "What's the hook?"

"I think the women who go there are in danger."

He frowned, restacked the photos. "You've got some interesting pictures here, Jeff, but you've got no story."

"You mean someone needs to be shot or the place has to be firebombed before the paper shows interest?"

He handed me the photos. "That's about the size of it."

I put the pictures back in the envelope, trying, without much success, to hide my disappointment. "Your burger's getting cold. Thanks for your time." I was on my feet, and started walking away when his voice stopped me.

"Why are these women in danger?"

I turned. "A couple of these protesters are certifiable."

He shook his head. "Not good enough."

"My sister-in-law has to face these jerks every day."

"So hire a guard."

"*I'm* her guard."

"You still haven't answered my question."

How could I? Eggs and lipstick were messy and inconvenient, but not particularly lethal.

He sipped his coffee. "This isn't like last time, ya know. As far as you know, there's been vandalism, but nothing concrete—like a dead body. I don't see the threat."

"Why does someone have to die to pique your interest?"

His piercing gaze appraised me. "Okay, I get it. This is something you feel strongly about or you wouldn't be here."

I stared right back. "You're damned right."

"Go to the cops, Jeff."

"Like you, they don't want to waste their time until someone gets hurt. I want to prevent that."

"Can you?"

I had no answer.

He studied me for a few moments before he grabbed a pad and a pen, scratched down a few notes. "All right. I'll look into it." He nodded toward my portfolio. "Can I hang onto them?"

"Sure." I handed him the envelope.

He took out the prints again, studying them. "This guy," he pointed, "is Robert Linden. Head of the Erie Country Assembly of Life. He emerged as the local pro-life superstar after the Spring of Life protests way back when. Years ago he broke away from Operation Rescue and that ilk."

"Is he dangerous?"

"He can inflame a crowd with his rhetoric. But we haven't had any incidents of note in a very long time."

I studied the photo. Dressed conservatively in a business suit and overcoat, Linden looked like the stereotypical fire-and-brimstone preacher. His short-cropped silver hair stood up to the brisk wind. His expression, in a face hardened by the years, was one of puritanical self-righteousness. The unease in my gut swelled, telling me to pay attention.

Sam looked at his calendar. "Unless something comes up, I can give you an hour or two on Wednesday. Would that be okay?"

"Sure."

"Bring your gear and a notepad. I'll put you to work getting names for the photos. That is, if you're willing to sell."

"I'm always open to negotiation."

ON MY WAY HOME, I drove past my father's house. The leaden sky did nothing to enhance the shabby little Cape Cod or the rest of the drab, lower middle-class neighborhood.

I didn't tell Richard or Brenda I'd been driving past Chet's house. I didn't tell them about my little photographic project, either. They had their own concerns.

But driving by on a daily basis was stupid. What was I hoping for, anyway? To catch a glimpse of the old man? To stake him out? Richard said he seemed to know an awful lot about me. How?

More than once I'd been tempted to pull in the drive, knock on the door, meet the old man—just to get it over with. Was I too chicken-shit scared of what I might learn, or that my anger might cause me to pick a fight with a man who could no longer defend himself?

Perhaps the best response was to just forget about him—as he'd forgotten about me for thirty-two long years.

I turned onto Kenmore Avenue, drove straight home, and spent the rest of the day contemplating the situation as I worked in the solitude of my darkroom.

"You really don't have to do this. I don't know why I made such a fuss the other day," Brenda said as we pulled out of the drive the next morning, but I could tell her bravado was all show.

"I don't mind. It's an excuse to get my lazy ass out of bed. Besides, I'm on stake-out duty today. It'll be just like old times."

"Old times?" she asked in disbelief. "You worked in a stuffy old insurance office."

"I was a field agent for almost four years," I reminded her. "I had my share of peeing in soup cans."

She scowled. I don't think she believed me.

Like before, we pulled into a parking space half a block from the Women's Health Center. I turned off the engine and we sat in silence for a few moments, studying the picketers. A new face had appeared in the crowd. He didn't look like the usual pro-life advocate—more like an aging hippie or biker. Clad in jeans and a grubby cord jacket, he had a gray-streaked, wiry beard, and his long hair was captured in a pony tail. His eyes burned—religious zeal or a drug-crazed glow, I wasn't sure which.

Getting out of the car, I placed myself between Brenda and the protesters across the street.

"Escort," the newcomer sneered as I walked her to the door, turning the word into a curse.

Once Brenda was inside, I returned to my car. As promised, I devoted the rest of the day to a half-assed stake-out. The picketers chanted, prayed, sang, and took every opportunity to shove leaflets at anyone who dared make eye contact. They took turns for lunch, and I followed a couple of them to a nearby strip mall where their converted school bus was parked. Did they all gather at the First Gospel Church and ride in together, or did some of them drive to the clinic on their own?

At three o'clock, I left my chilly car and walked over to the Niagara Realty Company, the clinic's next-door neighbor, to warm up.

"I wish the police would arrest every one of those bastards," the manager, Kathy Burton, said. "They're scaring my clients away. Lately, most of my agents have met prospective customers off-site to avoid the situation. Those protestors have been hanging around for almost a month now. I've still got two years left on a five-year lease. What am I supposed to do?"

"Call the cops?" I suggested.

"I have, but Bob Linden and his followers are always careful to act within the boundaries of the law."

Next, I spoke with Tim Davies, the heath center's security chief. He knew about the cars being egged and the messages in lipstick, but no one had seen the perpetrators. The clinic had beefed up its manpower with rent-a-cops, and had scheduled the installation of more security cameras around the clinic and in the parking lot by year end, but in the meantime what could unarmed minimum-wage guys with uniforms and brass badges do to stop violence aimed at the staff or patrons?

Right on time, I met Brenda in the health center's lobby. "Ready to run the gauntlet?"

She smiled, but seemed edgy.

We barely got down the steps before Brenda stopped short, distracted by a fracas across the street. Close to tears, an elderly woman, with a halo of snowy hair framing her drawn face, stood huddled in her drab gray topcoat, surrounded by a crowd of protesters.

"Don't go into that den of death! The Lord Almighty will forgive you if you turn away—condemn the child killers!" Bob Linden thundered.

"Leave me alone," the woman cried, shying away from the Reverend, who moved to block her way once again. The other picketers clustered around her, their shrill voices rising.

Brenda bolted across the street.

"Brenda, wait!"

"What the hell do you think you're doing?" Brenda hollered at Linden. "Leave this poor woman alone."

Linden turned, vexed. "The first amendment gives me the right to counsel anyone entering that slaughterhouse."

"It's a women's health center," Brenda bristled. "And the constitution does not give you the right to hassle this lady."

Linden straightened to his full height, and clutched his Bible to his chest. "I am here as God's messenger."

"You're no more God's messenger than I am," Brenda said.

"Brenda," I warned, grabbing her arm to haul her away. She shook me loose, her stance showing she was itching for a fight.

"You make your living murdering helpless babies," Linden accused.

"Come on," I grated, and tried to turn her away, but Brenda's and Linden's gazes were locked—brittle anger crackling around them like static electricity.

"I only came here to get a new prescription," the old woman

said, looking at me with pleading blue eyes. Her words caused Brenda to look away. She took the woman's left arm, while I grabbed her right, and we pushed through the circle of bodies surrounding us, leading the old lady away from Linden and his crowd of bullies.

"May God forgive you," Linden shouted as we guided the woman across the street and up the steps.

"What took you so long, boys," I said as two security guards opened the heavy glass doors to let us in. Behind us the picketers started singing a hymn.

"Are you all right, hon?" Brenda asked the elderly woman. I felt the old woman trembling under my grasp.

"Thank you for helping me. I've been coming here for over twenty years. I'm afraid to come back," she said.

"Who's your appointment with?" Brenda asked.

"Dr. Newcomb."

"Forget the waiting room. I'll get you right in," she said, and led the woman away.

The ineffective guards looked at me, embarrassed. I turned aside, and took a chair to wait.

Brenda stayed with the old lady until her son arrived to take her home. Linden and most of the protesters had disappeared by then.

I approached my car with some trepidation, remembering how years ago clinics down south had been firebombed. But these protesters were a church group. Surely they wouldn't condone that kind of violence.

Paranoia crept closer as I gingerly opened the driver's door, got in, and turned the key. The engine purred. I feigned a calm I didn't feel as I circled back to pick up Brenda at the center's entrance.

"What're you going to tell Richard?" she said, once we were on the road and heading home.

"What do you want me to say?"

"Nothing. Let me tell him. In my own way."

"You know him better than me," I said, hoping I wouldn't get the third degree later anyway.

I dropped her off and was only an hour late for work, and I busted my ass trying to make up for it. Between drawing beers and mixing drinks, I spent the evening pondering the absurdity of Linden and his followers harassing elderly women who weren't likely to get pregnant—let alone abort—any time soon.

Long ago, I found keeping busy the perfect way to distract myself from life—like thinking about Linden and his followers. Or Richard's next blood test.

Like thinking about my father.

I worked late on Friday, and got offered and took a last-minute job tending bar at a wedding reception on Saturday—even though it meant canceling a date with Maggie. I even managed to pick up an extra shift at the bar on Sunday. But by Monday evening I faced the silent telephone and decided to make the call I'd lost so much sleep over.

It was after nine when I finally dialed the number.

"Hello?" A young woman's voice startled me.

"I'm looking for Chet Resnick."

"Who's calling?"

"Uh . . . Jeff." I cleared my throat. "Jeffrey Resnick."

"Dad," she called, "it's *him*!"

Dad?

Did old Chester have a second family?

Did I have a sister?

An older man came on the line. "Son?"

Rattled, I almost hung up. "Chester Resnick? Married to Elizabeth Alpert?"

"That's right. What took you so long to call, boy?"

What took *me* so long? The old man had balls, I'll give him that. "I'm not even sure *why* I called."

"Things didn't work out between your mother and me. I don't know what she told you, but—"

"She didn't say much. Just that you were gone. I assumed you were dead."

"She wished I was," he said with bitterness and coughed, a loud, rattling sound. "Did your brother tell you I'm sick?"

"He mentioned it."

"I'm going to die pretty soon. But I'd like to know you first. When can you come see me?"

I didn't answer right away. "I dunno." I still didn't know if I wanted to.

"Tomorrow morning?"

Pushy bastard. Wary, I asked, "What time?"

"Ten. Bring doughnuts. I like the ones with chocolate on top and custard inside."

"Okay. I'll see you tomorrow."

He didn't say goodbye, just hung up.

I stared at the phone for a long time, wondering if I'd made a really big mistake.

3
____

I stopped at a Tim's Dairy, not some franchise place, for the best doughnuts in town. Don't ask me why. And don't ask me why I kept this visit from Richard and Maggie. I don't know that, either. Maybe because they'd been pushy about it. Pushy, like Chet. I was tired of being pushed into seeing this old man . . . even if curiosity drove me to do it anyway.

My father's house was on the outskirts of the city, only ten minutes from Richard's place. In the week since I'd found out my father was alive, I'd driven by some eight or ten times. Sometimes a white Mustang sat in the driveway, other times there'd be a battered old Ford Focus. The Focus was in the drive when I pulled up.

Doughnut bag in hand, I walked to the front door. I stood there, staring at the surname on the mailbox—my name. My stomach tightened in dread—like a kid called to the principal's office. Maybe I should just turn around. Go home. But I couldn't. Even if I didn't like what I found out, it was better than not knowing.

Maybe.

I closed my eyes—opened my mind—and got the same flash

of something I'd experienced days earlier when Richard first told me about Chet. Death. Still couldn't understand what it meant, but it had to relate to my father.

It had to.

My knuckles rapped against the door's flaking paint. Moments later an Hispanic woman in a white nurse's uniform opened it.

"I'm here to see Chet Resnick."

"You must be his son. Come in."

Son. It had been a long time since I'd been anyone's son.

The house smelled of fresh-brewed coffee and disinfectant. Though the furniture was shabby and dated, the place was clean. The woman ushered me through the tiny living room and kitchen to the back of the house, where a twenty-seven-inch TV blared. The cramped, paneled family room had been tacked on to the back of the little cracker box of a house.

Chester Arthur Resnick sat in a worn, oversized recliner, tethered to a green oxygen tank by a tube trailing from his nose. Dressed in flannel pajamas and robe, he looked like an older, sick version of the few pictures I'd seen of him. His sparse white hair was scraped across his head in a vain effort to cover his baldness. The energy-saver fluorescent bulb in the lamp nearby gave his skin a pale, greenish tinge.

I stood there, unsure of what to say, wondering if I'd be heard over the TV.

"Can I take your coat?" the woman asked.

"I'll keep it," I said, figuring it would be easier if I needed to make a fast escape.

"I'll get coffee. You like milk and sugar?"

"Just milk."

She nodded and took off for the kitchen.

Chet hit the mute button on the remote, the sudden quiet

jarring me. "Sit down," he said. "Did you bring my doughnuts, boy?"

He took the bag from me, taking out one of the chocolate-covered ones. He bit into it and the custard oozed onto his fingers. "Elena, bring some napkins."

A black cat appeared from out of nowhere, leaping onto the old man's lap. He let the cat lick the custard from his thumb, then wiped it on his robe.

"This is Herschel, he keeps me company," he said, stroking the cat fondly. It settled onto the old man's lap, glaring at me with yellow eyes.

"Richard says you know all about me," I said.

"Some. How come your wife got murdered?"

"She was into drugs."

He nodded, non-judgmental. "Too bad. You got a girlfriend now?"

"Yeah. She lives in Clarence."

His eyes wandered to the game show on the tube. "Is she nice?"

"Very nice. How do you know so much about me?"

He looked at me and shrugged. "I got friends."

I didn't like that answer, but I couldn't force him to give me a better one. I focused my attention on the cat, finding it easier than looking into my father's eyes. Though stray cat hair clung to Chet's hand, there was a noticeable lack of it on the furniture and rug. Elena kept the place spotless.

"Doctor says you got hurt last winter. That's why you come back to Buffalo," Chet said.

"I got mugged. They nearly killed me." Why'd I say that? I didn't need sympathy—or anything else—from him.

I decided not to volunteer any more information. If he wanted to know anything else, he could ask.

Dishes rattling in the kitchen caused Herschel to leap from Chet's lap. The old man shook his hand free of cat hair. "I was gonna get you when your mother died, but then Doctor took you in. I figured those people owed your mother, so I didn't bother."

"You could have let me know you were still around."

"What for? Your life's been fine without me, hasn't it? What could I offer you?"

Yeah. What?

"You got a sister," he said, and reached for a framed photo on the table next to his chair. The color dyes had faded on the high school senior picture. "That's Patty. She's twenty-six now."

I studied the young, smiling face. She was pretty, with muddy brown eyes—like mine—and dishwater blonde hair. She looked familiar somehow, but not because we shared a parent. She had some other quality I couldn't pin down.

"You remarried?" I asked Chet.

"Your mother was a good Catholic. She didn't believe in divorce. After Betty died, Joan and me never bothered to make it legal. Patty don't know that. Don't you tell her, now."

"Have you got any other kids?"

"Not that I know of."

Would he even care? He'd abandoned my mother and me and never bothered to marry Patty's mother. Typical.

"So, where's Patty?"

"Working."

"Does she drive the white Mustang?"

He nodded. "She wants to meet you. She's only seen pictures of you."

"Pictures?"

He reached for a shoe box on the table in front of him. He dug through it and came up with a couple of old black-and-white photographs and some color Instamatic shots, handing them to me.

I flipped through them. The black-and-white ones were me at two. My mother had had a duplicate set. I stared in disbelief at the faded color shots taken at my high school graduation. They weren't very good; I wasn't even the central figure in most of them, probably because they'd been taken from a distance. Though the focus was fuzzy, I recognized my sullen features, remembered feeling embarrassed in the black cap and gown. I thought Richard was my only family member to go to the ceremony. I thought Richard *was* my only family.

"Where'd you get these?"

"I took them."

"You were there?" I asked, my stomach tightening.

"You're my kid. It was your graduation day."

"Why didn't you say something? Why didn't you introduce yourself?"

He shrugged. "By then I had Joan and Patty. You didn't need me. Anyway, you done all right."

Yeah, right. Dumped on a brother I didn't know, whose family despised my mother—and me. Oh, yeah, living in the Alpert house was *real* pleasant.

I looked at that frail, sick old man, unable to let go of the anger. Yet this man was my father. Half of what I was came from him.

"You got any questions?" he asked.

Only one.

"Why did you leave my mother and me?"

The old man frowned. "All Betty ever thought about was getting her boy Richard back. That's all she talked about. That's all she cared about. After five years, I couldn't take it no more."

Something about that didn't quite ring true. I knew all about how Richard's grandparents had gotten custody of him after his father died and our mother had a nervous breakdown. She never regained custody of him. But I couldn't hold that against my brother, who'd been a pawn in the struggle between his rich old grandmother and my working-class mother.

I looked Chet in the eye, felt him take a mental step back as I connected with him. Unnerved, he looked away, but I knew something he wouldn't want me to know. My breathing quickened—anger rising as I registered a vague understanding of what he felt, and it sorted itself out in my brain.

"You . . . wanted to kidnap Richard. To extort money from the Alperts."

"That's a lie," he said, his face flushing "Whoever told you that lied!"

"I don't think so . . . ."

He leaned back against the chair, struggling for breath—his anger evaporating. "Believe what you want. I know the truth."

So did I. But after all those years, it wasn't worth pursuing.

He clutched the chair's arms, forcing himself to breathe slower.

"What happened to Patty's mother?" I asked.

"Joan died of cancer about ten years ago. That's a bad time for a girl to lose her mother. Patty's been a handful ever since."

"Tell me about her."

"She works at a medical supply house in Lockport. Makes good money, too."

"But she lives here?"

"When she's in-between boyfriends." That didn't set well with the old man.

I noticed the previous day's paper neatly folded at the side of his chair—reminding me of another question that needed to be asked.

"You told Richard you didn't know I was back in Buffalo."

"Yeah."

"What about the newspaper stories about us and that murder last winter?" It had been front page news, and my name

—and picture, as well as Richard's—had been prominently displayed in the paper, and on TV.

Caught in a lie, the old man looked appropriately guilty. He shifted his gaze, annoyed. "Elena, where's that coffee?" He called and dipped into the doughnut bag again.

"Are you supposed to eat those?"

He took a huge bite of a sugar-coated jelly doughnut, chewed, swallowed, and smiled. "No. But what the hell, I'm dying anyway."

Elena arrived with a tray of cups, napkins and assorted accouterments. "Don't you eat another one of those doughnuts," she ordered. "When your sugar goes sky high, I get in trouble." She took the bag from him, setting it in front of me. I prefer muffins, and had bought two of them. I took out an apple raisin one, and put it on the plate she provided.

Elena poured the coffee, then pointed a wagging finger at Chet. "No more," she warned once more and took her leave.

I doctored my coffee. "So what else have you been up to for the past thirty-two years?" He missed the dig.

"I had my own dry cleaning shop on Grant Street. I made good money. But then I got sick. Doctors said it was the chemical fumes and smoking. I had to give up both. Last I heard, you were in insurance."

"I got laid off. I was about to start a new job when I got hurt. Richard brought me back to Buffalo. He's been a good friend. He's done a lot for me."

"He *owed* you," Chet said. "What his people did to your mother—"

I tuned him out.

Richard and I had a rocky history. Some of it was his fault—some of it was mine. Since I'd moved back to Buffalo, he'd shown me nothing but kindness and generosity. I used to think he only acted out of guilt, and maybe at one time he had. We'd both come a long way since those days.

I lost track of what Chet was saying, but my ears pricked up when he said, "—and I hope you'll look out for her when I'm gone."

"Excuse me?"

"You'll be the man of the family. It'll be up to you to take care of Patty."

"But I don't even know her." Good Lord, what did the man expect?

"She wants to meet you. How about tonight?"

"I have to work," I answered automatically, anxious to avoid any further entanglements.

"What about tomorrow?"

"I'll call her later in the week."

"What's the matter? Is she not good enough for you since you live with those Alperts?"

"Did anyone ever tell you you're pushy?" I asked, trying not to lose my temper.

He frowned, but continued the interrogation. "Where do you work?"

"I tend bar at The Whole Nine Yards on Main Street."

"A sports bar, huh?"

"Yeah."

"Do you like it?"

"It's okay."

Our conversation continued in that vein for a few more minutes, bantering back and forth like a tennis ball in a tight match. Soon it became obvious the old man was tiring.

"I'd better get going." I rose from my seat and offered him my hand. He shook it, and I had to grit my teeth against the onslaught of emotions the old man broadcasted. Chief among them was regret, but I wasn't sure just what it was he regretted.

"You'll come back soon, won't you?" he asked, his brown eyes hopeful.

"I'll call," I said, making no definite promises. I headed back for the front of the house, but paused in the doorway. The old man smiled at me and I was overcome with an unwelcome guilt I didn't deserve to own.

Elena saw me to the front door. I could hear the TV blasting once again.

"You make him very happy, Mister."

"Is he good to work for?"

She shrugged. "Sometimes good, sometimes bad. This job won't last too much longer, I think."

I nodded. "Thanks for taking care of him, Elena."

She smiled and closed the door behind me.

I walked slowly back to my car and got in. I'd wanted to hate the old man. Instead, I felt pity—for the whole lousy situation. My mother had loved him, but she'd loved Richard more. And when my father left, it had nearly destroyed her.

What had she ever seen in Chet Resnick? He was nothing like Richard's father, in looks, temperament or social standing. Maybe she felt she'd married above her class the first time. Still, a part of me couldn't help but wish John Alpert had donated his sperm in my cause.

In that house, in front of the old man, I'd felt numb. But now I was out of that oppressive atmosphere and my anger bubbled over. He wanted me to watch out for Patty? What kind of reality did he live in, anyway? For *years* he'd ignored me. *Years!* And now he wanted me to be some kind of nursemaid to the child he *had* cared for? The one who'd had a father all that time.

Not likely.

· · ·

I DON'T EVEN REMEMBER the drive home, but eventually I found myself pulling into the driveway. A blue Altima with Pennsylvania plates sat in my usual spot. Something about that didn't feel right.

I headed straight for Richard's house with an unexpected sense of urgency. The side door was locked. I took out my key and opened the door that led to the butler's pantry.

"Richard?" Brenda called anxiously.

"No, it's Jeff."

I came into the kitchen. A black man in a bulky, dark sweater sat at the kitchen table. His bulging biceps and thick neck reminded me of a weight lifter. Brenda's delicate china cup looked ridiculous in his beefy hand.

"This is Willie Morgan. My ex-husband," Brenda said, her voice strained with tension. "Willie, this is my brother-in-law, Jeffrey Resnick."

I stood there dumbly until Willie got up, and offered me his hand. At six three or four, he towered over me. He probably weighed sixty or eighty pounds more than me, too. I'd heard how he'd beaten Brenda senseless countless times during their brief marriage. His size alone was enough to intimidate me. I didn't want to touch him—didn't want him to awaken my heightened awareness. But courtesy demanded I shake his hand.

Thank God I got nothing.

"Nice to meet you," he said politely. Knowing their past history, I expected his voice to be lower, menacing. It wasn't.

"Will you stay for coffee?" Brenda asked me hopefully.

"Sure." I shrugged out of my jacket, hung it over the chair and sat down at the round table.

Willie took his seat again.

"I noticed your license plates. What brings you to Buffalo?" I asked.

"I got a job with the Bisons."

"Coaching?"

"No, marketing."

I'd had the impression he worked more physical jobs. His imposing stature implied the same thing.

"How long has it been since you two have seen each other?" I tried again.

"Twelve years," Willie answered easily. "That was when Brenda moved to California and divorced me."

Brenda's mouth was tight; fear shadowed her eyes. "My mother gave Willie my address. She thought he might want to look me up."

Mrs. Stanley hadn't approved of Brenda living with Richard, a white man. When Brenda married him, her mother cut all ties.

Brenda set a cup of coffee and a plate of chocolate chip cookies on the table before me, but she didn't take a seat, instead retreating to the counter.

"Have you found a place to live yet?" I asked Willie.

"I'm staying at a residence motel. Most places I've looked at won't be available until the first of the month. I hope to find something permanent by next week."

I nodded. Now what could we talk about?

The silence lengthened. Finally Willie pushed his half-empty cup away. "I guess I'd better be going."

Brenda forced a smile but said nothing.

"Good luck in your new job," I said.

"I'll see if I can get you guys some free tickets for next season."

"Sure, thanks."

Willie got up, shrugged into his Bisons jacket, and headed for the door. "Nice to meet you." He looked past me toward Brenda. "I'll see you again sometime, Brenda."

Was that a promise or a threat?

Brenda remained riveted to the counter, radiating sheer terror. I followed and then closed the door on our guest.

I returned to the kitchen as Willie's car revved to life. Brenda stared at Willie's now-empty chair for a long moment.

We watched as the car passed the kitchen window as it backed out of the drive.

The quiet that followed was unnerving.

"Do you need a hug or something?" I asked Brenda.

A tear slid down her cheek and she nodded. I crossed the room in three steps, held her as she clutched me, let her tears soak into my shirt.

"You didn't go to the clinic with Rich this morning."

She shook her head. "I didn't feel well. My stomach's been upset lately."

"So Willie picked the one day you're home alone to come visit. Are you okay now?"

She nodded. "I'm so glad you showed up. I was so afraid."

"Come on, sit down." I led her to the table. "What happened?"

"I heard the doorbell, opened the door, and there he was. He barged right in."

"He wasn't overtly threatening," I said.

"He never was in front of other people. Believe me, under that quiet veneer lies a monster."

"Why did you ever marry him?" I blurted—a stupid question.

"I'm embarrassed to even remember." She took a cookie from the plate and nibbled at it. "My sister Ruthie was his girlfriend."

"She was killed by a drunk driver, right?"

She nodded. "We were twins," she reminded me, and her eyes filled with tears. "A few months after the accident, Willie and I started dating. At first, it was wonderful. He treated me like a queen. It was a whirlwind courtship. I was still in nursing school, but we got married anyway, for all the wrong—and obvious—reasons. It didn't take long for him to realize that I wasn't Ruth. He had loved *her*. And although we were twins, I wasn't *her*. Nothing I could do was ever right. It was like a nightmare when he lost his job and I was supporting us."

"And your mother would still prefer you to be with him?"

"He's the right color, if nothing else." She got up to pour herself more coffee, but the pot held only dregs. "Do you want another cup?"

"Sure." I glanced at the clock on the wall; it was almost lunchtime.

"Richard said he'd come home at noon. Do you want to stay?" she asked hopefully.

She was giving off weird vibes—still afraid, even though the object of her fear had departed. "Sure."

"Thanks," she said, relieved, and busied herself by getting a new filter for the pot and measuring the coffee.

"What did you guys talk about?" I asked.

"*He* talked—about the good old days. About the church where we got married. He said he still has the pictures. It gave me the creeps. I don't want to remember those times."

"How long was he here before I arrived?"

"Maybe ten minutes."

"What do you think he wants?"

"I don't know. I just don't know."

The coffee was almost ready when Richard's car pulled up. He came in, saw me sitting at the table then glanced over at Brenda, and took in her troubled face. "What's wrong?"

"Nothing. Now," she said.

Richard looked at me as he took off his coat, draping it on the back of a chair.

"Brenda had a visitor," I said.

His wary gaze traveled back to her.

"It was Willie. My mother gave him our address."

"And you let him in the house?" Richard yelled, quite uncharacteristically.

"Hey. It's cool. I was here."

"Right when he got here?" Richard demanded.

"No. Just after."

"No offense, Jeff, but from what I heard, you're just some little pipsqueak compared to this guy—he's like a linebacker. Right?"

"I wasn't in any danger," Brenda said.

"Oh, yeah? How many times did he hit you? How many bones did he break?"

I looked at Brenda, my stomach turning. She stared at the floor, on the verge of tears. "Please don't raise your voice, Richard. You sound just like *he* used to."

"I'm sorry. It's just . . . ." He moved to stand beside her, put his arm around her, and spoke gently. "I get so angry thinking about how he hurt you."

She looked up at him and Richard bent down to kiss her. "I'm sorry. Are you all right?"

She nodded. "Jeffy was great. He ran interference for me."

Richard looked over at me and I shrugged. "I don't do so bad. For a pipsqueak."

Brenda cleared her throat. "Who wants tuna for lunch?"

"Sounds good to me," I said, grateful to change the subject.

Brenda headed for the butler's pantry and Richard took a seat at the table, his voice low. "We'll drop this for now, but I want a full report later."

"I'm working tonight."

"Then I'll stop by the bar on my way home from the clinic."

"Suit yourself."

Brenda came back with a large can in hand. "Lunch will be ready in a few minutes."

Tension still filled that kitchen. Somehow I felt like *I* had done something wrong. I hadn't planned on mentioning my earlier adventure, but it seemed like a good distraction.

"I went to see my father this morning."

They both looked at me in wide-eyed surprise. "Great," Brenda said cheerfully, no doubt grateful for a change of subject. "That's great."

"Why?"

"Because you need family. Everyone needs their family."

"I have you guys. I have Maggie." What I wanted to say was, *I don't need any more.*

"How'd it go?" Richard asked, his tone neutral.

I shrugged. "He's a sick old man." I stared at the tabletop for a long moment. "It turns out I have a half-sister, Patty. She was at work."

"That's terrific," Brenda said. Her enthusiasm seemed strained. "When will you meet her?"

"I don't know. I'm not in a hurry."

She looked puzzled. "Why?"

"It's all happening too fast. I need time to get used to all of this."

"Don't take too long. At least, not if you want to get to know Chet. He hasn't got long." The quiet was ominous. Richard stared me straight in the eye. "I mean it, Jeff, he doesn't have much more time."

4

———

As promised, Richard stopped at the bar on his way home from the clinic that night. A lot of neighborhood regulars had dropped in for a few beers before heading home—not a good time for me to chat. I bought Richard a drink and he hung around until there was a lull in the action.

I noticed his glass was empty. "Can I get you another?"

"No. What did you get from Willie?"

So much for small talk. "Not a vibration, not a funny feeling. Nothing. In fact, he was kind of subdued. I know Brenda was afraid, but I get the feeling it'll be okay now."

"No, it won't. She's—" He stopped himself. "She's still pretty upset about it."

I thought about it for a moment. "Maybe you're right. Just thinking about her ex gets Maggie going. I'm the same about mine. You get the gold star as the only one of us without a failed marriage."

Richard's blue-eyed gaze bore into me. "I'll take that as a compliment."

A couple of women came in and I had to get back to work.

Looking grim, Richard gave me a half-hearted wave and headed for the door, looking as gloomy as when he'd arrived.

The happy hour crowd was long gone by nine o'clock. The place was dead, and Tom was about to let me leave when the phone rang.

"It's for you, Jeff."

I frowned. Maggie seldom called me at work, and since Richard had already dropped in, it wasn't likely to be him. "Hello?"

"Jeffrey? It's Patty."

Oh, wonderful.

"Hi. How'd you get this number?"

"You told Dad where you worked. I wanted to connect with you as soon as possible. How the hell are you?"

"Fine," I answered, wary. "How are you?"

"Great, now that I know you're home in Buffalo. I've been waiting my whole life to meet you. When's a good time? How about tonight?"

"I won't get out of work until late," I lied. I'd had enough emotional overload for one day.

"Damn. How about tomorrow? I can stop over at your place on my way home from work."

"It's not exactly on your way," I said, remembering Chet said she worked in Lockport.

"Don't worry about that—I just want to meet you. Is four-thirty good?"

"I suppose so. I live at—"

"Oh, I know the place. Dad's been driving past and swearing at it for years."

I didn't like the sound of that. Had he cased the house years before with the crazy idea of kidnapping Richard?

"I live in the apartment over the garage. There's an entryway on the left side. Just ring the bell."

"I'm sure I'll find it. This is terrific! I can't wait to meet you."

"Me, too," I said without enthusiasm.

"Well, see you tomorrow, brother."

"Bye." I hung up.

Brother.

I wandered back to the bar in a kind of uneasy fog, and automatically started washing the glasses piled by the sink.

"That didn't sound like Maggie," Tom said.

"It wasn't."

"Hmm, inviting a lady over to your apartment?" Something in his tone made me feel sleazy.

"She's my sister."

"I didn't know you had one."

"Until yesterday, neither did I."

I DIDN'T HAVE to tend bar again until Friday. Since Brenda went to the clinic with Richard, I wasn't on call to take her to work. I planned to spend the morning with Sam Nielsen interviewing the protesters in Williamsville. It gave me something to do besides wait for Patty's visit later that day.

Sam met me in the parking lot of a coffee shop a block from the Women's Health Center. We bought coffee to go and started walking. The brisk wind was at our backs and we talked as we went.

"I called Bob Linden's office. He's expecting us," Sam said.

"Why?"

"Showing up unannounced looks sinister. Like everyone in the movement, he's suspicious of the *liberal media.*"

"You don't look like a bleeding heart scumbag," I said.

"I work incognito."

I told him about Brenda's confrontation with the Reverend.

"Better let me do all the talking," he said. He got no argument from me.

Sure enough, Linden was on the lookout for us. Standing a head taller than most of his followers, he looked pretty much the same as when I'd photographed him; well-dressed, respectable—and definitely in charge. The hard glint in his gaze conveyed his stance as a man of uncompromising beliefs—yet my pictures hadn't captured the depth of his commanding presence.

Though several inches shorter than Linden, Sam met his intimidating gaze. He introduced us while I removed the camera's lens cap and snapped a few shots.

Linden listened to Sam, but scrutinized my face. "You walk the black nurse in a couple times a week."

I put the camera down. "So?"

"Why are *you* taking pictures of us?" someone else challenged.

"That's his job, and I'm here to listen to your stories," Sam chimed in.

"Why? So you can brand us as fundamentalist Christian jerks," another man said.

"No—to understand why you're so passionate about your cause," Sam said.

I let Sam take the brunt of their hostility. With notebook and pen in hand, I moved through the crowd to take down the names of people I'd already photographed. Picking the friendliest looking one, I approached the young woman dressed in a baggy green parka. Shoulder-length blonde hair framed her heart-shaped face under a white knit cap. She hefted a sign in one hand, clutched a little girl's mittened-hand in the other.

"I took your picture the other day, Miss. Can I have your name for the newspaper?"

She studied me for a moment before answering. "Emily Farrell." She spelled it for me.

"How often do you come down here to protest?"

"Twice a week."

"And who's this?" I asked the little girl. She clung to her mother's hand, and gazed at me through lowered lashes.

"Hannah's four. Why do you escort that nurse?"

"Because she's afraid of you."

"If she didn't kill babies, she wouldn't have to be afraid."

"She doesn't kill babies. She helps women with health problems."

"Being pregnant isn't a problem."

"For some women it is."

A frown crossed her features.

I didn't like being despised for helping my sister-in-law. "Look, I'm not here to debate the issue. Just to take pictures for the newspaper." I noticed she wore no wedding band. Maybe I could use that.

"I'm sorry," I said, softening my voice. "Would you like a copy of the picture?"

She brightened, suddenly looking all of seventeen. "Really?"

"Sure. I'll bring it next time I come."

I should've just gone on to the next person, instead I pushed my advantage. "My name's Jeff Resnick."

"Hi," she said, and smiled shyly. "You really think they'll use my picture in the paper?"

"Maybe—maybe not. They'll probably use one, maybe a couple of shots for the article—if it makes it to the Sunday paper."

She kept looking at me, an innocent smile playing at her lips. She looked back to the health center. "Is that nurse your girlfriend or something?"

"Just a friend." Emily didn't realize the opening she'd given me—one I took full advantage of. "How about you? Are you married?"

She shook her head.

"Dating?"

"No."

I gave her my most charming smile. "Do you think we could go for coffee or something some time?"

She drew back. "Oh, I don't know."

"Well, think about it."

A looming presence—Linden—entered my peripheral vision. He gave Emily a stern, paternal look.

"I have to get back in line. It was nice to meet you, Jeff." She gave me another shy smile, before she took the little girl's hand. "Come on, Hannah."

"Mommy, my feet hurt."

"Every step you take helps save a baby's life," she said, as she pulled the girl along.

I stood back, watching as she marched along her circular track once more.

Sam nudged my shoulder. "Don't you have a girlfriend?"

"Yeah. But it doesn't hurt to make friends with the enemy."

He smiled. "You would've made a great reporter." He thought better of it. "Then again maybe not. There's no story here, Jeff."

"Of course there is. If you can't come up with anything else, try a financial angle. The other businesses have called the cops a few times. That costs the taxpayers money."

"Get real."

"I'm telling you, Sam, something bad is gonna go down. Somebody's going to get hurt—or worse."

"Can I quote you on that?"

I eyed him warily. "Yes."

. . .

THE MORNING WASN'T a complete loss. I got some shots that promised to be good, while Sam went through the motions of interviewing Linden and several other protesters, as well as the clinic's PR Director. He as much as said he had no intention of writing a story, but it might be useful as background for a future piece.

The clock read one by the time I got home. The entire, endless afternoon stretched before me. I didn't want to get started in the darkroom, so I turned on the tube, tried to turn off my mind and watched Court TV for a couple of hours. But I kept thinking about those protesters, and Emily Farrell's earnest face in particular. I wasn't attracted to her, but her green eyes had a haunting quality. She warranted further investigation.

Restless, I got up and emptied the dishwasher, opened some of the mail, and dusted one of the end tables, but couldn't seem to accomplish anything of note.

A car pulled up outside the garage just after four o'clock. Patty was early. It wasn't the familiar white Mustang in the drive. A tawny-haired woman emerged from the passenger side of the blue sedan. I turned for the stairs and jogged down them to meet her.

Patty's hand was poised to knock as I opened the door. We studied each other for an uncomfortably long moment. It was the face from the high school graduation photo, but older, thinner. Who the hell did she remind me of?

I spoke first. "Hi."

"Hi, yourself." Patty's tentative smile broke into a joyful grin and she lunged forward, hugged me enthusiastically. I stood there, awkwardly put an arm around her, waiting for a flood of emotion to overtake me, but got no insight into her soul. Just like Richard—but unlike our father—she was a blank to me. She pulled back to inspect my face as I scrutinized hers once again.

Shorter than me by two or three inches, there was something about her that—

"You look like pictures of Daddy when he was young," she said.

"I always thought I looked like my mother."

She let that comment slide.

"What about your friend?" I said, indicating the man who sat behind the wheel of the rusting blue Ford. He raised a hand in a half-hearted wave.

Patty didn't even look over her shoulder. "That's just Ray—a guy from work. My car's in the shop for a new computer chip. He said he'd wait." She looked beyond me at the staircase. "So this is it, huh?"

"Not exactly. Come on up."

She followed me up the stairs and stepped into my living room, taking in the ten-foot ceiling, the newly sanded oak floors and refinished trim. Maggie and I had spent the better part of the summer renovating and redecorating the apartment. I closed the door and leaned against it, watching as she took in the place.

"Not bad," she said, admiration filling her voice. "How come you don't live in the big house?"

"I used to. When I was a teenager. And for a few months when I came back to Buffalo. I'd rather have my own space."

She nodded. "Nice little setup you've got."

"Sit down. Do you want some coffee?"

"A beer if you've got it."

I grabbed a Molson Ice from the refrigerator and a glass from the cupboard.

Her voice stopped me from pouring. "The bottle's fine."

I brought it over to her, setting it on a coaster. She rummaged through her purse and took out a pack of cigarettes and a lighter. "Have you got an ashtray?"

"No. My girlfriend has allergies. Even stale smoke makes her sick. I hope you don't mind."

"Oh. Sure," she said, but her expression reflected her annoyance. I'd just fallen a peg. She replaced the items in her bag and set it on the floor.

"I wasn't expecting you for another half hour."

"I skipped out of work early. They won't miss me." She took a swallow of beer, set the bottle down on the cocktail table, ignoring the ceramic coaster. "Dad says your brother's a millionaire." Why did her tone sound cunning?

"I wouldn't say that," I lied. "But he's comfortable."

"A lot more comfortable than me. They've got to have servants and stuff in a big house like that, right?"

I shook my head. "It's just the two of them. A cleaning lady comes a few times a month."

She looked skeptical. "So what's the story? Do you live here for free?"

"Not exactly. I'm sort of the caretaker."

"Does it pay well?"

"I work for my keep."

"I suppose that's not too bad. What do you do?"

"Yard work mostly. If something breaks, I try to fix it. If the cars need an oil change, I get it done."

"I wish I had such a cushy life." Her tone was wistful, with a touch of resentment.

"Did *Dad* tell you I got hurt earlier this year? I can't work full time. At least not yet."

She looked me over again. "What happened?"

"Fractured skull. I get bad headaches. I work when I can, but I can't make it on just that money. I'm grateful for Richard's generosity." Why had I told her all that?

Patty nodded, taking in the apartment once more. Dollar signs lit her eyes and I felt embarrassed for her. Maggie's decorating flair was evident by the prints on the wall, and arrangement of the furniture. We'd refinished my old coffee and end tables and she'd slip covered my crummy couch and chairs.

Patty picked up the bottle, took a long pull on her beer. "So when do I meet Richard?"

"What's the hurry?"

"He's sort of like family. Maybe I can work for him, too."

The hairs on the back of my neck bristled.

The sound of a car engine broke the quiet as another car pulled up outside. Patty got up and moved to the window. I followed and we both gazed down on the driveway to see Richard's silver Town Car.

"Nice wheels," she said.

Richard and Brenda got out of the car and looked up. They saw us and waved. I braved a smile and returned the gesture.

"Who's the jig?" Patty asked

I turned to glare at her. "I beg your pardon?"

"The jigaboo he's with? Is she the maid?"

"That's Richard's wife, Brenda."

"Wife?" She laughed.

"Don't ever call Brenda that again."

She pulled a face. "Sorry." Then she smiled. "Oh, I get it, you'd like a little brown sugar, too, huh?"

"What the hell is wrong with you, Patty?"

She laughed and punched my shoulder. "Can't you take a joke?"

"That wasn't a joke."

She scowled at me. "Dad was right. You *can* be grim. Lighten up. Life's too short to get upset over nothing."

Suddenly, I'd had enough.

"Listen, Patty, I can feel one of my headaches coming on. Maybe you should—"

"They get pretty bad, huh? Do you take drugs?"

"Prescription stuff."

"Do you get high from it?" she asked, eagerly.

"No. Usually I take them and go right to bed," I said, hoping she'd take the hint and leave.

"Too bad."

Was she sorry I got headaches, or sorry I didn't get high from the drugs I took *for* them?

She wandered through the living room again, pausing at the bulletin board over my desk. "Who took all these great pictures?"

"I did."

She leaned closer to study them. They were an eclectic mix of stuff I'd taken over the summer: the historic ships down at the waterfront, the Frank Lloyd Wright houses—even the backyard garden.

"You're really good. Why don't you get a job taking pictures?"

"I've been trying to."

"I've got a friend at the Sears portrait studio. She could probably get you an interview."

"That's not the kind of photography I'm interested in, but —thanks."

She shrugged.

I could've told her about my current project. I could've said so much more. But I didn't. Instead, I rubbed a hand over my temple. "I know you've only been here a short time, but I'm really not feeling well. Maybe we can get together another time."

"Oh. Sure." She chugged the rest of her beer, then set the bottle down. "How about Saturday? We're having kind of a family reunion. You can meet all the cousins. You can bring your camera and take pictures." She smiled sweetly. It probably worked on other men. "I'll call you Friday and let you know the details, okay?"

Not on your life, I wanted to say, but I didn't have the energy.

She rummaged through her purse again, found paper and a pen. "So what's your phone number?"

It was in the book, but I gave it to her anyway.

I walked her to the door, where she hugged me again. Her hair smelled of stale cigarette smoke.

"I'm so glad we finally met, Jeff. I always knew I had a big brother somewhere, I just never knew how to find you. You're everything I always pictured."

I forced a smile. "Thanks, Patty."

"I'll call you soon!"

She gave me a quick wave and started down the stairs.

I closed the door behind her. Good riddance.

As her footfalls faded on the stairs, I moved to the window overlooking the drive. Her friend stood outside the Ford, staring at Richard's house. He looked up, then turned, tossed his cigarette on the drive and crushed it under his heel. Then the two of them got in the car. Soon after, it pulled away.

For a long time I stared at the space where the car had been, trying to figure out what had passed between me and my . . . sister.

That still sounded strange.

I turned back to the coffee table. Grabbing her beer bottle, I placed it with the other empties under my sink. Good. Not a trace of her remained.

Unsettled, I turned and paced the apartment. I caught a glimpse of Richard's house out the window and suddenly craved company. Grabbing my jacket from the closet, I headed down the stairs.

Brenda stood at the sink, rinsing a Boston lettuce for a salad. Richard sat at the kitchen table, hiding behind the morning's sports section, the two of them looking like something out of a sixties sitcom when I burst into the kitchen.

Brenda looked up. "How'd it go?"

I took off my jacket, hooked it over the back of the closest chair. "Terrible. I hate her."

Richard folded the paper, and set it aside. "That's kind of a hasty judgment." He sounded just like Ward Cleaver.

"I don't think so." I looked at the glass in front of Richard. "What're you drinking, scotch?"

"Want one?"

I shook my head. "Got any beer?"

"In the fridge," Brenda said.

Grabbing a bottle of ice beer, I popped the cap, paused, then took a pilsner glass from the cupboard, and took great delight pouring it. Civilized. Like my sister wasn't.

I took a seat at the table.

"Well, what happened?" Richard asked.

"I had to get rid of her." I took a deep swallow. "Told her I had a headache."

"Then you know you shouldn't be drinking that."

"I lied. I just couldn't stand being with her another minute."

"What did she do that was so terrible?" Brenda asked.

"Nothing. It's just that she's so much like—"

I stopped dead as I realized just who Patty reminded me of. "Jesus," I murmured, sat back in my chair and took another long swallow of beer, wishing I'd taken Richard up on his invitation of a scotch.

"Who? Who?" Brenda asked.

"Shelley." My dead ex-wife. "Patty even looks a little like her —at least how she looked toward the end." Memories of those awful days came flooding back. I'd never told them all the crap my wife had put me through those last few months.

"Want to talk about it?" Richard asked, his voice gentle.

I looked into his worried blue eyes. How many times had he asked me that question in the last eight months? How many times had I refused to answer?

"Yeah," I said, half surprised.

"Why does Patty remind you of Shelley?" Brenda asked.

I turned to Richard. "She wanted to know about your money. Chet told her you were a millionaire. I told her you weren't. I don't want her asking you for a handout. If she does—don't give her anything."

"Jeff, first of all, she's not Shelley. I'm sure she wouldn't—"

"You don't know her. Hell, I don't even know her!" I downed the rest of my beer in a gulp, got up and took another from the refrigerator. I cracked the cap. This time I drank from the bottle.

"You're getting all upset over nothing," Richard said.

I let out an exasperated breath, tempted to tell them just what Patty said about Brenda.

No way. I wasn't about to hurt Brenda's feelings.

"What about Shelley and money?" Richard reminded me.

I took my chair at the table. "When Shelley left me, she cleaned out all our joint accounts. Three years we saved. Three goddamned years of brown-bag lunches, renting movies instead of going out. We planned to buy a house in Jersey—have a couple of kids. I really fell for the American dream. The quaint Cape Cod in the suburbs, white picket fence and all. I wanted it —probably because I never had it as a kid."

Anger always accompanied those memories. Or maybe it was betrayal—I was never sure.

"I probably pushed Shelley too hard. I tried to make my dream into hers. Maybe that's why cocaine appealed to her."

Richard looked uncomfortable. He hadn't expected me to spill the whole story. Me either, but I was on a roll.

"After Shelley got arrested, I found a lawyer who specialized in drug cases. He got her off, but it took almost five grand. I was stupid. I believed her when she said she quit using the stuff." God, how I'd wanted to believe her. "But one day I came home from work and the apartment looked like a bomb hit it. I thought we'd been robbed—until I found her note tacked on a cupboard door. She'd taken what she wanted and left. And she warned me not to go looking for her. I paid two hundred and fifty bucks to get the locks changed that night. I didn't know the check would bounce."

"What did you do?" Richard asked.

"I couldn't afford to hire someone, so I took a few days of vacation and found her myself. But I didn't trust myself to see her. I was afraid I'd beat the shit out of her. She was staying with one of her friends from work—the job she'd gotten fired from. I called. At first she hung up on me, but after a few days she told me we were through—that she had a new life. It turned out her new life was selling drugs."

"What did you do?" Brenda asked.

My anger drained. "Nothing. You can't make someone love you. So, I worked. Sometimes eighteen-hour days. I put my heart and soul into that job. That's why I was lost when I got laid off. It kept me from thinking about her and what she'd done. It kept me sane."

"Jeff, I had no idea," Richard said.

"I almost believed I was over her when the cops called me to identify her body." I took a breath to steady myself. The memories were still like acid eating at my soul—like it had happened yesterday. The lump in my throat grew. "The place smelled. Not of formaldehyde or anything, but like . . . death. You could almost taste it."

Brenda inched closer, frowning.

"The cop stood there, watching me as they flashed her picture on the video screen. It was unreal, like something out of a bad movie. There was my beautiful Shelley lying on a gurney."

I took a breath, forced myself to continue. "Because the top of her head was gone, they'd positioned her at an odd angle. They'd cleaned her up, but I was familiar with crime-scene pictures. I could tell it was bone and brains matted in her hair . . . ."

I stared unseeing at the beer bottle's label in front of me, remembering that dreadful scene. "Cops always suspect the husband first. I mean, I did own a gun. But she was shot with a nine millimeter and I owned a thirty-eight. It didn't take them long to figure out what really happened. Technically, I was still her husband—I'd never done anything about a legal separation. I guess part of me hoped she'd come back." I swallowed, trying to quell the anguish mounting inside. "Guess who got to pay for the funeral?" My voice cracked as I thought back to that awful day. The empty chapel—my empty life.

"She had no family that I knew of. I was too ashamed to tell my friends at work. Just me and a priest, and that damned casket—"

I lost it then—hunched over, fighting the tears that prickled my eyes. I couldn't bear to look at them.

Suddenly Brenda was hugging me, bathing me in the warmth of her concern. Richard stood behind me, his hand on my shoulder.

"Why didn't you call us?" he asked. "You didn't have to go through it all alone."

Hindsight. I should've done a lot of things different.

The ticking quartz clock on the wall was the only sound in that silent kitchen. I straightened, cleared my throat, and wiped my face with my sleeve. Brenda squeezed my hand. I still couldn't look at either of them.

"That's why Patty got to me this afternoon. She's just about Shelley's age. She does her hair the way Shelley did. And when she asked me if my medication got me high—" I took a breath, forced myself to continue. "I can't deal with her."

Richard sat down again, looked me straight in the eye. "First of all, she's *not* Shelley. Maybe she was nervous. People say and do dumb things when they're nervous. She's reaching out to you. Isn't there the slightest possibility she could feel something genuine for you? Look at the years *we* wasted."

What he said was true.

Okay, Patty had made a bad first impression. Suppose it was just a case of nerves.

"She invited me to some family thing on Saturday."

"Would it hurt to go for an hour or so?" Richard said.

"I'll bet Maggie would go with you. Or we could go with you for moral support," Brenda offered.

"No. I don't want her to—" *Insult you* was the first thing I thought of. "I don't want her to think she can impose on your generosity."

"Well, we're here for you," Richard said.

"Thanks." That one small word seemed incredibly inadequate for all I felt for them.

"Do you want to stay for dinner?" Richard asked.

I hefted the nearly empty beer bottle. "Yeah, I would."

"It's only chicken," Brenda warned.

I met her warm, brown-eyed gaze. "I love chicken."

She patted my shoulder, got up, and went back to the unfinished salad on the counter.

Richard punched my arm, and gave me an encouraging smile. "You're okay, kid."

That simple gesture made me feel better. No matter what Patty or Chet represented, Richard and Brenda were my family, and I loved them. Even if I couldn't say it out loud.

5

Thanksgiving: just another raw gray day in Buffalo. While the nation hunkered down for parades and college football, I spent a good part of the day outside, winterizing the three cars—filling the washer reservoir with blue stuff, and checking the oil and the tire pressure. To thaw out, I took a leisurely shower and found a pink-cheeked Maggie in my kitchen when I emerged in my bathrobe, with a damp towel draped around my neck. She greeted me with a warm kiss.

"What have you got there?" I asked, peering around her at the grocery bags she'd dumped on my breakfast bar.

"I didn't want the dessert to slide apart in the car so I'm putting it together now."

She gave me another quick kiss, slipped out of her coat, and went straight to work. A milk glass cake stand came first. Then, as if by magic, she produced four layers of chocolate cake.

"It'll be Black Forest cake," she announced.

I settled onto one of the stools at the breakfast bar, watching her fuss, trying to keep a grimace off my face. "I don't like gooey desserts."

"But Brenda and I do. And stop pouting, will you?"

I'm not big into holidays. They had never been a part of my past. But since most of Maggie's family had scattered to various in-laws, she'd been grateful for Brenda's invitation to join them for dinner.

"Have you noticed anything odd with Richard and Brenda?" she asked.

"What do you mean?"

"Something's going on."

"Such as?"

She rolled her eyes theatrically. "God, men are so obtuse. They've been looking at each other and smiling a lot. Doesn't that give you a clue?"

My gut tightened. Why did I feel such unease?

"To tell you the truth, I've been so preoccupied about Chet and Patty I haven't noticed a whole hell of a lot." I thought about it. "Brenda switched to decaf coffee."

"Big deal—I've been bugging her to do that for months."

Maggie sighed and finished putting the cake together, dotting the top with goo-covered cherries. It looked like a picture out of *Gourmet Magazine*, but it wasn't something I wanted to eat.

She looked at me with sympathy. "Don't worry, I made a nice, boring apple pie for you."

"Thanks. We can head over as soon as you're ready."

She rinsed her hands, dried them, then reached for her coat. "I'm ready."

A minute later we'd crossed the driveway and I opened the door, letting Maggie in ahead of me. The house welcomed us. The aroma of roasted turkey was like ambrosia.

Brenda stood at the kitchen counter, slicing carrots. "Come on in," she called. Maggie set the cake down on the counter and stepped forward to give Brenda a hug.

"Gee, you'd think it was months—not days—since you two last saw each other."

"Not to mention the fact they're on the phone for hours at a time," Richard said, entering the room. "Hi, Maggie." He received a peck on the cheek despite his greeting. "Who's thirsty?"

"I am," Maggie said. "Got any sour mix?"

"Whiskey sour it is," he said, anticipating her request.

"Beer for me," I said.

I watched Richard make the drinks, noticing he filled a glass with club soda for Brenda.

"Shall we adjourn to the living room?" Richard asked.

"Sounds good to me."

"I'll catch up in a minute. I want to finish this," Brenda said. Maggie hung back to help her.

I followed Richard, who set his drink on an end table by one of the leather wing chairs. He turned on a couple of lamps while I settled on the far end of the comfortable leather couch.

I sipped my beer and studied my brother's face. "Maggie says something's going on with you two."

"She's very astute."

"You going to tell me?"

His smile was enigmatic. "Not just yet."

I took a sip of beer. I don't like playing games. But this was his party. They'd probably finalized their Christmas vacation plans. Some exotic locale, no doubt.

I cleared my throat. "Are we going to the Bills game next Sunday?" He had season tickets.

"Sure." Richard sat down, took a sip of his drink.

Now what could we talk about?

Richard stared into his drink, looking thoughtful.

"Something wrong?"

"I got a call from an old school friend this morning. He's in private practice in Rochester." He took a sip of his drink.

"And?" I prompted.

He didn't look up. "A colleague of ours from the old days was killed recently. He wondered if I'd heard. The alumni bulletin will probably mention his passing."

I got a queasy feeling in my gut, reminding me of those disturbing dreams I'd been having. "How'd he die?"

"A hunting accident. Marty had a string of bad luck. His son died in a motorcycle accident last spring, then his wife was murdered—apparently in a robbery gone wrong. Jim said Marty had been drinking heavily and quit his job with the state."

Giggles from the hallway distracted me. Richard's face lit up as Brenda entered the room. Maggie placed a tray of veggies and dip on the coffee table, settling beside me. "Dig in," she said.

"It's that sun-dried tomato kind you like," Brenda told me, taking a carrot and gouging some out of the ceramic dish. She perched on the arm of Richard's chair.

I studied the two of them. They looked . . . smug.

"What's going on?" I asked.

Brenda's smile was radiant. "We've known for a while, but we didn't want to say anything." She looked to Richard, who nodded for her to continue. "We're pregnant!"

"I knew it!" Maggie cried and jumped up to hug Brenda.

I sat there, stunned, my stomach knotting.

Pregnant. This announcement didn't bring me joy—but what I felt was more than simple apprehension. The threat of HIV hanging over Richard's head—both their heads.

"Jeff?" Richard prompted.

"I thought you said you guys couldn't have sex. Not even with a condom—until six months after—" That terrible night flashed before my mind's eye. The shotgun blast—all that blood.

Richard, desperate to save a dying man—with no latex gloves to protect his bare hands.

"How?" I asked.

"Brenda laughed. "I must've become pregnant just days before our wedding.

In fact, they'd been married five months, but because of the threat of AIDS, they hadn't yet consummated their marriage. And yet Brenda didn't really look pregnant.

"You could say something positive," Richard said, eyeing me.

"Sorry." I laughed nervously, tipped my beer bottle in his direction. "Congratulations." I stood, reached over to shake his hand. "When?"

"About four months from now," Brenda answered.

"You're almost through the second trimester? If I gain five pounds—I look it," Maggie complained.

Brenda smiled. "Hey, I feel every pound of it." She patted her belly, her baby bump barely noticeable. "Too much can go wrong during those first few months. And because of Richard's situation—" She looked at him, her expression darkening. "I guess I didn't want to say anything to jinx myself."

I choked on my beer as a sick rush of fear coursed through me. Something told me Brenda would never carry her baby to term.

I couldn't stop coughing. Maggie slapped me on the back and Brenda and Richard were on their feet, clucking like concerned medical professionals.

"I'm okay," I rasped, took a few careful breaths and cleared my throat. Richard scowled but said nothing.

"Well, if the rest of us can all swallow our drinks," Maggie said, glaring at me good-naturedly, "I propose a toast. To Baby Alpert. Or should that be Baby Stanley-Alpert?"

"One name is enough," Brenda said. "Alpert."

That made Richard smile.

"May he or she be as happy and healthy as we are tonight," Maggie finished.

"Hear, hear," I said, raised my glass, and hoped to God it would come to pass.

Maggie settled on the couch again. "Have you picked out names?"

"I've been scanning the baby book for months." She laughed. "We've narrowed it down to maybe twenty."

"What room will you use as a nursery?"

"Jeffy's old bedroom," Brenda said.

"Wonderful. I've got scads of ideas for decorating it."

"I've got to check the turkey. Come on in the kitchen and tell me," Brenda said.

Once they left, the silence dragged. I drained my beer, unsure what to say. Subdued, Richard still worked on his Manhattan.

I forced a smile. "So, you're going to be a daddy?"

"Yeah. If I'm still around when the poor kid graduates from high school, I'll be—" He did a little mental arithmetic and frowned. "Oh, God, sixty-seven."

I swallowed the lump in my throat. "I thought Brenda wasn't interested in having children?"

"She wasn't interested in getting married, either. But here we are. It's a natural progression, isn't it?"

"How long have you known?"

"Since September. To tell you the truth, I thought you would've guessed—or rather, gotten one of your funny feelings."

I thought about it for a moment. "I have been getting funny feelings about Brenda. But I never put it all together. Damn slipshod of me."

"This doesn't change anything. I mean, I don't want to lose what we have. I value your friendship." He colored in embarrassment. "I need you—if only to play catch with the kid when I'm too old."

Or if he wasn't there?

I forced a smile. "Thanks." I leaned back against the couch. "First I find out my father's still alive, and I have a sister I never knew about. Now I'm going to have a little niece or nephew. Eight months ago I had no family at all."

"Have you and Maggie thought about getting married?" he asked.

"That's rushing it a bit. Besides, Maggie's not eager to tie the knot again. Besides, I'm not exactly a bargain. I can't support myself, let alone a wife." Maybe I never would.

Richard shrugged. "If she wants a family, time's getting away from her."

"It doesn't matter. She had a hysterectomy three years ago."

"Oh—that's right." He looked genuinely sorry.

"I'm sure she's already plotting how to spoil your kid. Has Brenda told her family?"

"She called her sister, Evelyn, last night. I'm not sure the news was well received. Her mother definitely wouldn't want to know. And since she gave Willie our address, Brenda doesn't want to speak to her anyway."

I shook my head ruefully. "Life's too short for that kind of shit."

"Tell me about it." He was quiet for a moment, then raised his glass. "No more somber talk. This is a celebration. We've— I've—got a lot to live for." He took a sip of his drink.

Richard's forced smile only increased the anchor weight on my soul.

What was I thinking? Thanks to medical science, being HIV-positive was no longer a death sentence. It was a big inconvenience to those who suffered from it, but with the right combination of drugs people like Magic Johnson had survived well into his second decade of good health.

Still, as I raised my empty glass in salute, I looked forward to later when I could go back to my own place, and get blissfully drunk, and not feel so damned responsible for the coming disaster. Because I couldn't get over the feeling that whatever happened to Brenda's baby would somehow be my fault.

Sophie Levin wasn't always home. Late at night I'd drive by the apartment where she lived above a bakery, and the place would be dark. If it wasn't, I'd drop in on my way home from work and share a cup of coffee or hot chocolate and shoot the shit with the elderly woman who'd come to be my friend. Much as I hated the word, I thought of Sophie as my "psychic" mentor. She saw colors—auras the new-age gurus call them. I tapped into others' emotions. But we were kindred spirits.

A quick look at my watch confirmed it was after three. I'd left a sleeping Maggie back at my place and walked the two miles to Sophie's place. As anticipated, the light was on in the shop's back room. I jogged across Main Street and moments later rang the bell. Sophie appeared within seconds.

"I've been waiting for hours," she scolded me. "An old lady like me needs her rest."

I followed her through the retail shop and into the back room where she held court. Two cups of steaming cocoa sat on the scared little card table, along with a plate of macaroons and a sheaf of paper napkins.

"I just put the marshmallows in. See, they're hardly melted."

I pulled off my jacket. "How'd you know I'd come by?"

She smiled. "It's a gift." She sat down and I took the seat opposite. "So. Talk," she said.

I took a sip of cocoa—wishing it was bourbon. "What do you

do when you know something bad will happen to someone you care about?"

She met my gaze, her smile fading. "You couldn't ask an easy question?"

"I'm serious."

Her gaze was grave. "What is it you know?"

I told her about my premonition of death for Brenda's baby, and the bad feelings I had about the Williamsville Women's Health Center.

"Losing a child is probably the worst thing a woman can experience," she agreed.

I thought about my mother. Losing Richard had just about destroyed her. But he'd been a living child.

"You could tell your brother," Sophie said, "but it won't do any good." She shook her head sadly. "People don't like hearing bad news. They blame you, when you have no control of the future. I tried so many times to warn people—to help. They resent you. Some hate you for it."

"I was hoping you'd tell me something positive."

"You know what you know. All you can do is be there and be strong for her—and your brother. Because they will be devastated."

I got up, paused at the doorway, and looked through the shop to the bakery's empty parking lot beyond. "I don't know how or when it'll happen. She could trip over a stair, have a miscarriage—it could be stillborn for all I know. I just know there isn't going to be a baby."

"Then you must keep her safe, and be there for her when she needs you. *You* can give her hope."

I let out a sigh. "There's a danger at that health center. But I'm not sure what."

"Then perhaps your brother is right. She should just stop working there."

"She won't."

"She'd believe you if you told her what's to come. She knows about these things."

"Even if she knows, nothing she or I can do will change the outcome. There will be *no* baby." I let out a breath. "Maybe that's what I really came here to talk about—fate." I turned back to face her. "There's nothing I can do to stop what's going to happen. It's not my fault. Why do I have to suffer with it? Why do I even have to know?"

Sophie toyed with the paper napkin by her cup. "You must believe that you *can* make a difference. And sometimes you have to try to change the world, even when you know you will fail. Otherwise, the cost would be your soul."

"I don't understand."

She pursed her lips. "I was safe, here in this country. I had my husband, my children. But I knew war would tear my homeland apart. My family sacrificed so that I could go back to Poland to bring my parents to America. I wanted to keep them safe, even though part of me knew it was hopeless. Once there, I couldn't leave. I couldn't save them from their destiny. My father died of dysentery in the camp. My mother . . . she died from the gas. They threw her naked body into the oven. This I saw—and more. Yet I was spared." Her voice cracked as tears filled her eyes.

"It took six years for me to come home to my children, my husband, but my life was never the same, never as good. I tried to save my parents and lost a part of myself."

Her voice broke—her anguish tearing at me. She stared at nothing, cleared her throat and continued.

"I always wondered . . . did I wait too long to go? Could I have made a difference some other way? Were their deaths easier because I was with them—or did I make it harder because they never knew I survived?"

"I'm so sorry," I murmured.

"There was a purpose," she said, nodding vigorously. "I survived. I helped others survive. My own mission failed, but a greater good came out of it. I have to believe that—and you must, too." Her brown eyes pierced me. "Family is *everything*, Jeffrey. Do what you must to protect those you love. *All* those you love."

Her words filled me with apprehension—and determination. "I will. I swear."

I AWOKE the next morning feeling surly. I couldn't decide if my migraine was the usual post-fractured-skull type or that tumbler of Mr. Jack I'd had after talking with Sophie.

Maggie knows I'm no fun under those conditions. After a make-shift breakfast of toast and tea, she left with a feeble excuse about a shopping date with her sister.

To make it to work later that day, I needed to get rid of the pain in my skull. I swallowed a couple of pills, heading back to the bedroom when the telephone shrieked.

"Jeffrey? It's Patty."

The last person I wanted to talk to. "Oh. Hi."

"Are you okay? You sound funny."

"Just another one of my headaches."

"Do you think you'll be better by tomorrow?"

"Tomorrow?"

"Yeah, Aunt Ruby's having a party, remember? We all want you to come."

Oh. That party. Richard's warning about my father's health had finally sunk in. I realized I had a lot of unanswered questions I wanted—needed—to ask before he died. Much as I didn't want to go . . . .

"Okay. Where and when?" I jotted down the address and the

time. "Can I bring my girlfriend?"

"Oh, sure. The more the merrier. Bring your brother Richard if you want."

A flicker of annoyance coursed through me.

"I'm so glad you'll be there," Patty continued. "It means a lot to Dad. Now, don't forget to bring your camera."

"I'll see you tomorrow."

I hung up, stared at the note on the pad, trying to decide what kind of impressions I'd received.

None.

My head ached and I crawled back to bed to hide from it in sleep.

THAT EVENING, the bar was filled with men whose wives or girlfriends had spent the day shopping, leaving them to watch football games on the tube. Escaping from leftover turkey, they scarfed up happy hour wings and pizza.

It was another early evening—only midnight—when I got home. I showered, sat in my robe in front of the tube with a beer, letting myself unwind with CNN. It must've been a slow news day. My eyes glazed over during an item on the state of the Japanese yen. I dozed off, but when I awoke with a start a couple hours later, the same financial clip was playing. Though groggy with sleep, I had a vague feeling something was wrong.

The clock on the wall read three twenty one. My back ached, either from standing for hours behind the bar or lying scrunched on the couch. I got up, stretched, and wandered into the kitchen, trying to pin down the feeling of unease. I put the empty beer bottle under the sink, went back into the living room and looked out the window toward Richard's house where lights glowed. The place had been dark when I'd gotten in from work.

I grabbed the phone and dialed.

"What the *hell* do you want?" Richard demanded, before it even rang once.

"I saw all the lights on. What's up?"

He exhaled loudly. "Sorry. Some prankster's been calling and hanging up. Calling and breathing. I was about to unplug the damn phone."

"Have you pissed off anyone lately?"

"No. At least I don't think so."

"It's probably just a kid fooling around. Is Brenda all right?"

"Just frazzled—like me. Why would anyone do this?"

"Do you think maybe Brenda's ex—?"

His voice grew cold. "I thought of that, too. Caller ID said it was a blocked call."

The answer seemed simple. "Forward your calls to me."

"What good will that do?"

"You'll get some peace and maybe I'll pick up something from the caller."

"Did you ever get anything over the phone before?"

"No. But there's always a first time. And if it's an emergency with one of your patients, I'll come over and get you. Okay?"

"I'd appreciate it."

"Don't sweat it. Now hang up and do the magic with the phone."

"Okay." There was a sharp click. About a minute later, the phone rang. "It's me," Richard said.

"Okay, it should be set. Go back to bed and I'll see you tomorrow, okay?"

"Thanks again, Jeff."

"Go to bed." I hung up the phone.

Wide awake and restless, I wandered the apartment, wondering if the phone would ring. I grabbed a writing tablet, my box of contact prints, and settled on the couch to sort through the photos.

I studied the shots I'd taken a week before outside the Women's Health Center, remembering that I still hadn't gotten back to the darkroom to process the last roll. One shot in particular looked interesting. Though taken on an overcast day, I figured I could burn in the clouds and—

The phone's jangle broke the silence. The clock read three forty six. The phone rang again before I grabbed it. The caller breathed loudly, in an exaggerated way. I shut my eyes, willing myself to connect with the person on the other end of the line.

Long seconds passed.

Was that muffled traffic in the background? Caller ID gave me a number, which I jotted down.

Heavy breathing isn't an original idea. I did likewise and the sound abruptly stopped. The connection broke.

I hung up the receiver, grabbed the tablet and pen, wrote down the time and approximate length of the call. A good investigator writes down everything. That I was no longer an investigator hadn't dulled my instincts or training.

I sat back, thinking. No insight, not that I'd really expected any. But it bothered me that someone was playing this prank on my brother.

Could it be Willie Morgan? After twelve years, was the man petty enough to aggravate the woman who'd left him? I thought back to our brief meeting. I'd gotten no impressions, intuition—whatever you want to call it—from him, either. Was that why the call had given me no insight, or was the telephone a poor conductor? One thing was certain, I could never work for a psychic hotline.

I puttered around the apartment for another hour, but the phone didn't ring again.

It was nearly five when I finally hit the sack, hoping I wouldn't be plagued with dreams of the dead, white-haired old man.

6

———

"I don't think those calls were a prank."

Richard looked up at me from his seat at the kitchen table. The phone book was open before him. A pad with notes scribbled on it sat beside it.

"Here's what I got last night." I plucked a sheet of paper from the large Kraft envelope I held, and gave it to him. "Mind if I bum a cup of coffee? I'm out."

"Help yourself. How many calls did you get?"

"Just one." I got a mug from the cabinet and poured the coffee, took a sip and remembered they'd switched to decaf.

I explained what I'd heard in the background the night before. "I'd guess each was made from different public phones. The phone company should be able to verify that Monday. That could make it hard to pin down the bastard."

Richard's grim expression hardened as he stared at the paper.

"Take a look at this," I said and tossed him the envelope.

He sifted through the stack of photographic prints—duplicates of those I'd given Sam Nielsen, only these had Post-It notes identifying each person. I told him what I was up to—and why.

"I appreciate you looking into this, Jeff."

"No sweat."

He cleared his throat. "Are you available Monday morning? I need another favor."

"Sure, what?"

"Unless they can get someone to cover for me, I have to be at the clinic every day this week. But I've called a couple of companies for estimates on security systems for the house. We're probably the last holdout on the street."

He was right. Every other home in this expensive neighborhood boasted a sign for the firm protecting it from mayhem.

"Has this got anything to do with those calls last night?"

"Everything. That and the fact Brenda's ex is in town. What do you think?" He looked like he expected an argument.

"It's a good idea. Amherst may be one of the safest towns in America, but why take chances? I could handle the whole thing for you—it would be a piece of cake."

"Thanks. I don't care what it costs. I want Brenda to feel safe here at home. I'm also getting an unlisted number. Now all I have to do is get her to quit that job. She respects your opinion. Do you think you could talk to her about it?"

"Sure. But I doubt she'll listen." I studied his guarded expression. "She's worried about you, you know—besides the crap that's already hanging over your head."

"Making sure she's safe is more important than anything I've got going."

I wondered if I should push him for a better explanation, but he looked like he didn't need another problem right then.

While I drained his coffee pot, we discussed various security options. It stroked my ego to know he trusted my judgment.

"In the meantime, do you think Maggie would let us borrow her dog? Just until we get a system installed," Richard said.

I thought about Maggie's Golden Retriever. "Holly's not what I'd call guard dog material. Guard your refrigerator maybe."

"She'll bark—that's all we really need," he said.

"It's a good idea. Sometimes the best security system *is* a dog." I considered the extra yard work that accompanied a large dog—which would be my responsibility.

He closed the phone book, and put it back on the counter as Brenda came in with a stack of mail. "Hey, Jeffy, what's new?"

"Looks like I got suckered into going to that party tonight."

"The one Patty told you about?" she asked, sorting through the envelopes and opening one.

"Yeah. I'd rather have a tooth pulled."

Richard smiled. "You'll survive."

Brenda stared at the paper in her hand, suddenly radiating tension.

"Is something wrong?" I asked

She frowned. "Look at this." She handed me a creased sheet. A chill ran through me as I studied the one-word message in large type: YOU.

Richard sidled closer, his expression darkening. "Who was it addressed to?"

"Me, I guess." She handed him the envelope. It said: Brenda Alpert.

"But that's not your name," he said.

"Whoever sent it obviously didn't know she kept her maiden name."

"What do you think it means?" Brenda asked.

"I don't know. But I don't like it."

"Me, either," Richard agreed.

I studied the cheap business-sized envelope that could have been purchased in just about any store. A Buffalo postmark canceled the stamp. No return address, of course. The note looked like standard twenty pound copier paper. The font was common, from a computer laser printer, also standard in any office. Neither the note nor envelope gave me any kind of impressions. Damn.

"If you get another one of these, wear latex gloves to open it," I warned her. "Just in case there're any fingerprints." Or Anthrax, or some other nasty substance manic pro-lifers have sent to pro-choice doctors and nurses in the past.

"Do you think this could be something serious?"

"I don't mean to scare you, love, but yes, I do."

She stared at the sheet of paper, chewed at her lower lip. "Why would somebody do this?"

"It's that damn health center you work at. Those protesters are dangerous," Richard said.

"We all know your opinion on that subject," she said.

"Well, now will you take it seriously? These nuts have targeted clinic staff before."

"Not in a long time." She turned away from him. "Jeffy, should we call the police?"

"Right now you haven't got enough that'll interest them. They'd rather wait until someone gets hurt before they waste valuable tax dollars on protection. But I'd definitely tell your supervisor at the clinic. You're probably not the first to get a note like this."

She nodded and I felt her tension ease. Apparently being a singular target was more frightening than sharing that privilege. But how did the protesters know her husband's name? And if they did, would using it divert suspicion from them? Or was Willie Morgan playing games?

"Brenda, why don't you call Maggie, ask her about the dog. Maybe she'd bring her over this afternoon," Richard suggested.

"Okay," Brenda said, forcing a smile. "I'll call from the phone in the living room—this could be a marathon session and I may as well be comfortable."

"I have to go out for a while," Richard said. "Will you be okay for a couple of hours?"

"Sure."

"Don't open the door to anyone while I'm gone, okay?" She nodded, gave him a quick kiss, and headed down the hall.

I waited until she was out of earshot before speaking. "You've got a stand-up lady, there, Rich."

"I know. Come on, let's take a ride."

"Where to?"

"First the Women's Health Center. I don't want to wait 'til Monday to find out if other staff members have received one of these letters. Then I want to pay a visit to Mr. Willie Morgan."

"It's an awful big city. How do you plan to find him?"

"We can start at the Bison's main office downtown."

"On Saturday of a holiday weekend?"

"Why not? He's new in town. What else has he got to do?"

"All right. But we're only going to talk to him, right? We're not going to accuse him of anything. We're going to stay nice and calm."

"Of course."

I scrutinized his blue-eyed gaze, unsure I believed him.

THE WILLIAMSVILLE WOMEN'S HEALTH CENTER was about to close for the day when we arrived. Their head of Security, Tim Davies, remembered me from our talk a few days earlier. He hadn't heard of other employees receiving similar letters, but he took the implied threat seriously and copied the letter for their harassment file. Richard promised to keep him posted.

The ballpark was located on the opposite side of the city. The holiday shopping season was officially underway. It seemed like all of Buffalo had hit the road, heading for the malls. The stop-and-go traffic didn't help my rising anxiety. Confronting

Willie might not be smart, but I couldn't blame Richard for wanting to protect his wife—especially now.

Richard stared pensively out the car window, his face a concentrated frown. I can't read him at all, but I didn't need empathic insight to know his anger was building.

"Rich, this doesn't feel right."

He looked at me across the bench seat. "What am I supposed to do, let someone hurt or kill Brenda? That letter's proof she's being targeted, not me."

"You can't exactly call it a campaign of terror. I mean, it only started last night. And we don't have any proof it's Willie. Not even circumstantial evidence."

"I realize that. But if we don't at least ask—"

"*We* shouldn't ask. I should. I'm trained to do this. You shouldn't even be there—you're too upset."

"Don't you think I have a right to be?"

"Yes. But we don't want to antagonize someone with a history of violent behavior."

"I don't intend to antagonize him."

"Oh, yes you do."

Richard turned his guilty gaze back out the window.

We drove the rest of the way in stony silence.

I parked the car in the ramp garage closest to the stadium. The place was nearly empty, although prominently parked near the exit on the first level was the blue Nissan Altima with Pennsylvania plates.

"You were right," I said, pointing the car out to Richard. "Now all we have to do is get into the office."

We headed down the sidewalk toward the stadium's main entrance. Not being much of a baseball fan, I'd never been to Dunn Tire Field, although Richard and Brenda had gone to several games over the summer. The place seemed deserted. Dried leaves, styrofoam cups, wadded fast-food wrappers and other trash had blown against the grandstand's locked gates.

"This way," Richard directed.

As expected, the doors to the business offices were locked, but the lights were on inside. Richard hammered on the glass until he got someone's attention.

"We're closed," the woman mouthed. She pointed to the office hours stenciled on the door.

"We're here to see Willie Morgan," I said. I had to repeat myself several times, but eventually the woman understood. She unlocked the door, ducked her head outside.

"Is he expecting you?"

"No. But it's important."

She considered it for a moment. "Wait here. I'll get him." She locked the doors once more and disappeared down an aisle.

I shoved my hands into my jacket pockets, stared at the floor, trying to figure out a tactful way to approach the impending conversation.

Richard tapped the glass with his knuckle, and pointed to the equipment at the receptionist's station. "Here's proof he's got access to a computer and laser printer."

"So have about a million other people in Erie County."

Richard ignored me, and strained to see down the aisle.

A minute later, Willie appeared from around the corner and unlocked the doors.

"Let me do the talking," I reminded Richard.

Willie gave us the once-over. If anything, he looked several sizes larger than when I'd met him days earlier. And he had to be at least two inches taller than Richard.

"Jeff, right?"

"Yeah."

His gaze went to Richard, instantly sizing him up. "You must be Brenda's husband. What can I do for you?"

"This is kind of an awkward situation," I explained. "But Brenda's been—"

"She's not hurt, is she?" Willie asked, concerned.

"Now why would you think that?" Richard demanded.

I raised my hand to stave off more comments. "No, but she's being bothered. Telephone calls. Threatening letters." It sounded silly—even to me. What the hell were we even doing talking to the guy on such flimsy evidence?

"Are you accusing me?" Willie asked.

"Of course not," I said.

"Maybe," Richard said over me.

"Now wait a minute," Willie started, "I've only been in town a week."

"And the harassment started after you got here. Isn't that a coincidence?" Richard taunted.

"Richard!" I glared at him, but he didn't back down. I tried again, struggling to hold onto my patience. "Mr. Morgan— Willie, we know that you and Brenda didn't part under the best circumstances, and—"

"Did Brenda ask you to come here?"

"No."

"And she wouldn't, either. Look, I've done nothing wrong. I visited an old friend. That's all."

"How can you call yourself a friend after what you put her through?" Richard challenged.

Willie's gaze was menacing. "I think you'd better leave — now. Before I call the police."

"I'm the one who should be calling the police!"

Willie stepped forward, pointed his finger in Richard's face. "I know about rich folk like you. Think you can shove everybody around—take what you want. You got money and now you got my woman."

"Brenda divorced you years before she even met me. Your

former woman is now legally my wife. And she's carrying my child," he threw in as fuel for the fire.

"I'm surprised you got it in you, old man."

I grabbed Richard's arm as he drew back to throw a punch. "Let's not get crazy," I said, hauling him away. Willie could've pulverized us without breaking into a sweat. I wasn't used to playing the sane, rational brother. This role reversal was downright scary. "Rich, why don't you wait for me downstairs."

Richard glared at Willie for endless seconds. I'd never seen such fury in him. Finally he tore his gaze away, stalked over to the exit, let the fire door slam.

I turned back to the angry man. "Sorry, Willie. My brother's a good man. He loves Brenda and he's worried someone's trying to hurt her."

Willie exhaled a long, deep breath. "Yeah, well, I guess I can understand that. She's a very special lady."

I offered him my hand. "No hard feelings?"

He frowned, but we shook on it anyway.

"Sorry to have bothered you," I apologized again.

He nodded, looked back at the door where Richard had disappeared, then turned, went back into the office. I watched as he locked the doors, then vanished into the corporate land-scaping.

I stepped off the elevator, but Richard wasn't around. None of the bars in the area looked open this early, so I headed back for the parking garage. Sure enough, Richard leaned against the passenger side of my car, an air of defeat surrounding him. I opened the doors and we got in.

I paid the parking attendant and drove off before Richard finally spoke.

"Sorry, Jeff. I don't know what came over me back there."

"It's okay. I probably would've done the same thing in your

shoes. Of course you realize we're no closer to knowing who's behind all this."

"That's what's making me crazy."

"You can't afford to be crazy. Brenda needs you. Besides," I said, lightening my tone. "I'm just some little pipsqueak, remember? I can't keep bailing your ass out of trouble from giants like Willie."

"Am I ever going to live that down?"

"Unfortunately, we failed to consider the piss-off factor. If Willie is the one bothering Brenda, our visit could provoke him into something more dangerous."

"And if it isn't him?"

"Then we've annoyed an innocent man, and we've still got a problem." I made a right, palming the wheel. "It doesn't even have to be someone she knows. Someone could've just picked Brenda at random. It happens."

"Do you think Willie's responsible?" he asked pointedly.

"I don't know. I don't get any kind of vibe, aura—whatever from him."

Richard looked even more depressed.

"What next?" I asked.

"Go home. I don't like leaving Brenda alone. Besides, you need to get ready for your family reunion."

"*You're* my family."

"Don't be so negative. Sometimes you have to leave your comfort zone."

"Now you sound like some corporate asshole."

"Thanks. I needed to hear that."

"Admit it, bro," I said. "It's a shitty day, and it ain't going to get better."

"Let's go home," I said to Maggie, as I parked the car behind a rusty Toyota in front of my Aunt Ruby's house.

"You made it this far," she said.

I switched off the engine and looked at the well-tended, white frame house with its neatly pruned shrubs. Though located in one of Buffalo's older neighborhoods, it had never fallen into decay. Cars lined the narrow driveway and were parked along the road in front.

"What if it's smoky? You know how your allergies—"

"I took an antihistamine before I left home." She studied my face. "Come on, Jeff, what's the worst that can happen?"

I thought about it for a moment, remembering Patty's tacky comment about Brenda. "You'll judge me by them."

She frowned. "I'm not that shallow—and I doubt these people are out to hurt you."

I looked away. I'd changed my clothes three times before deciding on a sweater and Dockers. No point trying to impress anyone, this crowd probably knew I was only a bartender. But then, I doubted there'd be any nuclear scientists present, either.

I faced Maggie. "I don't know what I think."

"Then turn it around—what's the best thing that can happen?" she said.

I thought about it for a moment. "Maybe . . . I might like them."

Maggie reached for my hand, squeezed it. "Come on."

She opened the car door and got out. I hesitated. Like confronting Willie, this felt wrong. But I grabbed my camera and slipped out of the car anyway, took Maggie's hand and led her to the house. Although it wasn't quite dark outside, all the lights were ablaze. To anyone else the place would've looked friendly, welcoming.

I climbed the concrete steps and rang the bell. In seconds the door swung open, banging into the wall behind it. "Yeah?" said a breathless boy of about ten.

"I'm Jeff Resnick, and—"

"Gramma!" He took off, letting the storm door slam in our faces.

An elderly woman padded to the door. Her hair was dyed a brilliant shade of red—much too bright for her age of seventy-five or more. Thick cherry lipstick covered her lips, complementing her floral print dress and pink slippers. "Jeffrey? My God, you haven't changed a bit!" she squealed. "Come in, come in!" She ushered us inside and kissed me on the cheek. "Remember me? I'm your Aunt Ruby, Chet's younger sister."

"Sorry. I'm afraid I don't."

"Don't worry. You'll have plenty of time to get to know me and the rest of the family." She touched Maggie's arm. "Now, who are you, dear?"

"This is my girlfriend, Maggie Brennan."

"My, what a lovely dress. Did you get it out of the Penney's catalog? They have the nicest clothes." She didn't give Maggie a chance to answer, but took our coats and disappeared into a room off the hall.

We waited in the entryway, taking in the small living room. Its pastel pink walls were sweating with condensation, seeming to glow in the incandescent light. The couch and every chair was occupied, with people engaged in lively conversation. I gave a self-conscious nod to those who'd noticed our arrival. One of them I recognized: the guy who'd driven Patty to my place a few days earlier.

Ruby reappeared and turned toward the kitchen. "Everybody. Chet's boy is here!" She grabbed my arm and tugged me along.

Maggie and I were paraded in front of a long succession of cousins, aunts, uncles, and old family friends. I tried, without success, to attach a name to every face. My fears about being on display were vastly overblown. Dinner was a bigger priority.

With no dining room, chairs were pushed back, making room for a folding table set up in the living room. Older ladies fussed with food preparation, setting out dishes and bowls. A haze of steam and cigarette smoke filled the kitchen, and I tried to hurry the introductions to steer Maggie clear. When I mentioned Maggie's allergies to Ruby, she guided me to the family room tacked on at the back of the house, which was kept smoke-free for Chet's sake.

My father sat huddled in a recliner in the corner, looking like a sad, sick Jabba the Hut, still tethered to his little green oxygen tank. Ruby plunked me in a folding chair next to him, handed me a bottle of no-name beer.

"Did you have a nice Thanksgiving?" a plump old lady asked me before I could even greet the old man. I'd met her less than three minutes before and couldn't remember her name or her relationship to me.

"Uh, yes, thank you. And you?"

"The turkey was very dry this year." She risked a glance at Ruby across the room, lowered her voice. "Some people don't know what a baster is."

I nodded, not knowing what else to say.

"I'll get you a plate, Chet." She patted my father's hand, then waddled off in the direction of the kitchen.

I glanced at my father. His skin tone was ashen, his lips were a blue line: oxygen starvation. "How're you feeling?"

He shrugged. "Not good. But I'm still here." He studied me, and slowly a smile crept across his puffy, wrinkled face. He held out his hand and I took it. Cool and dry, his grip was surprisingly firm. He held on tight, and I was flooded with a relentless fatigue. And yet, the old man felt happy because I'd come to his family's party. Tears filled his eyes—and suddenly mine, too. But they were his tears—I was just a mirror of his emotions.

I disentangled my hand, patted his arm and turned away.

Maggie caught my eye and bent low. "Overloaded?" she asked.

I couldn't catch my breath, and nodded dumbly.

She smiled. "You'll live."

I wished I could be so cavalier.

"You must be Maggie," the old man said.

She reached over to shake his hand.

"You're very pretty," he said.

Her smile was genuine. "Thank you."

"Are you going to marry my son?"

I nearly choked on my beer. "Hey—!"

Maggie smiled. "So far he hasn't asked me." She looked at me speculatively. "How 'bout it, sport?"

"I—I hadn't thought about it yet today."

She leaned toward my father. "You just scared him silly."

The old man laughed and started to cough.

"Jeffrey!"

Patty shouldered her way through the crowd, with a beer bottle clutched in her hand. I stood, taking in her dark velvet slacks and the low-cut, clingy, gold lamé blouse that accentuated the contour of her full breasts. I felt like a pervert for noticing. She was my sister, after all.

She hugged me. This time she smelled like perfume, cigarette smoke, and beer. "Glad you made it."

"Patty, this is my friend Maggie."

"Hi, nice to meet you." She gave me the once-over, saw the camera beside me on the floor. "Oh good, you brought it. Take lots of pictures tonight. Can you do a portrait of me?" she said, showing off her profile.

"They're not my specialty, but—"

"Dad, you should see the pictures in Jeff's apartment. They are the best."

"Thanks," I murmured.

Patty tipped back her beer bottle, paused, squinted at it. "Damn. Empty. Are you ready for another?" she asked me.

"I'm fine."

"The food's getting cold!" Ruby called from the kitchen.

"I'll be right back," Patty said.

Chet shook his head, his mouth drooping as he watched her stagger back to the kitchen. "She drinks too much."

"She's young yet," I defended her, instantly wondering why. Maybe because the old man looked so worn out. Like he saw his daughter on a collision course with a bad fate and was unable to steer her away from a danger he knew too well.

"Who was the woman that went to get your dinner?" I asked, changing the subject.

"My sister. Your Aunt Vera."

"Do you have any brothers?"

He shook his head. "You're the last of the Resnick line, boy. When are you going to have kids?"

Not any time soon. I just shrugged.

Vera returned with a plate of food, and set it on Chet's lap. "You'd better get something to eat before it's all gone," she advised us.

I looked back toward the kitchen, where Patty motioned us to join her. "We'll be right back."

Most of the family sat on folding chairs at the table in the living room, while another group crowded around the kitchen table. Bowls and serving dishes heaped with meat and vegetables covered the worn Formica counter, buffet style. Several cakes stood waiting to be cut for dessert. We served ourselves and rejoined Chet in the family room. Vera had set up TV trays that wobbled precariously but made a better table than would a lap.

Patty joined us, followed by her friend, Ray. He settled on a folding chair, with his plate on his lap. Patty set another beer down for me, sucking back one of her own. She ignored the half-empty plate on the tray before her. My father had no appetite either. He shoved the plate of food away, and leaned back in the recliner.

Conversation stayed at a minimum. Ray didn't join in, but alternately stared at me, my father and my sister. It was probably just my imagination.

"Mr. Resnick, tell me what Jeff was like as a child," Maggie said at last.

The old man quirked a smile. "He was a good kid. Almost never cried. He never woke me up at night. Not like this one." He jerked a thumb in Patty's direction.

"Mom said I had colic," she whined.

"What else?" Maggie prompted.

His face screwed up in thought. "For a while he used to sing some damn ABC song—all day long. Thank God that didn't last."

Maggie beamed and I felt my face flush.

Chet's smile faded, and a far-away look entered his eyes. "But he didn't laugh much, either."

"Still doesn't," Patty said, and took another swallow of beer.

"Eh . . . we didn't have a very happy home," Chet admitted.

A fragment of memory flashed.

My mother and father, screaming at each other, me crawling behind the couch to get away. Hands pressed tightly over my ears, I'd curled into a ball of fear, willing myself to just disappear.

After the yelling came—

My hand tightened around the beer bottle.

I didn't want to remember any more.

"He didn't even play with his toys much," Chet continued. "We took him to some fancy doctors 'cause someone told Betty he was probably autistic, but they said he was okay. Just a quiet kid. Doctors told us we should be grateful."

Yeah, a quiet kid, who even as a toddler had known not to rock the boat. Because if you did, you'd hear that voice that could cut you down to nothing. That could—

The anger flared anew. I couldn't look at the old man, feeling cowed—like I was as a kid again. More embarrassing was talking about it in front of strangers—Ray and Patty. Hell, except for Maggie, they were all strangers.

"Can't we change the subject?" The edge to my voice was unmistakable, the silence that followed was awkward.

"So where did you get the nice camera, Jeffrey?" Patty asked.

"My brother, Richard, got a new one, so he gave me this one."

"Why didn't he buy *you* a new one?" Chet demanded. "He can afford it."

I felt an unreasonable need to defend my brother. "He wanted something digital. I used to have one just like this, but it was stolen."

"Jeff's sold some of his pictures to a magazine," Maggie said.

"Then why are you still a bartender?" Chet accused.

"It takes time to build a new career," Maggie answered for me.

The anger I'd never been allowed to show as a child threatened to erupt. Who were these people to judge me? To judge Richard?

"Take pictures now," Patty said. She smoothed her hair and plucked at her blouse.

I didn't want to take any pictures of *her*, yet I couldn't see a graceful way out of it. I picked up the camera and attached the flash, glad to hide behind it.

"How do I look, Dad?" she asked.

The old man gazed at her with pride. "Like my little princess."

I snapped a couple of shots, started to put the camera away.

"We have to have a family photo," Patty insisted. "Just the three of us. Maggie can take it."

"I'd be glad to," she said, reaching for the camera.

I hesitated, but reluctantly handed it over. Patty and I perched on opposite arms of the old man's recliner.

"Lean in closer," Maggie instructed, looking through the viewfinder. "Closer."

I reached out a hand to steady myself against the back of Chet's chair, unwilling to touch him. His very proximity drained my soul, dragging me to depths I hadn't visited in thirty-two years.

"Say cheese!" Maggie encouraged.

"Whiskey," Patty said, and I forced a smile. The flash momentarily blinded me. "Take another," Patty said.

Maggie cocked the shutter, advancing the film, then waited for the flash to light ready. "Nice big smiles!"

Take the fucking picture, I mentally ordered.

Why was that damned Ray staring at us so intently?

Ruby and Vera had seen the flashes and bustled into the room, demanding to get into the act. I suffered through several more shots until Maggie finally surrendered the camera and I could lose myself in a familiar task.

Patty dragged me into the living room and I ended up shooting the rest of the roll on the assembled relatives, with Patty promising prints to people I didn't even know. She enjoyed being the life of the party, a feat I'd never been able, nor wanted, to accomplish. Her laugh was golden—she basked in the attention.

It took twenty minutes to extricate myself from the crowd. Now that they'd eaten, my cousins had more questions for me. Part of me would rather have spoken with my father—I had a lot of questions, although I wasn't really sure I wanted to know the answers.

By the time I got back to the family room, Chet was dozing in his chair, his rattling breath uncomfortable to hear. I set my camera down and faded into the background, nursing a warm beer, letting Maggie take up the conversational slack. I half-listened, smiling when appropriate, but not actively participating. Ray had finally wandered off, probably bored.

I stared at my father, trying to remember him as he used to be. Fragments of memories drifted into my mind—fuzzy faces and indistinct events that hadn't entered my thoughts in years. Yet I hesitated to embrace them. All these years later it was still all too painful.

I vaguely noticed Patty in the background. Her voice was getting shrill, her laugh became a cackle. My half-drunk beer suddenly tasted sour. I set it aside.

Ruby glanced toward the kitchen, and looked distressed. "I think Patty's had a little too much to drink."

"Eileen and Michael said they'd take Chet home and get him settled. It's on the way," Vera said.

"Does this happen often?" I asked.

Ruby nodded, lips pursed. "I'm afraid so."

An embarrassing silence fell among us, as though we shared in a conspiracy.

Chet woke from his uneasy doze, his watery gaze settling on me. He managed a smile. "Still here."

Did he refer to me or himself?

Chet straightened in the chair but his breathing didn't ease.

"Can I get you anything?" I asked.

He shook his head and a coughing spasm overtook him. Ruby was instantly at his side, steadying him as she rubbed his back. He couldn't seem to catch his breath, the choking noises growing—his distress radiating like a smothering blanket. My own unease verged on panic. Suddenly there wasn't enough air in the room.

Then Maggie stepped in front of me, and took my hand. Her calm, blue-eyed gaze, and the tranquil she projected, was a counterforce against the anxiety building inside me. She smiled, squeezed my hand, and my breathing eased. She edged closer and pushed me away from my father.

A gaggle of relatives surrounded the old man, deciding it was time for him to leave. Vera pushed through the crowd, Chet's coat draped over her arm.

Vera's son-in-law must've pulled chauffeur duty before, because he took charge, guiding the old man and his walker to his car. Maggie and I followed, and stood watching in the frigid stillness.

Chet paused at the open car door, his gaze riveted upon me. "Are you gonna call me, boy? Will you come see me again?"

"Sure," I said, not looking forward to it.

We watched the glow of taillights recede into the distance. I put my arm around Maggie's shoulder and walked her back to the house to say our good-byes to Ruby. We found our coats and

I snagged my camera. I heard Patty's shrill laughter from another room. Her friend, Ray, could take her home.

"We'll see you at Hanukkah, won't we?" Ruby asked hopefully.

I'm a lapsed Catholic—I didn't know anything about Jewish traditions. "I haven't made any plans yet. I'll let you know," I hedged.

"I'm so glad you could come," she said, and I got the feeling she had restrained herself from pinching my cheek. "We are your family. We love you," she said and threw her arms around me, radiating unconditional love.

"Thank you," I murmured.

As we headed down the walkway, I turned to see her wave. Framed in the doorway, she suddenly looked liked someone else —someone very familiar.

I put the thought out of my mind. I had too many other things to think about just then.

8

The ride back to my place had been quiet. Maggie doesn't push me when I fall into one of my contemplative moods. Confusion battered my mind and soul. I wanted to get shitfaced—a condition I found myself in too much lately.

Like my sister?

The lights were still on in the big house when we pulled up Richard's driveway. Maggie glanced at the glowing clock on the dash. "It's early. Do you want to stop in to see Brenda and Richard?"

"Why not," I said, trying to sound nonchalant. I'd rather get the inquisition over with.

We went in through the back door. Only the stove's hood light illuminated the kitchen. Maggie followed me down the hall. "Anybody home?" I called.

The big old house felt gloomy and empty after Ruby's tiny little Cape Cod overflowing with people. I called out again and we headed for the study, which was where Richard and Brenda tended to end up after dinner. A trail of lights led to the front of the house, and the soft sounds of Vivaldi from the stereo broke the quiet.

"In here," Brenda called.

Holly barked and danced wildly around Maggie's legs. "Did you miss your mommy?" she asked, making a fuss of the dog. "Is she being a good girl?"

"I may not give her back," Brenda said. Stretched out on the leather couch, she was surrounded by stacks of catalogs and brochures, all featuring baby products. "You're back early. How'd it go?"

I shrugged noncommittally. "Not bad."

"Everybody was very nice. And the food was de-lish," Maggie gushed, taking off her coat and setting it on the opposite side of the couch.

"How's your father?" Richard asked from his seat behind his grandfather's big old mahogany desk.

"Not good."

Brenda studied us, waiting for more. "Is that it?"

I nodded. "Essentially."

"Of course it isn't," Maggie said, clearing a space on a chair and sitting. "I'll be glad to fill you in on *all* the details."

Brenda's gaze was still fixed on me. "I don't think Jeffy's ready to talk about it."

"I think you're right." I turned to Richard. "Got any beer?"

"As a matter of fact, no."

"What kind of a host are you?"

Amusement lit his eyes. "One who didn't make it to the grocery store today."

"I've got a twelve-pack in my fridge. Want to head over there?"

"What about us?" Maggie asked.

"You don't drink beer," I said.

"It's possible male bonding is about to happen," Brenda said.

She knew me well. I did feel a need to talk to Richard, although I hadn't realized it until that moment.

"Then by all means, don't let us interfere," Maggie said.

"There's some wine in the fridge if you want it," Brenda told her. "I'll bet we could polish off the last of your Black Forest cake, too."

"Sounds like a plan," Maggie agreed, and Holly wagged her tail enthusiastically.

"Hang on, I'll get my coat," Richard told me. He grabbed a jacket from the hall closet and followed me across the driveway to my place.

I HIT the switch and the warm glow of incandescent light filled my living room. I hung my jacket in the closet before heading for the kitchen.

"Drinking buddies," Richard mused, peeling off his coat and setting it on the back of the chair. "I haven't had one since college."

"I've just opened up your life." I crouched before the open fridge, tore open the cardboard carton and handed him a bottle of beer.

"On the contrary, I like to think I've opened yours." Richard settled on the upholstered wing chair, stretching his long legs out before him.

I took the south end of my couch and sipped my beer.

It was quiet—too quiet. I thought about turning on the radio, but that would mean getting up and walking all the way across the room.

I took a few more sips of my beer.

Richard didn't look happy. "Jeff, why'd you invite me over here?"

I couldn't look him in the eye. "My head's filled with a lot of crap and it doesn't feel good."

"You're still not used to letting yourself feel anything. That's why everything hits you so hard."

I didn't comment—maybe because what he said was absolutely true.

He took another sip. "Did you enjoy yourself tonight?"

"No. I felt like an outsider. There were so many people, and so much emotion spilling out. Obligation to be there—duty to family, yet everyone seemed at ease. They all knew every detail of each other's lives—a history I have no part of."

"Didn't it ever occur to you that Chet could have relatives in town?"

"No. All I ever heard growing up was 'your brother Richard this—your brother Richard that.' Even though Mom didn't know you, I could never measure up to her ideal of you."

His smile was ironic. "My grandmother used to talk about my father the same way. I couldn't measure up to him in her eyes."

I took a deep swallow of beer, emptied the bottle, and got up for another. "Why'd he fall in love with our mother—she wasn't in his league. Was he out to spite the old lady?"

"I don't know. I don't remember him at all. Grandmother only spoke of his life prior to marrying Betty. Our mother was a forbidden subject. But sometimes Grandfather would tell me about my mother. He didn't despise her the way Grandmother did."

I brought back four bottles, and set them on the coffee table. "How'd you find out about me?"

He frowned and studied the label on his beer. "I hired a private detective."

"You're kidding?"

He shook his head. "It only took him a couple of days to find out Betty had remarried, where she worked, where she shopped. He took pictures of her with a little boy. You were about seven at the time."

An unreasonable anger filled me. "Why didn't you contact us?"

He exhaled a long breath. "I was going to Paris to study and —" He shrugged, and avoided my gaze. "I didn't want to give Grandmother a reason to cancel my plans."

"I assume you needed her money to go?"

"At the time, yes."

Why did it feel like he'd sold my mother and me out?

"When I came back a year later, I was in med school and . . . life continued. I thought there'd be plenty of time. There wasn't." He gave me a faint smile. "But at least I still have you."

I sipped my beer, feeling like a shoddy consolation prize.

"Last Easter you said you didn't have any pictures of Mom. What happened to the ones the detective gave you?" I asked.

"They disappeared while I was in Paris."

"Your grandmother found them?" I guessed.

"They were gone when I came back. I knew better than to ask about them."

I thought about it for a few moments. "How come you showed up the day Mom died?"

"We've been over this before," he said quietly.

"Not in over twenty years."

He sighed, and looked uncomfortable. "I was with her when she died."

I leaned forward, disbelieving. Why hadn't he told me that before now?

"She called me a few days before and asked me to come see her." He paused. "She wanted me to take care of you."

"Kind of last-minute, wasn't it?"

He took a sip of his beer. "Yeah, it was."

Maybe I really didn't want to hear the rest of the story. I didn't like to revisit the past—living with my mother or those few years with Richard. The memories were just too painful. And yet, I asked anyway. "She didn't make any kind of provision for me—did she?"

Richard's cheeks colored in embarrassment. "Look, she didn't really believe she was dying—not until the last couple of days."

"What about Chet? She knew he was still alive."

"She was adamant—she didn't want him in your life. She said she'd rather see you in a foster home."

The anger inside me intensified. "Did she know I'd be living with your grandparents?"

"I guess so."

I frowned. "She must've been pretty pissed at old Chester, because I know for a fact she hated Mrs. Alpert."

"I don't know what went on between Betty and your father. She wouldn't say." Richard stared at some point beyond his hand, which was clamped around the long-necked bottle.

Our mother died on a cold, sunny Wednesday in March. I was leaving school about three o'clock when I saw Richard standing on the walk outside the main entrance. I'd only met him once before, but I remembered his face. Remembered that grown-up moustache.

"I've got some bad news," he said by way of greeting.

"She's dead. Isn't she?"

He nodded, avoiding my gaze. "I'm sorry, kid."

A group of teenaged girls passed us, giggling. He motioned for me to follow him to the parking lot. The sky was bright blue on that raw March day. How could someone die on such a beautiful winter's day? I slid into the passenger side of Richard's red Porsche two-seater. I'd never sat in an import before. The dashboard looked strange—as foreign as the controls on a space ship.

Richard took papers from the breast pocket of his topcoat and showed them to me. "As of today, I'm officially your legal guardian. You're going to come live with me."

Anger flashed through me. "What if I don't want to?"

"I'm afraid you've got no choice."

I swallowed my pique, and tried to be grown up. "What about school?"

"You can finish the year here if you want. You'll be going to Amherst Central next fall."

No choices. Just commandments. My mother was dead and a stranger was calling the shots.

"What about my stuff?"

"We'll go pack a bag now. We can get the rest later."

I ground my molars so hard, I was sure they'd crack. "What about Mom? Can I see her?"

"Tomorrow. The service will probably be Friday."

I nodded, and stared ahead at nothing.

The silence lengthened.

"Do you want to talk about it?" he asked finally.

I looked into his blue eyes and saw fear—as if he was wondering what the hell he had gotten himself into.

I shook my head. What else was there to say?

A group of stragglers exited the building. What was the point of finishing the school year there? I had no close friends. Why delay the inevitable?

Richard turned the key in the ignition and we drove away.

I never went back.

"Anyway," Richard said, bringing me back to the present. "My lawyer drew up some papers. Betty signed them the day before she died."

"You were twenty-six. Why would you take on that kind of responsibility?"

"Because you were my kid brother, and I had the enthusiasm and energy to take on my work, and you, and the whole world. And maybe I thought it would be a kick."

"Was it?" I asked, although I already knew his answer.

"No."

I took another sip of my beer. "Sorry to be so much trouble."

"If it weren't for my grandmother bitching, I would've hardly known you were there."

Of course not. He'd been so busy building his career, sometimes weeks passed and we didn't see each other.

"Taking care of you was the only thing my mother ever asked of me," he continued. "I couldn't turn her down."

I wasn't sure how I felt about that. 'Not good' came close.

"Why did you bring me to live with your grandparents? You must've had your own money by then."

"I worked crazy hours at the hospital. You needed a stable home. Besides, I had an unspoken agreement with Curtis to watch out for you."

Curtis had been Mrs. Alpert's chauffeur—a neat old black dude with a soft spot in his heart for kids.

"Let's face it, you liked him—and you didn't like me." Richard paused; he wouldn't look at me.

What he said was true. Why did I feel bad hearing it now? Maybe because it was no longer true.

"I couldn't get you to open up," he continued. "One morning I came home from an all-nighter at the hospital and Curtis was playing Solitaire in the kitchen. He looked up at me and said, 'The boy likes basketball.' I was going to rush out and get you a backboard, but Curtis said you wouldn't use it if I gave it to you outright. He said to wait for you to ask. So I bought it, and I'd go out and shoot baskets every night . . . rather badly, too, as I recall."

"Yeah. Go on," I urged.

"It took two weeks before you asked if you could play."

"Ten days."

He smiled fondly. "Curtis was a wise man. The closest thing I had to a father."

"Me, too." I cleared my throat. I couldn't talk about it anymore. I didn't want to remember any more, especially since that incident was probably the only good memory I had of my nearly four-year stay with the Alpert family.

I changed the subject. "Speaking of fathers, I got some screwy impressions from old Chester the day I met him. Tonight I got more unpleasant images. I don't know if they're my own memories or his. One thing I'm sure of, Mom and Chet argued about you—a lot."

"Me?"

"Chet said she was obsessed with getting you back from your grandparents. He keeps remembering a plan to kidnap you. What do you know about that?"

Richard frowned. "I never heard it."

"The old man denied it, but it's something he felt strongly about."

Richard looked thoughtful, like the possibility bothered him. He raised the bottle to his mouth and drank.

"So, what do I do about old Chester?" I asked.

"Nothing. You don't have to love him. You don't even have to like him. But would it hurt you to just accept him?"

"He comes with years of baggage and he broadcasts it like a transmitter. It hurts, Rich. It really hurts to be near him."

His expression softened. "I can't imagine what you go through with this psychic stuff. I wish I could help you, kid. I honestly do."

I looked away. Acknowledging his compassion would only foster another round of painful memories I wasn't up to facing.

As though sensing my unease, Richard tipped his beer bottle upside down. "Got any more?"

I glanced at the empties on the table. I had a good buzz working. I usually do a better job of pacing myself. I got up, staggered to the refrigerator, and got him another cold one.

He cracked the screw cap and took a sip. "What do you think those women are talking about?"

I shrugged. "Baby stuff."

He smiled, and leaned back in the chair. "Can you believe I'm going to be a daddy?"

"You like the idea."

He nodded, but the smile faded. "Yeah, but unfortunately racism isn't dead in this country. It'll be tough on him . . . or her."

"That was true a generation ago. Not now. Not when a kid of mixed race can grow up to become president of the country."

"I hope you're right. I'll tell you this, no child was ever wanted more. My kid." His expression could only be called sappy.

I looked away, unable to bear the guilt. I couldn't tell him what I feared, couldn't be the one to shatter his dream.

"Maybe I'll have just one more," I said and got up again, and steadied myself on the furniture as I walked. No matter how much I drank, it wouldn't obliterate what I knew. There'd be no baby. Why the hell did I have to know this? Why couldn't I be blissfully ignorant like the rest of them?

I opened my beer and took a long pull.

Richard looked at his watch. "Christ, is that the time?" He got up, and grabbed his jacket to leave.

"Send my woman home, will you?"

"Sure thing."

The phone rang before he reached the door. I grabbed the receiver. "Resnick's Pizza."

"Jeffy?" Brenda's voice was small, frightened. "It's started again."

My comfortable buzz-on evaporated. I didn't need to ask what she meant. "Sit tight, honey. Rich is on his way. Bye." I hung up the phone. "She just got another one of those calls."

Richard's face twisted with anger. "Dammit."

"Look, see if the phone recorded the number and write it down. Then forward the calls over here for the night."

"Then you and Maggie will be bothered."

"It's the least I can do for you guys."

He stared at me for a long moment, his expression an odd mix of gratitude and apprehension. Then he headed out the door.

THE PHONE RANG four more times during the next two hours. By the third call, Maggie was in tears. I methodically wrote down the time and duration of each call, silently listening while my anger boiled.

After Maggie had gone to bed, I sat on the couch nursing a bourbon and soda and stared at the phone, daring it to ring again.

Tomorrow I'd hit the Internet to review New York's anti-stalking laws. I already knew it was a crime—with mandatory jail time—to make threatening or abusive calls. One for our side.

I took another sip of my drink. Had our visit with Willie set him off? Was he the most likely suspect? It would be a tidy solution, but what if he wasn't? Bob Linden, the pro-life group's leader, wouldn't stoop to petty harassment, but other members in the organization might not be as savvy about the legal ramifications of such acts. I'd promised Emily Farrell a copy of her photo. It wouldn't hurt to cultivate her friendship. To do that, I needed to get in the darkroom and finish printing in the morning. Then later I'd commandeer Richard's computer for some research.

The fear in Brenda's voice came back to haunt me. She didn't deserve that kind of persecution. She was more than my friend, she was my family.

There was that word again. I thought about the bizarre evening at Aunt Ruby's and realized with some surprise that I'd wanted to belong. Was it the feeling of familiarity, of kinship, that warmed me in those cramped rooms, or the unexpected yearning to feel connected to a shared past?

My end of the family tree had certainly been dysfunctional —my blue-eyed mother the odd one out. I never thought about her eyes until I met Richard and saw his were blue, too. My father and Patty had brown eyes. Me, too. Every time Mom looked at me, did she see Chet? Had I been just a painful reminder of their unhappy life together?

Although I didn't actually meet my brother until I was a teenager, I'd heard about him all my life. Finding out about Patty had shaken me. The old man's love for her was strong— her presence gave him joy. His feelings for me were laced with guilt.

I drained my glass and realized with some irony that I was a snob. Though employed in white collar jobs most of my adult life, I always thought of myself as a working stiff. Probably because Mom waitressed and we lived in a cramped apartment over a bakery. Patty seemed entrenched in the working class stereotype of getting drunk to prove she was alive. Seeing my mother's downhill slide into alcoholism affected the way I look at drinking. With all Shelley put me through, it would've been too easy to find solace in a whiskey bottle. Instead I'd thrown myself into my career, choosing one form of addiction over another.

The ice in my glass had nearly melted. I put the glass in the sink.

It was after two when I crawled into bed beside a sleeping Maggie—my island of peace in a chaotic world. Putting my arm around her, I nestled my chin against the warmth of her shoulder, and felt her steady breathing.

And somewhere out there, some asshole with nothing better to do was stalking Brenda.

9

———

After Maggie left the next morning, I headed straight for my darkroom and developed the roll of black-and-white film I'd taken the night before. While the negatives dried, I made several prints of Emily Farrell and her daughter outside the health center, the best of which I enlarged and mounted. Emily had a sweet, natural presence, and her engaging personality made me wonder why such an attractive woman was alone.

I made contact prints from the new negs, dried them with a hair dryer, then sat down with a ham sandwich, trying to figure out if any were worth printing. One shot Maggie had taken of me with my father and sister was pretty good. I didn't look half as uncomfortable as I'd felt. The question was, did I want to bother enlarging any of them?

The answer was no. But my father and Patty would probably like copies. There was a nice one of the three of us with Chet's sisters that Ruby and Vera would probably like, too, but that was it. I'd make only those prints and file the negatives away forever.

I studied the sheet, frowning. How had Patty's unsmiling friend, Ray, gotten in so many of the shots?

The phone's jangle interrupted my musing. "Hello."

"Jeffrey? It's Patty."

My hand clenched the receiver. "What's up?"

"It's Dad. He's real sick. It wasn't a good idea to take him to Aunt Ruby's last night. I know your brother's been his doctor for a while. Do you think he could come over and see Dad?"

That's right. Put me in the middle.

"Why don't you just call an ambulance," I said.

Silence.

"He won't let me," she said finally. "Please, Jeff?"

I let out a long breath. "I'll see what I can do. I'll call you back in a few minutes."

Grabbing my coat, I scooped up my notes on the calls from the night before and headed out.

"Anybody home?" I called as I opened the back door to Richard's house. Holly, barked, jumping up to lick my face.

Brenda was in the kitchen, emptying the dishwasher. "Hey, there."

"Is Rich around? I've got a big favor to ask."

"I think he's in the study. What's wrong?"

"My father's really sick."

Brenda nodded, like she'd expected it. For an awkward moment we just looked at one another. I figured if anyone could understand my mixed emotions about my father, it was Brenda.

"Well, I better find him."

Richard looked up from his computer screen when the parquet floor creaked under my sneakered feet. "What's up?"

"I got a call from Patty. She says Chet's pretty sick. She wondered if you could come over to see him."

He frowned and clicked the print button. "I'm not surprised. Especially after what you said last night."

"What're you up to?" I asked,

"Checking out local anti-abortion Web sites, looking for Brenda's name. Other health center staff are there—but not her. You can't believe the crap they post. Decomposed, full-term fetuses passed off as abortions—more likely stillbirths. Anybody with a computer and good software can manipulate images to suit their twisted purposes. I tried to find what I could on the protester's names you gave me yesterday, too."

The last of several pages rolled out the printer. I picked up the top sheet, scanning it. "What the hell?" I looked Richard in the eye. "This looks like Linden's medical records."

He didn't say anything, and just logged off the Internet.

"You hacked into his medical records?" I asked.

"I learned a thing or two about systems in my job at the Foundation." He didn't look the least bit concerned.

"That's illegal," I sputtered. "And you're Mr. Straight-And-Narrow."

"Linden harasses women entering family planning centers, threatens clinic staff, and condones violence, which is immoral." He crossed his arms over his chest. "I'm willing to stand before God's judgment, just the same as him."

I glanced at the type. "The Reverend suffers from PTSS?"

"Post Traumatic Stress Syndrome. On some pretty strong medication, too. And if he doesn't take it—"

"Paranoia, subject to violent outbursts," I read. "Just the kind of guy you want preaching to pro-life protesters."

"Exactly."

He switched off the computer and got up. "I'll get my bag."

I nodded. "Oh, here's the log of the calls from last night. We can talk about it later, okay?"

"Sure." He tucked it under the edge of his blotter. "I'll meet you by the back door."

I threaded my way through the house, and used the phone

in the kitchen to call Patty. Brenda watched as I hung up, her expression filled with compassion.

"Do you need a hug, Jeffy?"

"Sure." I let her put her arms around me, soaked in her genuine regret—her need to comfort. "He's dying, Brenda."

"I know."

Holly gave a pathetic whimper, tried to insinuate herself between us, her wet nose nudging my hand. I pulled back, crouched down to scratch behind the dog's ears. "Have you met Chet?"

Brenda shook her head. "No, but Richard pointed him out to me at the clinic."

I stared at the floor. "This pisses me off. The old man's not my responsibility." I risked a look at Brenda. Her intense gaze unnerved me, made me feel guilty. "And now I have to get Rich involved, too. A week ago I didn't know him or Patty, and now they're jerking me around."

Brenda's silence only enhanced my guilt.

Richard appeared wearing his oversized navy pea coat, with his little black bag in hand. "I don't know when we'll be back," he told Brenda.

"I'll be okay."

"If you get lonely, call Maggie. If Willie shows up, call nine-one-one."

"I'll be okay," she repeated, and patted Holly's head.

"Lock the doors," I said.

"I *will*."

Richard kissed Brenda goodbye and we headed out.

The deadbolt clicked behind us.

I DROVE, my fingers clenching the wheel, my knuckles white. As each minute ticked by my frustration mounted.

"I'm sorry I dragged you into this, Rich," I said finally.

"I *am* his doctor," he pointed out reasonably.

"I know, but—" I didn't know. My thoughts were spinning. I wasn't sure what I was saying or thinking or feeling. And I didn't like that sense of impotence one bit.

"This could be the beginning of the end," Richard said.

I refused to look at him.

"You should be prepared," he said.

"For what? To lose him? What's to lose? I just met him." I was lying. I was scared and I didn't even want to think about why.

"If nothing else, you might want to mourn the lost years."

"Fat chance," I bluffed. He was probably right, but I didn't want to admit it to him—or even to myself.

I pulled up the driveway and we got out. Richard took in the rundown little house with its peeling paint and untrimmed shrubs. Embarrassment washed over me. This was all my father had to show for seventy-plus years on the planet.

Patty opened the storm door, her face taut with worry. "Dr. Alpert? Thanks for coming," she said, ignoring me.

"Hi. Patty, right?" he said.

She nodded, ushered us into the house. "Sorry to call you over on a Sunday, but Dad's so sick."

"Where is he?"

"The bedroom."

"I'll wait here," I said as they headed down a darkened hallway.

I parked in a chair and looked around the shabby living room. It was an old man's house. The walls needed painting; the faded, threadbare carpet was probably older than me. Grocery-store prints of scenic landscapes hung over the couch. My father's lover—common-law wife?—had been dead for ten years. It stood to reason there'd be nothing new in the way of furnishings. But there didn't seem to be any semblance of Patty in the house, either. Her time between boyfriends was probably brief. Maybe the house had become more a way station than her home.

Patty came out a few moments later and flopped onto the chair opposite me.

"How is he?" I asked.

"Richard's examining him now."

They were on first-name terms already.

"He sure is good looking."

"Who? Richard?"

She nodded, her expression far away, a slight smile crossing her lips. "He seems real nice. Like he's got a gentle way."

"He does have a good bedside manner," I agreed warily.

"How long has he been married?"

"Since the end of June."

She counted the months off on her fingers. "Five months— not long at all."

"What exactly is wrong with—" I still had trouble using the title. "—Dad?" I asked impatiently.

"He's having trouble breathing. He said he had pains in his chest. I tried to talk him out of going to Aunt Ruby's yesterday, but he was determined."

"He's pretty much house-bound?"

She nodded. "He's hardly been out at all lately, except to go to the clinic. Elena usually takes him." She changed the subject. "Richard looks different than he did the other day. Kind of hunky." That wistful smile was back.

"It's the coat." I hoped she caught the meaning behind my deadpanned words.

Patty frowned, and looked away.

We ignored each other for several long minutes until Richard came out—much sooner than I'd anticipated.

"I'm going to call for an ambulance," he said. "Your father needs to be in a hospital until we can stabilize him."

"Is he going to be all right?" Patty asked.

Richard frowned. "I don't foresee any great improvement. Emphysema is a progressive illness."

"He's going to die, isn't he?"

"Let's not anticipate anything. And we don't want to upset him. Can I use the phone?"

"It's in the kitchen," she said and pointed the way.

Richard left us to make his call.

Patty's face had gone pale. "I—I guess I'd better go pack a bag for him." Dazed, she nearly bumped into a chair on her way out.

I turned, shoved my hands in my pockets and stared out the window at the bleak sky. A dull ache of foreboding settled in my gut. The air, stale with sickness, seemed to grow heavy. We were going through the motions of prolonging the old man's life, though all of us knew the inevitable outcome.

Richard paused on his way to the bedroom. "Do you want to see him?"

I shook my head, surprised at the fear growing within me.

"He asked if you were here."

I let out a long breath. "Then I guess I better go in."

I followed my brother down the hall to the bedroom on the right. Crammed with dressers, night tables and a double bed, the loud, old-fashioned floral wallpaper made the room seem even smaller. A forty-watt bulb in the overhead light did little to dispel the gloom.

The old man's face was gray. He looked ancient. Struggling for breath, he argued with Patty. "No, the blue one. The blue one —" He pointed at a drawer.

"But, Dad, it's got a hole in it," she said and showed him the pajama leg.

"Pack it," he said.

Chet noticed Richard and me crowded in the doorway, and sank back against the pillows that kept him propped up. His breathing was a rattling wheeze. I took a few steps forward and he reached out, waving me closer. I stopped short, unwilling to touch him, but he leaned forward, clasped my forearm with a grip that surprised me.

A tidal wave of pain, suffering, and regret washed over me, stealing my breath. Panicked, I backed into Richard at my heels. The old man's failing condition yawned before me like a black abyss. Richard lunged forward, breaking the connection.

Gasping, I turned aside, holding my arm as though it had been scalded. Patty stared at me, her face a mix of irritation and puzzlement. Richard covered for me, asking Chet how he felt, and taking his pulse, but I saw in the old man's troubled eyes that even he knew something had passed between us.

"Jeffrey?" he wheezed.

I coughed, straightened, buried my hands in my coat pockets. I had to clear my throat twice before I could speak. "Yeah?"

"Sit here, boy." Chet patted the edge of the bed.

I threw Richard a wary look, but he only shrugged.

I perched on the end of the mattress, as far from my father as possible. The cat suddenly appeared, jumped up on the old man's lap, keeping a narrow gaze on me. Patty finished stuffing clothes into the bag, slammed the drawer, and fled the room.

"I'm supposed to see the lawyer tomorrow," the old man said, gasping.

"What for?" I asked.

"To add you to my will. It's only right. You're my first born. You ought to get half—"

"No, Patty—she should get everything."

He shook his head, determined. It wasn't worth arguing

about. There was no way he'd make it to any attorney's office. Better to let him make his plans.

"Okay. Just take it easy."

"I made a mistake, Jeffrey. I should've had you come live with me when your mother died. I never forgot you, boy. I always loved you. It just wasn't meant to be. You understand that, don't you?"

"Sure . . . Dad."

Of course I didn't understand, but what was I going to say to a dying man?

Richard collected his stethoscope and blood pressure cuff, pretending he hadn't heard the exchange. My father scratched the cat's head. Herschel purred loudly, greedily nuzzling his hand.

Brisk footsteps announced the arrival of the ambulance crew. Grateful for the opportunity to escape, I sprang to my feet, and sidled past them.

Patty waited for me in the living room. She looked at me with suspicion. "What happened to you in there?"

Embarrassed, I avoided her gaze. "It's a long story."

She studied me like I was some kind of freak. "Tell me some time, okay?"

"Later." Yeah, right. Tell you my secrets? No way.

Long, awkward minutes later, the paramedics wheeled the gurney through the living room.

"We'll follow in the car, Dad," Patty said, donning her jacket and grabbing her purse.

"Don't forget to feed Herschel," the old man cried feebly as they whisked him through the door.

"You don't like me much, do you?" Patty asked, as I backed out the driveway.

"Why'd you say that?" I asked, feeling her penetrating glare cut through me.

"Just the way you act around me."

"It takes me a while to warm to people."

"I guess I'm not surprised," she said, staring straight ahead. "What with the way you were brought up and all."

I kept my mouth shut—didn't want to start an argument. The silence that followed was unnerving. I wished Richard hadn't ridden in the ambulance with my dying father. I tuned the radio to a rock station to fill the void.

The ambulance pulled into the emergency entrance. I dropped Patty off before parking the car. Inside, a nurse directed me to the waiting room. Patty knew the drill. She'd grabbed the first empty chair, paging through out-of-date magazines. Restless energy kept me on my feet, pacing.

I glanced at my watch. I'd already killed more than an hour. I'd probably have to hang around until Patty was ready to leave. Great. That meant I wouldn't get online or finish my darkroom work. I wondered if I should call Maggie, warn her I might not make it for dinner.

The doors to the treatment rooms remained closed. My father was in one of the sterile cubicles, probably wired for sound and attached to IVs. I tried to think of anything but that.

"Will you sit down?" Patty said. "You're making me jumpy."

Reluctantly I took the seat beside her, stared at nothing, and thought about death. Tried not to think about death. Tried not to think.

"Is this Richard's second or third marriage?" Patty asked, thumbing through another magazine.

"What?" I asked, stunned by her question. Our father was dying down the hall. Where the hell was her head?

"Was he married before?" she asked again.

"No. Why do you care?"

"I'm just making conversation." She put the magazine down, picked up another—and didn't look at me. "How long did they know each other before they got married?"

"I don't know. Maybe ten years."

She frowned. "She's younger than him, isn't she?"

"Thirteen years." Time to end her nosy questions. "Brenda's pregnant."

Patty paused in her page-turning. "Oh."

I glanced at the other worried faces around me and remembered the hours I'd spent worrying when Richard was in the hospital earlier that year.

Had I just admitted I cared about my father? God knows I didn't want to. But, yeah, I guess I did. Mourn the lost years, Richard had said. Yes, I could do that at least.

I got up, found a coffee machine, bought myself a cup and took my time drinking it. After a while, Patty gave up on the magazines, and stared out the window at the cars in the parking lot.

I was on my third cup when Richard reappeared, his expression a mix of worry and compassion—a look that made my stomach tighten. Instantly on her feet, Patty reached for his hand, looked into his eyes with puppy-dog devotion. I felt like a fifth wheel.

"We're going to keep your father here at least overnight," he said.

"Is he going to die?" Patty asked.

Richard pointed to the chairs and we sat down again. His voice was gentle. Patty kept hold of his hand.

"We can make him comfortable," Richard said, "but that's about all. Have you thought about hospice care?"

"Yes, but . . . I thought we had more time."

"Now's the time."

"Does that mean he can't stay here?"

"He can stay for a day or so—but he'll need constant care from now on. He'd prefer to be at home."

Patty thought it over. She was remarkably controlled. I'd known the man less than a week and I felt panicked.

"What should we do?" I asked.

Patty looked at me, annoyed. "I'll handle it," she said, all business. She looked up at Richard. "Will you help?"

"Of course." Richard rose. Patty followed, and wound her arm around his.

"Thank you, Richard. I feel so much better knowing you're here for Daddy." She closed her eyes, and rested her head on his shoulder, a small smile of satisfaction on her lips.

He patted her back, oblivious of her little performance. He was made for the role of caregiver.

Me?

I wanted to hurl.

CHEERFUL CHRISTMAS LIGHTS illuminated the gloom on Maggie's street. I'd forgotten Thanksgiving weekend was traditional for holiday decorating. I promised Maggie I'd put lights along the roof and around the windows of her house. Buffalo's unpredictable weather may have put an end to those plans. If it snowed tomorrow, there'd be no holiday lights at Maggie's home this year. Yet another of my unfinished projects.

By the time Chet was admitted and moved into his hospital room, it was already dark. I'd driven Patty home, then dropped Richard back at the house. My gas gauge hovered near empty and my reserve of civility was in just about the same condition.

I pulled up Maggie's driveway and wondered what kind of reception I'd get, not that I needed to worry. Maggie wasn't a stickler for promptness and I'd already called to warn her I'd be late. Still, it irked me that the best part of my weekend had been disrupted by Patty and by my father's illness. These people hadn't given a damn about me for decades—*decades*—and now they were sucking me into a tragedy I didn't deserve to own.

Maggie must've heard my car pull up, for she met me at the door. She eyed me, as though assessing my mood. "Should I get out the bourbon?"

"Yeah. But I'll only have one. I've got to drive home later."

"You won't be staying tonight?" she said, and took my coat, sounding disappointed.

"I've got to be home for the security guys tomorrow morning. Besides, I want to be there in case Brenda and Richard get more screwy calls tonight."

"I'd want to be there, too," she agreed. "But you can't blame me if I'm lonely."

I'd almost forgotten her dog was at Richard's house. I gave her a smile. "What do you know, for once I have you all to myself." I took her in my arms and gave her a long, intense kiss.

"Wow," she said, coming up for air. "You're welcome any time." She pulled away from my embrace. "Sit down and I'll bring you that drink."

"Is dinner ruined?"

"It's on hold. We can sit and talk for a few minutes. It'll give you a chance to unwind." She disappeared into the kitchen.

I settled on the couch, kicked off my shoes, and stretched out my legs. Some new age piano CD played softly on her stereo. Restful. Just what I needed after the emotional roller coaster I'd been on all afternoon.

Maggie returned with my bourbon and soda and a glass of wine for herself. She snuggled up beside me and I put my arm around her. Maggie exudes an aura of peace that envelops me like a soothing cocoon.

"Is your dad going to die?" she asked.

"Yeah."

"I'm sorry."

"So am I. It's like a nightmare. People I didn't even know a week ago are calling the shots, involving me in stuff I never could have anticipated."

"Your father, or Patty?"

"Patty," I admitted. "Everything she says—does—pisses me off. You should see the way she looks at Richard. Like she's got the hots for him."

"He's married."

"That doesn't seem to bother her. She's a bigot, too." I told her what Patty had said about Brenda days before. "I *don't* like her. I never will."

"You're judging her too hard and too fast."

"What do you mean?"

"Some women fall in love with their doctors," she said, playing devil's advocate.

"Richard's not her doctor."

"No, but he's a genuinely nice man. And he's damn fine looking." For a moment her expression was wistful, then she caught herself, and hurriedly explained, "Not that you aren't."

"Thanks," I deadpanned. I thought about what she said. "You could be right," I admitted. "But her admiration of him almost borders on incest."

"He's not *her* brother," Maggie reminded me.

I sipped my drink.

"You're worrying too much about the long-term impact Patty will have on you," Maggie said. "Once your father's . . . gone," she said gently, "she'll go back to her old life, which didn't include you. She'll probably find another boyfriend and leave both you and Richard alone."

"Since when are you such a prophet?"

She shrugged. "School of hard knocks." She took a sip of wine. "You and Richard aren't like most siblings."

"How so?"

"You're closer now than when you were growing up. Me and my sisters were close—especially in our teens and early twenties. We had so much in common—men; minimum-wage jobs; men. But they both fell in love, married, and lived happily ever after. The little house, the kids, dogs—the works."

"It bothers you that you missed out on some of that, doesn't it?"

"They treat me differently," she admitted. "Like they're members of some secret society I'll never be a part of, simply because I can't have a child."

"It hurts, doesn't it?"

"I have my life and my job and my friends. But sometimes it does feel like I'm missing out on a whole big part of life."

"You have me."

Her smile warmed me. "You're the best part." She brushed a kiss against my cheek, snuggled closer. "It's a pretty good life, too."

"Yeah, this year's been good."

"Except for the whack on the head that almost killed you," she reminded me.

I forced a smile. "Yeah. That wasn't much fun."

She stood, and held out a hand to me. "Come on. Let's eat. Afterwards we can do something else."

"What did you have in mind?"

She glanced in the direction of the bedroom. "As you noticed, we are quite alone."

"That's right." I rose, leaned closer, pressed my lips against hers then gently covered her mouth. "Are you really all that hungry?" I whispered.

Her smile was seductive. "No."

"Neither am I."

As Maggie pulled me to the bedroom, I noticed the photos on the wall. Maggie and her two sisters, their two parents, her nieces and nephews. She missed a life she didn't have. So did I.

So did I.

10

Richard's house was dark when I pulled up the driveway after leaving Maggie sound asleep. I wondered if he'd call-forwarded their phone. My answering machine wasn't blinking, so I hit the sack. The phone never rang to wake me, either. Richard, on the other hand, would've made a fine alarm clock. He called before he left for the clinic the next morning to remind me the security people were coming out that morning. He'd had no prank calls the night before and was grateful for a night of undisturbed slumber.

I sat down at my kitchen table to call the phone company. Passing myself off as Richard, I learned all the phone calls had been made from public pay phones. I took down the addresses to check out later, then arranged for a new phone number to take effect the next day, changing the designation to unlisted.

I hung up and scrounged a map to pinpoint the pay phones, which were scattered in a circular pattern downtown. I'd take a drive and check it out later, but I suspected they'd either be inside or near bars. Our prankster probably had a drink, made a call, and moved to another location. I'd have to ask Brenda if Willie was a heavy drinker.

The first batch of security guys arrived precisely at nine a.m. Ken Tyler, the sales rep, and I discussed motion detectors, lasers, adding more lights around the house and placing an electric gate at the bottom of the drive.

The second team wasn't as impressive, so I went with the first company, although they couldn't do the installation until Friday. Tyler also offered me a discount for one of their private security guards. I told him I'd think about it.

With a couple of hours to kill, I decided to check out Reverend Linden's church. I had no time for a stake-out, but drove around the lot and wrote down all the license plate numbers of cars parked there. An uneasy feeling settled in my gut when I noticed a pick-up truck with an empty gun rack in the back window.

The mail hadn't arrived by the time I got home, which meant I was looking out my window every five minutes for almost an hour. When I saw the carrier walk away, I headed for the mail-box, grabbed the mail and opened Richard's door—letting the dog out as I went in.

I sorted through the stack of letters and my heart sank when I saw that familiar envelope. Richard had left me a pair of latex gloves. Normally I don't open other people's mail. But then, normally Brenda didn't receive prank—possibly threatening— letters. I sat at their kitchen table, carefully slit the envelope and unfolded the sheet of paper. It read: WILL. Putting both letters together read: YOU WILL

You will what? Win a Rolls Royce? Not likely. I had a hunch I knew what the next envelope would contain. I didn't want to think about it.

I called the Williamsville Women's Health Center and told Tim Davies about the second letter, then placed it and the envelope in a folder on Richard's desk. Grabbing my coat, I headed out the door. I had to work that evening, so decided to make my duty visit to my father at the hospital beforehand. Since the clinic was nearby, it made sense to stop in and see Richard first.

The waiting room was stuffed with coughing children, wheezing oldsters, and every make and model in between. The receptionist told me Richard was with a patient. I stood near the door and breathed shallowly for nearly fifteen minutes before he could see me.

I almost didn't recognize my own brother. Dressed in a white lab coat, with a stethoscope slung around his neck, he looked different from the every-day Richard I was used to. His eyes were weary. I hated to dump more bad news on him.

"We got another letter," I said.

"Damn." He snagged my arm, and pulled me into the doctor's lounge—a misnomer for the cramped room containing a coffeemaker, a cot and a couple of tables and chairs.

"Tell me everything," he said.

"It was the same type of envelope, the same paper and font. A decent lab might get a DNA signature from saliva from the seal, but until we have a suspect—"

"I've got one: Willie!"

"Okay, he's a credible suspect. But we haven't got anything concrete we can pin on him."

"How would we find it?"

"If I had his Social Security number, I could make some inquiries. Your best bet is to hire a private detective in Philadelphia."

"Do you know anyone?"

"A year ago I could've given you a couple of names. Since the mugging, my memory's shot. Your attorney can probably arrange something."

"I'll call him. Should we tell the police?"

"There's still no real threat. This whole thing could be an elaborate prank."

"But you don't think so."

I shrugged and avoided his gaze. My gut instinct said no, but I had no impressions to rely on, either. "Are you going to tell Brenda?"

"Not unless she asks."

I nodded, and felt bad for him. Next, I told him about my conversation with the phone company and gave him a quick rundown on the security system. He agreed with my decision to schedule implementation, said he'd think about hiring a guard. He kept looking at the clock.

"I won't keep you," I said.

"Are you going to visit your father?"

"That's where I'm headed now. Have you seen him today?"

"Yes." His solemn expression made the knot in my stomach tighten. "Your father did his legal homework. He requested—and I agreed to post—a do not resuscitate order. The paperwork's already on file at the hospital."

Stunned, I stood there, blinking at him. "What did Patty say?"

"She understands the situation. She's been to hospice counseling. She wants to make this easy on your father."

"Then I guess it makes sense," I heard myself saying, although I wasn't sure I liked the idea. Richard kept looking at me, like he expected an argument. As a newcomer to the extended Resnick family, I had no right to voice an opinion either way.

We stood there, not saying anything. I could tell he had something else on his mind, but he wasn't willing to talk about it. At least, not yet.

"I'd better go," I said.

"Thanks for everything, kid. I'll talk to you later." He clapped me on the shoulder, and started for the door.

I followed, and watched as Richard headed down the hall to the treatment rooms. Hands thrust into his coat pockets, his stooped shoulders and hanging head made him look older than his forty-eight years.

At that moment, I felt older.

PEOPLE SAT CLUSTERED in knots in the hospital's lobby. I sailed through without checking in. When my mother was dying, they wouldn't let more than two people visit at a time. Did those rules still apply? If anyone was already with my father, I figured he would still want to see me no matter what the rules said.

I found his private room—Richard's doing?—with no trouble, and paused at the open doorway. Patty leaned against the wall, staring at the ceiling. Ruby occupied the room's only chair, her coat slung over one arm, her pocketbook securely seated on her lap. The bed was cranked to a full, upright sitting position, and the TV was on.

I knocked on the doorjamb. "Hello."

Chet fumbled with the TV control, and pressed the off button. "Jeffrey!" The timbre of his voice conveyed his pleasure, reinforcing my sense of guilt.

Patty gave me a funny look—a cross between irritation and relief. I couldn't guess what she was thinking. Ruby's smile was welcoming, sympathetic.

"Hey, Dad. How're you feeling?" I said, feeling self-conscious, keeping my distance.

"Good. Good," Chet said, an obvious lie. He looked worse than he had the day before. His lips were a blue line, the ever-present nasal cannula hung from his nose, encircling his head like a fallen halo. But a spark of life still lit his brown eyes.

Ruby gathered her purse and coat. "Let's get some coffee, Patty, and give these men time to talk."

"Sure," Patty said, her tone wary. "We'll be back in a while, Dad."

Ruby bustled her out of the room.

I took the chair my aunt had just vacated, and stuffed my hands into my jacket pockets. Left alone, my father and I looked at each other for an uncomfortable moment.

"I'm glad you came, Jeffrey."

I gave him a wan smile. Duty alone had prompted the visit. Why? Why did I owe anything to this person?

Maybe it was time to find out.

"How're you feeling?" I asked again. Talk about a dumb question.

"Awful," he answered truthfully this time. "Will you come to my funeral?"

I blinked. "That's a terrible question."

"Why? We both know I'm dying. Maybe today. Maybe next week."

"Yeah, but—"

"I had a good life. Maybe it could've been better. Maybe I shoulda done things different."

The sentence hung between us.

His mouth drooped, his eyes growing watery. "Patty says you don't like her."

"She thought I'd be a different person."

"I tried to tell her. You're more like me—you keep to yourself. She's like Joan—outgoing."

"Joan was a lot different than my mother, wasn't she?"

My father looked away, took a breath and coughed. He moved his legs restlessly under the covers and gazed out the window.

"What happened with you and my mother? Why did you leave?"

"That was a long time ago. It doesn't matter any more."

"It does to me."

"I'm an old man. I put that stuff out of my head years ago. I made a new life with Joan. That's the only life I remember."

My fists clenched in my jacket pockets. After all these years, what the hell did he have to hide?

"I saw you early last summer," Chet said.

I looked up, had to work at keeping my voice steady. "Where?"

"Your brother's house. Elena drove me. You were planting begonias in the yard. Do you like to garden?"

"Yeah." It was a new hobby. It had been Brenda's idea to transform the yard, but I found solace in the task. "How long were you there?"

"Maybe ten minutes."

"Why didn't you come over, introduce yourself?"

He waved a hand. "What for? You'd have just been mad—like you are now."

"I'm not mad at you." Okay that was a lie. "I'm disappointed. It's too late now."

"Too late for what? You didn't have to know me for me to love you, boy."

"Why are you telling me this? You're making it so hard."

"It doesn't have to be hard. I've been sick a long time. I'm ready to die. You don't have to feel bad."

"But I do. We could've been friends."

"That wasn't necessary."

Maybe not for you, I wanted to shout, but what was the use? Nothing I could say would change him. If I was going to get answers, they wouldn't come from him.

Our brief conversation had drained the old man. He leaned

back against the pillows, his breathing a hoarse whistle. I didn't know what to do, so I sat, staring at my shoes, wishing Patty and Ruby would return so I could leave.

I hated the place, its smell, the lingering aura of suffering. Memories of the week I'd spent in the hospital in New York City after the mugging were still too fresh. My life had changed since then. Some things were worse—the frequent headaches and the damned annoying insight I sometimes got. Some things were better. I had a family—Richard and Brenda—and a woman who loved me.

Family.

What if this was the last time I saw my father? What if I never got answers to all my questions? Maybe what I really needed was to make peace with that.

I turned my gaze to the old man sleeping in the bed and wished to God Richard had never told me about him. I could've been blissfully ignorant when it came time for him to die. Yet I couldn't work up anger toward my brother. Richard longed for family and he wasn't going to get his wish. Was keeping that truth to myself a blessing or a curse? Eventually I'd have to face that, too.

The guilt just piled higher and higher.

The featureless walls seemed to be converging. I got up, stared out the window at the ugly gray sky. Bleak—just how I felt.

Voices at the door caused me to turn. Ruby's and Patty's conversation stopped abruptly when they saw Chet asleep.

I met them in the hall. "I have to go to work," I whispered. "Tell Dad I'll . . . see him tomorrow."

Ruby's eyes filled with tears. "God willing." She drew me into a hug. There was nothing of her. A gust of wind could blow her away.

I pulled back, then nodded at Patty. "See you later."

"We should talk," she said. "There's things that need to be decided."

"Yeah." What else could I say? I looked back at my father, frowned, then turned and headed for the exit.

I'D LIED TO PATTY. I didn't have to be at work for a couple of hours. Instead, I took a drive, needing the distraction.

Like old times in my job as an insurance investigator, I checked out the addresses the phone company had given me. Just as I'd thought: the crank calls to Richard's phone had been made from taverns, bars, and strip joints. I needed a picture of Willie to flash to the bartenders—a description alone wouldn't cut it. I was pretty sure Brenda hadn't saved photographic souvenirs from her brief marriage. Too bad. It wasn't likely anyone working the day shift would've been at the bars when the calls had been made, anyway. I'd have to come back at night.

The afternoon evaporated. I headed back across town to go to work.

The Whole Nine Yards was busy for a Tuesday night, usually the slowest night of the week. It had been a long day, and I was wiped by ten o'clock, with another two hours—minimum—before I could leave. I needed the money and was damned glad it had been days since I'd had one of those incapacitating headaches. That was about the only thing to keep me from being gainfully employed. And keeping busy kept me from thinking about other unpleasant situations—like my father dying.

I was in back, getting a case of beer, when a coarse, familiar voice called out, "What's it take to get some service around here?"

It was the pony-tailed man from the protest line.

He wasn't the same social scale as the rest of the bar's clientele. Still dressed in the same grubby, grease-stained jacket, he sat on a stool at the bar, resting his arms on the polished oak surface.

I set the case of Labatts on the floor beside the fridge and straightened. "What can I get you," I asked, reminding myself that the customer's always right.

"What you got on tap?"

He didn't recognize me. Good. "Molson Golden, Budweiser, and Coors Lite."

"Gimme a Bud."

I turned for the tap, poured the beer, and gave it a generous head. He tossed a five on the bar. His nails were bitten down to the quick, grime embedded in the skin. What was he, a mechanic? I rang up the sale, set the change in front of him and turned away, started putting the bottles in the fridge.

"Hey, I know you," Pony-tail said, lighting a cigarette — strictly illegal in public places in New York State.

"I don't think so. And please put out your smoke."

"Yeah. You're that Ass-cort I see at the clinic couple times a week," he said, ignoring my request. "The nigger lover."

The muscles in my arms tightened and I straightened. My aversion to the phrase must've been plastered on my face— which was just the reaction he'd hoped for.

"Yeah, you're a big man taking care of that baby-killing whore. Is she a good fuck?" he said, taking another drag and exhaling. Heads turned in his direction, eavesdropping.

I leaned over the bar and kept my voice low. "Finish your beer and get your redneck ass out of here."

He exhaled smoke into my face. "You can't tell me what to do, *nigger-lover*."

"Have we got a problem here?" Tom, my boss, asked. Though in his fifties, his years as a bouncer in other people's taverns had served him well. He was still capable of beating the shit out a troublemaker. "Hey, pal, don't'cha know it's illegal to smoke in a public place."

"The gentleman was just getting ready to leave," I said.

"Am not. I haven't drunk my beer yet."

"Sir, we've got ladies at the bar. Your language is not appreciated," Tom grated.

Pony-tail straightened his shoulders and stubbed out his cigarette on the oak bar. "Who's gonna make me leave?"

Tom grabbed his elbow and lifted him off the stool. "Me."

"Hey!" Pony-tail dug in his heels, but Tom had no trouble dragging him to the exit.

"You asked for it!" he yelled at me over his shoulder. "You shouldn't a messed with me, man! I'll make you sorry!"

I went back to work, cleaning up behind the bar, ignoring the other patrons' stares and whispers. I studied the glass and the cigarette butt sitting before me, hesitant to touch them. But I couldn't afford to lose the opportunity to gain some insight into one of the protesters' souls.

The glass had nothing. He hadn't held it long enough to leave a psychic signature. I dumped the beer down the drain and left the glass to soak. I grabbed the cigarette filter between my thumb and forefinger. Anger. Stupid, petty, fury. But I couldn't focus on the source. Maybe there was none.

I tossed it in the trash.

Tom came back in. "He got in his truck and left. He won't be back."

I nodded, hoping he couldn't see how the jerk had shaken me. Of all the bars in Buffalo, why had Pony-tail chosen to quench his thirst here?

When the basketball game ended after eleven, the bar cleared out. A few stragglers watched a rerun of a middleweight title fight while I washed glasses, then wiped down all the tables. Near the end of the fourth round, Tom told me I could leave.

Huddled in my jacket against the cold, I headed for the bar's tiny parking lot. It was twenty-three days until the official start of winter—but what did Mother Nature know about calendars?

My car was in the farthest spot but even in the dim light I could make out the garish red lipstick against its white exterior. The message wasn't inspired. Pony-tail's vocabulary was extremely limited. The aura left behind was the same unfocused anger. I kicked aside the glass from the smashed headlight, grateful he'd taken his petty revenge out on the car and not me.

I spent the next hour in a self-serve car wash, scrubbing away the evidence. I was supposed to drive Brenda to the Women's Health Center in the morning. I didn't want her to see how low some asshole would stoop to show the depths of his hatred.

MY PHONE never rang in the middle of the night with prank calls or bad news from Patty. I got up at the usual time, ready to take Brenda to the health center.

I tossed the envelope of prints I'd made over the weekend onto the back seat of my car and started the engine. If Brenda noticed the broken headlight, she didn't mention it. Instead, she chatted about the furniture she'd chosen for the nursery. The words were right, but there was a forced cheerfulness in her tone. Likewise, it was getting harder for me to fake a smile of encouragement.

Emily Farrell was back on the protest line—Pony-tail wasn't. I parked the car and walked Brenda into the clinic. On my way out I waved to Emily, received a shy smile from her and hateful glares from other protesters on line who shouted promises of fire and brimstone to the damned who entered the clinic.

I hiked to the coffee shop down the street, got a couple of cups of hot chocolate to go, and headed back to the line.

"Can we talk for a few minutes?" I asked.

Emily's smile was tentative. "Sure."

Some of the women glared at her—like she was fraternizing with the enemy—but Emily set her sign down on the ground as I handed her a cup. We walked down the block to a bench that overlooked Main Street.

"The whipped cream is probably all melted by now."

"That's okay," she said, removing the cover and taking a sip of the steaming cocoa. "Mmm. Good."

"Where's Hannah?"

"Preschool. She loves playing with the other kids." She eyed the envelope on the bench beside me. "Is that for me?"

"Oh. Sorry. Yeah. I hope you like it."

She opened the clasp and took out the photo. I'd dipped it in sepia toner, shading it a warm brown, and then mounted it on black art board.

"Oh, it's beautiful. Thank you." She studied the picture for a long moment. It was good, but then I'd had an equally good subject. My lens had caught Emily as she'd crouched to adjust her daughter's hat, her smile filled with a mother's love.

"You're welcome."

She replaced it in the envelope, and set it beside her.

Traffic whizzed past and we sat for long moments in awkward silence. I cleared my throat. "Why do you come to the health center?"

She swallowed, her mouth going slack. "A few years back I almost made a terrible mistake."

"Hannah?"

She nodded. "My parents wanted me to have an abortion. They said I was ruining my life. The truth is they were embarrassed. They didn't want their friends to know how their daughter had shamed them."

"But you didn't go through with it."

She shook her head. "It would've been easy. Just make an appointment and show up. But I wanted to keep my baby. I was a sophomore in college. Old enough to know better. My boyfriend dumped me. My father threw me out of the house and I ended up on welfare."

"Things are better now, though, right?"

She nodded. "I finished my degree last semester, but I haven't found a decent-paying job, yet. I get some child support from Hannah's father. Right now I work part time in a book store."

"Sounds like a busy life."

She nodded. "Not half as exciting as working for the newspaper."

"I'm just freelancing," I said, kind of the truth. Had Pony-tail told the others he'd seen me?

She sipped her cocoa as I gave her a much abbreviated version of my life history. If I could figure out a way to touch her, I might get more information out of her.

"You're here on a regular basis," I pressed, hoping my tone seemed casual.

"It's part of our prayer vigil. Some of our older members can't take the cold, that's why I've been here more lately."

"Just how organized is your group? Do you have regular meetings?"

"We meet weekly at the church. Then there's the phone chain," she answered. She looked at me with sudden suspicion. "We're not a bunch of kooks. And we're not dangerous."

"Are you sure of that? Have any of those people ever been arrested?"

"We take that chance every time we picket. Being arrested doesn't mean you're violent."

"I guess that depends on why you're arrested. Your movement hasn't always been violence free. Acid drops, clinics bombed, doctors and nurses shot. And it's insidious. It starts out with small things—like writing slogans in lipstick on people's cars. Egging their windshields."

"I heard about that, but I don't know who did those things. It wasn't any of us."

"Are you sure?"

"No one in our group believes in violence. We believe in the sanctity of *all* life!"

"What about that guy with the Pony-tail?"

"Lou Holtzinger?"

"Yeah. He vandalized my car last night."

"How do you know it was him?"

"He came to the bar where I work part-time. He left me his calling card. Is he really a member of your church?"

She looked away. "He hasn't been with us long. Just since he —" She lowered her voice. "—got out of jail."

"For what?"

She wouldn't look at me. "Stealing cars. Something like that." She stared at her quickly cooling cocoa. "He joined us in good faith. If he's breaking the law I'll . . . I'll have to tell Reverend Linden. He'll have to decide what to do."

"Maybe the police should talk to Bob Linden."

Emily stood, her cheeks flushing. "Look, I'm tired of being branded a nut just because in the past some people in the movement got carried away. Hannah's the best thing that ever happened to me. I just want to make sure other women don't make a terrible mistake."

"And I admire your conviction."

She looked away, biting her lip as her eyes welled with tears.

"Hey, I'm sorry. I'm only here because I'm worried about my friend. Maybe we're here for different reasons, but we can still be friends, can't we?" I held out my hand to her, willing her to take it.

Emily looked down at me under her fringe of blonde bangs. "I guess so." She reached for my hand, wrapped her cool fingers around mine.

I opened myself to her fading anger, embarrassment, and curiosity—about me. Her pulse was racing, her sudden smile shy. Too soon she withdrew her hand, sat down again, and avoided my gaze.

I'd pushed her too hard, too fast, and I hadn't gotten any information on Bob Linden—but I did have Pony-tail's name.

It was time to make nice once again.

"I'd like to take your portrait sometime. It's not my specialty, but I think you'd make a great subject. I could take one of you and Hannah. Sort of an early Christmas present. What do you say?"

"I'll think about it."

"Fair enough."

She looked to where her friends were still shuffling in a circle on the sidewalk across the street from the Women's Health Center. "I'd better get back."

"Sure." I stood, tossed our cups into a nearby trash barrel. "Can I see you again?"

She looked at me shyly. "I'll be here Thursday. Maybe we could go for coffee."

I gave her a smile. "I'll plan on it."

Sam Nielsen was at his desk at the newspaper. After a little persuasion, in the form of coffee and a vending machine candy bar, he did a search of the paper's database and let me read everything they had on Robert Linden. He'd been married to the same woman for thirty-seven years, had four children, and six grandchildren. He was an expert marksman, a decorated Gulf War veteran—no doubt the cause of his Post-Traumatic Stress

Syndrome—active in his church and the Boy Scouts. Not very helpful.

Notes attached to the file indicated Linden had once been considered militant, but after some of the more publicized violence, he'd softened his rhetoric and was now considered a moderate.

I didn't find anything on Lou Holtzinger. I needed to get to the courthouse and look up his criminal record and see if any of the other protesters were ex-cons, too. But I didn't have time that day. I hoped I wouldn't have to visit every township to gather complete information. The thought of all the upcoming legwork made me realize how much I missed my resources at the insurance company.

I wasted another hour getting my headlight replaced. By the time I got home, the mailman was heading down the street. I parked the car and jogged to the mailbox. Sure enough, at the bottom of the stack of junk mail was that familiar envelope. Holly was waiting behind the pantry door, her tail wagging with excitement as I entered the house. I let her out before settling at the table. I didn't bother to remove my jacket but quickly donned a pair of latex gloves and slit the envelope.

The one-word message chilled me: DIE!

11

Detective Bonnie Wilder of the Amherst Police Department studied the three letters. I guessed her to be in her early forties, looking more like a sedentary librarian than a cop. A gold band encircled her left ring finger and silver roots graced the base of the part in her dark hair.

"This is unusual," she said, looking up at me over the rims of her gold-frame glasses. "You say you're the target's brother-in-law? Why didn't she come in herself?"

"She doesn't know about the last two letters. She's pregnant. My brother and I didn't want to upset her."

"She's going to be pissed," the detective predicted.

Despite the knot in my stomach, I managed a weak smile, appreciating her laid-back attitude. "Yeah."

"Of course by opening these, you've tampered with the U.S. Mail. That's a federal offense."

"Are you going to arrest me?"

She shook her head and proceeded to bag the letters and envelopes separately. "I'll send these to the lab and see what they come up with. What else have you got?"

I handed her an envelope with copies of my photos. Post-It notes identified each of the subjects. While she scrutinized them, I unfolded the list of license plate numbers I'd taken at the First Gospel Church and the record of the prank phone calls. I told her about the incidents at the clinic's parking lot, Brenda's run-in with Reverend Linden, and my own encounter with Lou Holtzinger the night before. Tom said he drove a truck. I was willing to bet it was the same one I'd seen at the church—the one with the gun rack.

"You said you're a bartender?" she asked.

"I used to be an insurance investigator."

"A pretty good one by the look of this stuff."

"I knew I'd eventually bring it to the police. I had to wait 'til I'd collected enough to interest you."

"Oh, I'm interested—and the FBI may be, too. But I need to speak with your sister-in-law before I can open a case file."

I glanced at my watch. "How about right now? She's at the Williamsville Women's Health Center."

"Dammit, **Jeffy**, why didn't you tell me about this? I'm a grown-up, too," Brenda protested, glaring at me. As Wilder had predicted, she was pissed.

Brenda and Detective Wilder sat in the visitor chairs in Tim Davies' stark office, while I held up the wall next to a file cabinet. The clinic's security chief's small office reminded me of prison cell, thanks to its gunmetal furniture and walls.

Photocopies of the three letters lay on the edge of the desk before Brenda. She turned her worried gaze back to Detective Wilder. "What happens now?"

"Tell me everything."

Brenda recounted what I'd already told the lady cop, giving it a different spin, but essentially the same information.

"Could the letters, phone calls and other incidents against you be racially motivated?" Wilder asked.

I looked up, suddenly remembering Patty's stupid remark the week before. I'd forgotten to mention that.

"No," Brenda answered and sighed. "I haven't had any trouble. Neither has my husband—at least not that I know about. We keep a pretty low profile."

"I'd advise you to stay that way until we figure out what's going on," Detective Wilder said. "Have you had problems with neighbors? Kids? Any traffic mishaps? Perhaps a death in the family?"

"No."

"What about your ex-husband?"

"It could be him. I haven't talked to him since last Tuesday."

"What precautions have you taken?" Davies asked.

"Jeffy walks me into work," Brenda said.

"We're having a security system installed on Friday," I added. "The phone number was changed as of today, too."

"We'll have a talk with your ex-husband," Detective Wilder said. "And I'll see if we can get a patrol car to pass the clinic every hour or so during the day, and around your house in the evenings. A police presence should keep the protesters from getting cocky. It's possible someone's just trying to scare you. But I'd advise on the side of caution."

Brenda's smile was tight. "Thank you."

"Have you mentioned these calls and incidents to other staff members?" Detective Wilder asked.

"No. They're just as nervous as me. I figured if clinic security knew about it, that would be enough."

The detective nodded. "Is there a reason someone would single you out?"

"Nothing I can think of."

"What about that TV interview?" Davies said.

Brenda blinked. "I'd forgotten all about it."

"What interview?" Wilder asked.

"When the school year started, I went to several high schools to talk to pregnant teens about prenatal care."

"Not abortion?" Wilder asked.

"No."

"We got flack from several churches, including The First Gospel Church," Davies said.

"I knew there had to be a connection," Wilder said. "Otherwise why would Reverend Linden be here?" No one had an answer. "I'd like to speak to some of the other women on staff."

"No problem," the security chief said. "I'll take you around now, if you like."

"I'll keep in touch," Detective Wilder promised, placing her business card in front of Brenda on the desk, then she and Davies left us alone.

Brenda stared at the worn carpet, nervously twisting her wedding band.

"Are you okay?" I asked.

"I'm just really annoyed."

"Then why not do us all a favor and resign."

She looked at me. "I did—this morning. Friday's my last day."

"Good."

Her expression soured.

"Hey, Rich and I aren't just being bossy, overbearing men. We care about you."

"Don't you think I know that?"

"Well, do you?"

She glared at me, then her angry expression melted into an ironic smile. "Of course I do. But what am I going to do, sit at home all day worrying that some kook is out to get me?"

"Rich will be working at the clinic full time for the next few weeks. I'm sure they'd be glad to see your smiling face every day, too."

"I suppose. But I *like* this job. I feel like I make a difference here."

"You can make a difference in a safer place." I handed her her coat. "Now, come on. Let's get out of here."

WE BOTH SAW the long white florist's box sitting on the front doorstep as we pulled up the drive. "They'll be for you, of course," I said, as I shut off the engine and withdrew the key. "No one ever sends me flowers."

"Richard's such a romantic," she said, her eyes shining with excitement.

"You get them. I'll let the dog out."

Holly was happily sniffing the grass in the back yard—no doubt on the trail of a squirrel—by the time Brenda retrieved the box from the step and headed for the back door. I didn't even have a key to the front door, I realized, and wondered if she did.

I held the door for Brenda and wondered why Richard had ordered the flowers to be delivered instead of giving them to Brenda himself.

I switched on the lights while Brenda shrugged out of her coat, tossing it onto a chair. She stood over the box on the kitchen table, wriggled the ribbon off the end, removed the lid, and drew back the green florist's tissue. She gasped.

"Gorgeous, huh?" I asked, taking off my jacket.

She shoved the box aside as though scalded and turned away—a wave of her shock smacked me headlong.

I looked into the box and felt cold. A dozen black roses, with wicked thorns still gracing their slender stems.

YOU WILL DIE, was the message on the letters she'd received. Now this.

I snatched the envelope from among the tissue, and yanked out the card: "Who's sorry now?" No signature.

"My God, who's doing this?" she managed, voice hushed to almost a whisper, and sank into one of the wooden chairs.

I snatched the box lid and turned for the phone, punched in the numbers under the gold-embossed logo. I waited as it rang: one, two, three, four times.

"Castlerock Florist. Can I help you?"

"Yeah. What kind of sick bastard sends black roses?"

There was a pause. "There is no true black rose," the woman said. "But I think I know the order you're talking about. Would you verify the address, please?"

I gave her the information. "Who ordered them?" I demanded.

"Please hold while I look it up."

Brenda stared at the ceramic tile floor, her right hand covering her mouth, eyes wide with fear. I'd almost swear she'd paled.

The woman came back on the line. "They were ordered this morning by a Mr. W. M. Morgan."

"Have you got an address?"

"Sorry, sir, I can't give out that information."

"Thanks, anyway." I hung up the phone and stared into the box. The florist was right. They weren't really black—more a deep purple.

"It was Willie, right?" Brenda asked.

"Yeah. Who's sorry now?" I repeated. "What the hell is that supposed to mean? His not-so-subtle reminder that you and he are black and Richard isn't? Or a thinly veiled threat?"

Brenda wasn't listening. "I didn't think I'd have to call Detective Wilder so soon."

"I'll do it," I said. She retrieved the card from her purse and gave it to me.

The lady cop hadn't yet returned to the station. I left a message, asking her to get back to us.

I hung up the phone, heard Holly barking, and went to let her in. Brenda got up from her chair, drew the kitchen drapes against the deepening twilight.

"Did you hear from Patty today?" she asked, as Holly trotted in and planted herself in front of the fridge, waiting for a snack.

"No. I guess I'd better check my messages," I said, and turned back for the phone. I called my own number, punched in the retrieval code. One message. I had a feeling I didn't want to hear it.

"Jeffrey? It's Patty." Her voice sounded flat, resigned. "Dad slipped into a coma this morning. You'd better come to the hospital if you want to see him before the end. Bye."

I replaced the receiver.

"Shit."

"Bad news?" Brenda asked.

"Yeah."

I tried reaching Richard at the clinic, but he'd already left and had apparently hadn't turned on his cell phone.

"Will you be all right on your own?" I asked Brenda, pulling my jacket on again.

"I've got Holly to protect me," she said, and smoothed the silky hair on the dog's head, setting Holly's tail thumping against the floor. "And Richard will be home any minute now. Go," she said.

"I feel rotten leaving you alone right now."

"Willie sent roses, not a bomb."

"This time," I said.

She frowned. "Go."

.   .   .

THE LATE AFTERNOON traffic was heavy. I kept thinking of Brenda all alone in that big house, yet I found myself welcoming every red light or other delay that would keep me from the hospital.

Why did this have to happen now?

I didn't know who'd be with my father or what I'd say to them. I had a premonition of what I'd experience upon entering that room: being sucked into some dark miasma of misery. My hands clenched the steering wheel.

In the lobby, I pressed the elevator button and the doors obediently surged open. Upstairs, the nurses' station was empty. No geezers with walkers blocked the oddly quiet corridors. I headed for my father's room.

Patty wasn't around. The old man was alone. Why wasn't anyone keeping a death vigil? Had they all stepped out for an early dinner?

Propped up in bed, Chet looked asleep. His waxy complexion had a grayish tone. Without his dentures, his face seemed thin—caved in. Each breath was a struggle.

"Dad?" I called, still uncomfortable with the title—not expecting an answer. "Dad, it's Jeff."

I stood over him, feeling self-conscious. Incredibly, I thought about Star Trek's Mr. Spock and Vulcan mind melds. After being clunked on the head with a baseball bat, I could sometimes absorb others' emotions like a sponge. I found myself suddenly envious of those fictional, unemotional aliens who'd learned to turn off all feelings.

I clenched my hands to keep them from trembling. If I touched the old man, would I gain a whole new understanding of him? Would I learn something to make up for all the years I hadn't known my father? Would it give both of us peace of mind? So far I'd only gotten sadness and regret from him—and an inkling of the depths of his ravaging illness.

I went back to the door, shut it, craving privacy, somehow

knowing this would be my only chance to say good-bye. As I neared the bed, I reached out—stopped, afraid. I had to force myself to rest my fingers on the gnarled knuckles of his puffy hand.

The skin was cool, but I got nothing. No sense of him remained. The body lived, but his mind, his life essence, was ebbing, already inaccessible to me.

I pulled back my hand—disappointment building to anger.

"Can you hear me, old man?"

No reaction.

"You got pissed at my mother and left us. You *never* came back. *Never* saw me grow up. Never let me know you were even alive. You came to my high school graduation, but you never let me see you. Strangers in Manhattan spied on me for you. You knew everything I did—every move I made."

I paced back and forth, yelling at this stranger—I couldn't stop myself.

"How could you do that to me? How could you cheat me like that? Then you had the nerve to tell me you always loved me. You didn't spend an hour of your time with me in thirty-two years. God, I hate you for that."

Chet's eyes snapped opened.

I jumped back, and smacked into the wall.

His gaze wandered to the ceiling, his forehead furrowing as his jaw fell as though in wonder.

I swallowed down terror, unable to look away. He was half of this world and half gone.

"Dad?" I whispered.

His hand reached out, searching for mine, but I was terrified--convinced he'd drag me with him on his final journey. Pinned to the wall, I watched him, like a rubbernecker at a car wreck, as his gaze traveled from left to right and back again as though tracking something—someone?

"Dad?"

Chet's expression grew vague and distant, his eyes drifted shut. His chest rose and fell. The breath rattled through him then abruptly stopped.

"Dad? Dad!" I stepped close, put my ear to his chest, and listened.

Nothing.

Had he heard my tirade, or was he blissfully ignorant of my anger?

Had he known I was there? Had he reached for *me*?

It didn't matter.

My father was dead.

Holy Mary, Mother of God, pray for us sinners—even the Jewish ones who don't believe in you—now and at the hour of our death. Amen.

My vision blurred. I brushed the tears away.

I should've pressed the call button for a nurse—but what for? Richard had signed the no resuscitation order.

Richard.

The room had a phone. I didn't use it. I had to get away—I needed some space.

I cleared my throat and headed out, letting the door whoosh shut behind me. The fluorescent lights in the corridor seemed incredibly bright. I stumbled past the nurse's station and found a pay phone nearby. Dropping coins in the slot, I punched the newly memorized number.

"Hello?"

Relief swept through me. "He's dead."

"What?" Richard asked.

"Chet just died."

"I'm sorry, Jeff. What can I do?"

"Nothing. I just . . . I guess I should've called Patty. But I—"

"Are you okay? You sound funny?"

"It hit me harder than I thought it would."

"Do you want me to come up there?"

"Do you mind?" It sounded like a plea.

"I'll be there in fifteen minutes."

"Thanks." I hung up the phone. Other visitors passed me. Dinner carts rattled down the hall. A voice over the hospital P.A. system paged a doctor.

I took my time walking back to my father's room. A young nurse, no more than twenty-three and dressed in scrubs, smiled at me as she taped garland around the doorway of the meds station. The cheerful Christmas decorations seemed out of place where people came to die.

Chet was just as I'd left him. I sat down to wait in the straight-backed, uncomfortable chair. I knew I should do something, so I picked up the phone, and dialed Patty's number. It rang eight times before I hung up.

A harried-looking nurse's aide poked her bleached-blonde head into the doorway. "I'm a little behind," she said breathlessly. "I'll be back in a few minutes to take his vitals."

She didn't look like she needed another problem, so I nodded dumbly. She propped the door open and walked away.

Numbness crept through me. No more opportunities to get to know the old man. No chance to talk. No more anything.

I hadn't expected to feel such an acute sense of loss.

I looked beyond my father's body to the window. Headlights cut through the gloom outside. People heading home after work, going out to dinner, stopping at the corner store for a quart of milk or a newspaper. Life went on pretty much as usual, but for the first time in seventy-plus years Chet Resnick wasn't around to witness it.

"Jeff?" Richard stood silhouetted in the doorway.

I looked away, feeling embarrassed. He approached the bed, felt for a pulse, and listened for a heartbeat before pulling the sheet over Chet's face. My father was now officially dead.

"Did you call Patty?"

"She wasn't home."

He studied me, making me feel even more uncomfortable. "Are you okay?"

"Yeah."

Was I?

He glanced back at the sheet-shrouded corpse. "I'll tell the nurses. They'll get things started."

"Okay."

He grabbed my arm and pulled me to my feet. "Come on. You can wait down the hall."

PATTY SHOWED up while Richard was signing the death certificate. "I was just down at the cafeteria." Her gaze went from me to Richard. "Daddy—he's gone, isn't he?"

Richard reached for her hand. "I'm sorry."

Dressed in tight jeans, knee-high boots, and a waist-hugging white rabbit jacket, her hair puffed and perfect, she locked her watery gaze on Richard's and held his hand longer than absolutely necessary.

Why did she remind me of a cheap hooker?

"Let's go somewhere more private," Richard said, and led us to an office down the hall. He switched on a couple of lamps, obviously familiar with the room, although another doctor's name plaque was attached to the door.

Patty sat on a couch, dabbed her eyes with a tissue as Richard explained what happened. I didn't say anything, and never felt more useless.

"At least he isn't in pain any more," Patty said. "I just didn't think it would happen this fast." She cleared her throat and straightened in her seat. "Can I use the phone? I have to call Aunt Ruby."

"We'll give you some privacy," Richard said.

We retreated to the hall.

"I need to finish the paperwork." Richard nodded toward the office. "Why don't you hang around in case she needs you?"

"Why would she need me? We don't even know each other."

"Then now's a good time to remedy that." He turned and started down the hall.

I resented his tone—his inference—but I nudged the door open wider, and quietly reentered the office.

Patty hung up the phone, took out a card from her purse, and dialed another number. Perfectly composed, she finalized the arrangements she'd started earlier that day. I quickly learned the differences between Jewish and Catholic death rituals. Chet would be buried the next day. I needed more time—two or three days—to get used to the idea of losing someone. Time for a wake, a funeral Mass—time to grieve.

Richard returned as she replaced the receiver.

Patty wrote down the Temple's address, tore the page from a small spiral notebook, and held it out to me. "You'll be there, of course."

I took the paper. "I'll be there."

She nodded and collected her purse. "I guess I'd better get going. I have a lot to do tonight."

"Is there anything I can do to help?" Richard asked.

She shook her head, but reached for his hand once more. "Thanks for taking care of Dad. He liked you. He said your mother would've been proud of you."

Richard looked thoughtful. Had it occurred to him that Chet was the last link to the mother he never knew?

Patty stepped close, brushed her lips against my cheek. "See you tomorrow." Then she was gone, and I put her out of my thoughts.

I stood there in that silent, dimly lit office, feeling dazed.

Richard shrugged into his jacket. "We'd better head home."

"Yeah, I don't like leaving Brenda alone."

"She's downstairs in the lobby. I wasn't about to leave her alone—not after getting those flowers."

I thought about what happened earlier in the day. "Did she tell you about the letter?"

His eyes narrowed. "What letter?"

I told him as we headed for the exit.

"Why didn't you call me?" he demanded.

"What could you do about it?"

"Be there for Brenda—for one." The edge to his voice intensified.

"Well don't yell at her—or me, either. We both had a shitty day." My voice sounded harder than I'd intended.

"I'm sorry. I just feel . . . frustrated."

I saw a pay phone and had one of my more brilliant ideas. "Let's call Maggie. Let's all go out for dinner. Somewhere noisy, with lots of people."

We ended up at a quaint little Italian restaurant near Maggie's house. The checkered tablecloths and dripping candles in Chianti bottles were about as clichéd as you can get, but the food was good and the drinks were generous. Maggie and Richard made polite conversation while Brenda's distracted gaze remained fixed on her untouched plate. I watched her, kept downing doubles, and tried not to think about the absoluteness of death, black roses, and threats in the mail.

The fresh air hit me like an icy brick as we left the restaurant. The next thing I remembered was Richard helping me up the stairs to my loft apartment. He was talking, but I wasn't listening.

I ended up in my bed, the lights winked out and my queasy

stomach shuddered, making me wish I'd stopped before that last round. I closed my eyes in the silence, knowing that all the bourbon in the world would never obliterate the memory of my father's sightless eyes or the groping hand that had reached for mine.

12

———

The dead man had a face. Roman nose, thin lips and a two-day growth of beard. Haunted eyes. Not an old man as I'd first thought, but past mid-life. Not white, but salt-and-pepper hair hung below his collar.

He opened the screen door and came out of the white frame house. A stiff breeze whipped the tails of his untucked flannel shirt. Thumbs hooked on the empty belt loops of his jeans, he sauntered down the drive. His lips moved as he walked, but I couldn't hear him.

Did he speak to me?

He paused, looked up sharply, and backed away as fear captured his features. Hands raised in submission, he mouthed the words, 'Not my fault.'

Turning, he started to run. The air was fractured by gunfire. His left leg buckled, shattered. He rolled over, his face twisted in agony —terror.

Wordless ranting, then a final shot. Blood spattered across the man's face and onto the grass around him. The wind played with his hair as his brown eyes dulled, staring unseeing at the gray sky.

He was dead.

Again.

. . .

I AWOKE, heart—and head—pounding, knowing I had witnessed a murder. The man who'd haunted my dreams was not my father.

But who the hell was he?

RICHARD SHOWED up on my doorstep about eight o'clock the next morning, forcing me from my bed. I'd awakened with one of my skull-pounding headaches. On a scale of one to ten, this one rated an eight. Not a good start to the day.

Richard made tea and toast, then sat me down at the breakfast bar. I took a sip from my mug, swallowing my migraine medication. The quiet was unnerving.

"You should be taking care of Brenda, not nursemaiding me."

"She understands."

I looked away. Being an object of pity sucked.

The memory of my father's sheet-covered corpse filled my mind. Dread welled up in my chest—making me feel like an asthmatic. But wasn't that a normal reaction to losing a parent? Chet's death was just another of life's passages, a grim reminder of my own mortality.

And what about the dream? The last time I'd been plagued with dreams of death, I'd gotten involved in a murder investigation. No way did I want to repeat that experience. But it bothered me.

I cleared my throat. "Remember when I first came back to Buffalo, I had that recurring dream about a murder?"

"Yeah." Richard's tone said he didn't want to remember, either.

I told him about the most recent nightmares. "At first I

couldn't see the man's face. He was old, with white hair. I thought it had something to do with my father. But the dreams have gotten more detailed. It's no one I recognize."

"Go on."

"It's unsolved. The man was shot twice. First in the leg, from a distance, then point blank in the gut." I couldn't explain it better. I barely understood it myself.

"When did this happen?"

I shrugged. "I don't know."

He set his mug on the table. "Those other dreams brought unpleasant emotions. What do you get now?"

He was beginning to sound like a shrink, but I hadn't really thought about it. "The creeps—like any other nightmare. I'm starting to think I might have a personal stake in this."

There. I said it—making it real.

Richard looked thoughtful. "Dr. Marsh, on our staff, has a good reputation. She might be able to help you figure out what's going on."

I shook my head then wished I hadn't. "No, thanks." I looked away to hide my disappointment at his willingness to just pass me on to a colleague. Then again, the dreams related to Matt Sumner's murder had been the first link in a chain of events that led to Richard being shot. No wonder he wasn't eager to repeat the exercise.

Besides, he had enough on his mind.

"I guess I'll just wait and see what happens." I stared at the crumbs littering my plate. "Will you go with me to the funeral?"

"Of course, we'll be there. I've already got someone to cover for us at the clinic."

"Not Brenda."

He frowned, his brows narrowing. "Why? Are you ashamed of her?"

"How can you even ask?" I took a shaky breath. How could I

convince him? There was no easy way to say it. "I don't want people I don't really know or care about to say something that could hurt her."

His eyes bored through me. "Do you have reason to believe someone might say something?"

"Maybe."

He looked away, stared into his own mug for a moment, then exhaled. "Okay. I'd better get changed." He pushed back his chair, and grabbed his jacket. "I'll be back in twenty minutes."

"Thanks, Rich. Thanks for everything."

He managed a smile. "Don't mention it."

I took my time getting dressed. I even gave my shoes a fresh coat of polish. I wanted to look good—a useless gesture. My father was dead. My appearance wouldn't make a damned bit of difference to him.

By the time Richard returned, I stood in front of the mirror in my bedroom and finished tying my tie.

"Have you ever been to a Jewish funeral?" he asked from the doorway.

I shook my head and winced at the stab of pain it brought.

"At the grave site, Orthodox Jews rip their clothes to show sorrow. Especially for a parent."

I looked at my suit jacket and considered how much such a repair would cost. "Do I have to?"

"It depends. Take your cue from Patty."

I donned the jacket, fastening the center button. "How do you know so much?"

"I've lost several Jewish friends over the years. Believe me, I'd rather I didn't know the customs."

"The family's not Orthodox. Patty told the undertaker they were Jewish Lite." It didn't sound funny. I stared at the reflection of my brown eyes flecked with gold. My father's eyes. "It never hit me before. I'm half Jewish."

"Technically, the mother's religion defines the children's, and Betty was Catholic."

"A good Catholic, too. She went to Mass at least twice a week—sometimes more."

"Did she?" he asked, truly interested.

I nodded. "Your grandmother was Catholic. How come Mom being the same religion didn't mean anything to the old witch?"

"Grandmother wouldn't have approved of any woman my father brought home. She thought *she* should be his life."

"Too bad." If things had worked out different, I might be looking at a reflection of the same blue eyes Richard had inherited from John Alpert.

I stared at myself in the mirror, standing so straight in my somber suit. I hadn't worn it since Shelley's funeral. Funny, I'd worn it to our wedding, too. Bad luck seemed to dog that suit.

"Shelley and I got married at City Hall," I said, still staring at my reflection.

Richard's gaze moved to the mirror, his expression darkening at this comment from left field.

"Dan McNeil, a guy from work, was my best man. Some woman Shelley worked with was our maid of honor. I don't even remember her name. We went out for Chinese afterwards. We had a weekend honeymoon at a B and B in Cape May. It was off-season, so the rates were cheap."

It seemed like so long ago.

Tears threatened and, ashamed, I looked away. "God, I feel awful."

Richard's voice was gentle. "You'll be okay."

"I suppose Chet could've loved me." I looked at my brother for confirmation, feeling pathetic.

"Yeah." Richard grasped my shoulder, and gave it a squeeze. "Come on. We don't want to be late."

. . .

WE DROPPED Brenda at the hospital's clinic and headed for the temple. I tried to decide if my discomfort resulted from not knowing what to expect or not knowing the people who'd be there. Or was it only the remnant of a hangover?

I followed Richard up the steps and paused to straighten my tie. The old brick building looked seedy, run-down on the outside. Inside, the interior was spotless, with polished wood and freshly waxed floors. I had to force myself not to greet the few familiar faces I knew by name—Patty, Ruby, and Vera. Richard said it was a Jewish custom. No one greeted me. Still, Patty reached for Richard's hand, and told him how pleased she was that he'd come. He looked flattered, which annoyed me. Or maybe it was the admiring look he gave her. Dressed in a black knit mini-dress with dark stockings, Patty could've been going to a cocktail party instead of a funeral.

A wizened little man in a shiny black suit gave us yarmulkes. Why hadn't I asked her to come instead? As the oldest child, and only son, I sat up front, next to Patty, with Richard on the other side of me. I would've preferred to blend into the background. My aunts, Ruby and Vera, and their families, were close behind me. So close, I could hear Vera's heavy breathing. Had she been a smoker, too?

The closed casket sat at the front of the room, sprays of flowers flanking it. Richard gave me my cues when to stand and when to sit. Thanks to him, I didn't look like a complete yutz, yet I didn't feel part of the service, either. I was a good Catholic boy in the middle of a Jewish funeral, feeling like I should recite the rosary.

The scent of gladiolus filled the air. Faces around me were twisted with emotion. Watching others grieve is difficult. Experiencing their grief is unbearable. Sorrow, despair and even boredom bombarded me from all directions. I could tell that some of the mourners came out of family duty. The children were happy for a day off school. Only Richard and Patty were blanks to me, but their presence was no shield against the onslaught of emotions the others broadcasted.

I had to force myself to listen as the young rabbi spoke of my father and his lasting effect on all of us. One by one family members rose to tell how my father had impacted their lives.

Patty stood. Clutching a tissue, she wiped her nose. "When I was ten, I wanted to skate like Oksana Baiul. Daddy once closed the shop to take me to the Ice Capades. Then he paid for lessons and pretty sequined outfits, even though he really couldn't afford it. That's the kind of Dad he was."

She brushed against my arm as she sat down, but I couldn't look at her. Clamping down on my envy, I stared at the coffin. She'd at least had a life with him--he'd abandoned me.

Vera was next. "I remember," she said, her voice cracking. She pressed a hand to her lips while she composed herself. "I remember how Chet helped so many friends and relatives down on their luck. Giving them jobs at his dry cleaning store."

"He was always generous," Ruby added. "He'd give you the shirt off his back."

No one mentioned his drinking or gambling—the only things I'd heard about while growing up. No one mentioned my mother or the life he led before he straightened up—before he met Joan and started his second family.

Ruby beamed when she spoke of Chet's reunion with me. She turned her tear-filled gaze toward me. "You brought such joy to his last days."

I looked away, feeling uncomfortable.

A long silence followed.

I didn't get up. I had no stories to tell.

While the relatives sniffled or sobbed through more prayers, I sat hunched over, rubbing my throbbing temples, feeling limp from the pain of their grief. I couldn't make it my own. It attacked my brains like a jackhammer through concrete. Even blinking hurt. The pills I'd downed at breakfast hadn't helped a bit.

Maybe what I needed was time to put some perspective on just what it was I thought and felt about a man who hadn't been a father to me in thirty-two years. But it didn't help at that moment.

Another funeral shadowed my thoughts.

St. Michael's Church had seemed cavernous with so few mourners attending my mother's funeral mass twenty-two years before. A spray of pink roses covered the silver coffin. Richard probably paid for everything. I was fourteen then, and didn't worry about such things.

I remembered Richard clearly—a stranger I'd only known for two days—and how odd it felt to sit next to him. I didn't cry. No way would I show weakness in front of him. Now I realized I'd been numb—there'd been too many changes for a kid to absorb in such a short time.

I tried to remember more of that day, of the vaguely familiar faces of neighbors or my mother's co-workers from the restaurant where she'd waitressed the breakfast and lunch shifts for almost seven years. Most of the faces were a blur, but I remember turning in my seat to see a lone man enter the church. He knelt and genuflected before sliding into one of the pews. He'd known the Mass, recited every prayer.

Until that moment, I hadn't realized that the man was a thinner, dark-haired version of Chet Resnick.

My father.

Preoccupied with the past, I hadn't noticed the ceremony had ended. Richard stood. I stayed seated as everyone else headed for the exit, like passengers on a plane, eager to end the journey.

. . .

A BRIEF CEMETERY SERVICE FOLLOWED. Patty played the role of the bereaved like an Oscar contender. She lost no opportunity to drape her hand over Richard's arm like an ornament. Maybe her long, wistful gazes were filled with genuine grief. Was it cynical of me to think otherwise? Meanwhile, Richard seemed comfortable in his role as her unofficial escort, leaving me to silently fume.

I walked behind them from the grave. My quiet, darkened bedroom beckoned, a haven from that pounding headache, but as we reached the line of parked cars, Ruby turned and sought me out.

"You'll come to the house, won't you?"

Richard looked at me quizzically.

I wanted to tell her 'no' and get the hell out of there, but my aunt's watery, familiar-looking eyes did a number on me. I gave her a weak smile. "Sure."

She squeezed my hand.

Always the consummate gentleman, Richard helped the ladies into the waiting limo. Patty hit the electronic window control to lower the glass, raising her hand in a coy wave as the Lincoln started off down the narrow strip of asphalt.

Richard pulled up his collar against the wind. "Are you sure you're up to this? You don't look well."

His sudden concern irked me. "Is that a professional opinion?"

"Yes, actually, it is."

I exhaled a shaky breath. "I have to go. It would look bad if I didn't."

"Since when do you care what people think?"

He was right; doing something for appearance's sake had never mattered to me before. I didn't answer.

The rest of the mourners were already in their cars, driving away. I glanced back toward my father's grave, reminded of other unfinished business.

"I've been back in Buffalo for almost nine months and I haven't visited Mom's grave. How about you?"

Richard shook his head. "Let's go."

We made it to Mt. Calvary Cemetery in minutes. It had been years since either of us had been there. We traveled around the same section three times before Richard remembered where to find the grave. We parked the car and walked the slight incline.

Tall, dried grass obliterated the base of the simple, white granite monument. Only our mother's name and the years of her birth and death marked the stone. It gave no hint of who she'd been or the life she'd lived. Or those she'd left behind.

Wind rustled the naked branches of a nearby maple. I stared at the carved words, feeling empty. Losing her had changed my life, probably for the better. What a pathetic epitaph.

"She would've been sixty-eight now," Richard said.

I huddled into my raincoat, annoyed I'd forgotten my gloves. "She had a shitty life. It may as well have ended the day your father died."

"I wish I'd known her better."

I looked up at him. "You might not have liked what you'd have seen."

"What do you mean?"

"Her drinking, mostly." I looked away and hoped he wouldn't press me for more. I didn't have the words to tell him. "What did your grandfather tell you about her?"

He shrugged, and stared blankly at the headstone. "That she was a sick woman who deserved our pity."

Old Mr. Alpert had been right.

"You don't realize how damn lucky you are," Richard said. "You've found a family that wants to welcome you—something I always wanted. I used to daydream of having brothers and sisters. The reality was a small boy with elderly grandparents, no one to play with, and a very, very quiet house."

I stared at the grave. "I had no one, either." And I'd lived with a mother who'd loved him, not me.

Until that moment, the depth of my childhood jealousy toward Richard had never fully registered. Here was that phantom brother who'd commanded all my mother's love, even though he wasn't there, leaving nothing for me. For an instant I wanted to haul off and hit him—to make him pay for the years of neglect I'd had to endure.

He stared at the marker—at the name carved into stone; a woman he'd never known. Maybe it wasn't so much anger I felt as frustration. Richard had wanted our mother's love and she'd longed to love him. We'd all been scarred by the experience.

I felt stupid and ashamed and suddenly quite unwell. I cleared my throat, took in a deep breath of cold, fresh air. "You're not alone any more, Rich. You have Brenda and me."

"And soon I'll have a son or a daughter." A weak smile brightened his features.

I didn't even want to think about it.

13

———

The ride to Ruby's house took forever. Richard drove my car—I was too far gone by then, which should've warned me. The closer we got, the worse I felt.

Cars lined the road in front of the little Cape Cod, which seemed forlorn in the wan December sunlight.

"Are you sure you're up to this?" Richard asked again as he parked the car.

"No. We'll have a cup of coffee then leave. Okay?"

He nodded. We got out, and headed for the house.

A steaming pitcher of water sat on the front step. Clean towels were draped over the iron railing.

"You have to wash your hands," Richard advised.

"Another custom?"

"It's an act of purification after being in close proximity to the dead."

I followed his lead, washing my hands before we entered the quiet, crowded house. The atmosphere seemed charged, not so much with grief, but with a sense of relief. The funeral was over; it was time to regroup. Black fabric draped all the mirrors in a show of respect for the deceased. After such a loss, the living don't need to be concerned with their appearance.

Patty made a beeline for Richard, taking his coat before whisking him off to be introduced to all the relatives, and leaving me to fend for myself.

Shucking my raincoat, I wandered into the kitchen, and saw a lavish spread of food covering the kitchen counter. Ruby had donned an apron to protect her black mourning dress. She pushed a plate into my hand. "You're so skinny. Doesn't your Maggie feed you?" she asked, and stood on tiptoe to kiss my cheek.

I attempted to smile. "She tries."

"And you're so pale. You should take vitamins—with minerals. Now sit, sit." She ushered me to one of the chairs around the Formica table. "Will you have some tea?"

"I'll have coffee if you've got it," I said, more interested in a strong caffeine fix for my pounding head. It was a big mistake for me to come. I took a bite of bagel, chewed, and struggled to swallow it.

My gaze wandered to the family room, where Richard and Patty stood conversing. She smoked a cigarette, holding an ashtray. He nodded sympathetically, his face a study in kindness. Nearby, the chair my father had sat in less than a week before was empty. Seeing it left a hollow feeling in my gut.

Ruby set a cup of coffee in front of me. "There you go, dear. Let me know if you need anything else." She patted my shoulder, transmitting another blast of unwelcome emotion.

I fumbled in my pocket, found my vial of pills, and downed two of them with a sip of black coffee.

Images from the past bombarded me: three funerals meshing, superimposed. Three coffins. Three deaths. My mother, my dead ex-wife—Shelley—and Chet. Three people who could've shown me love—three people who'd chosen not to. What was it in me that was so unworthy?

Then again, my father's dying moment would always haunt me. The one time he'd reached out for me, I'd rejected him—let him die alone, without another's touch.

My throat closed as guilt set in again.

Voices in the living room distracted me. Ruby turned away from the sink, her brow furrowed as she looked from the front of the house back to Patty.

I got up. "Is something wrong?"

"It's Ray, that friend of Patty's." Disapproval filled her voice. "They had a terrible fight after you left the other night. He's *not* Jewish," she muttered, as though that explained his rudeness. It reminded me, too, where I stood.

"I just wanna pay my respects," said the voice. "Patty!"

Patty looked up as Ruby gestured for her. She gave Richard a tight smile and hurried into the kitchen. "What is it?" she asked Ruby.

"Patty!" Ray hollered.

"Oh, God!" Patty groused, recognizing the voice. She stamped out her cigarette, slammed the ashtray onto the table, and stormed off.

I followed.

Walking into that living room was like penetrating a bubble of corrosive anger. It radiated from all around, and made me stagger back. Vera's son-in-law, Michael, stood near the doorway, blocking the way. Ray's thinning brown hair was combed back. The bright blue ski jacket he wore was zippered half-way, revealing a dress shirt and tie underneath. His eyes, fever bright, were filled with accusation.

"What the hell do you want, Ray?" Patty grated.

"I just came to pay my respects," he said, lowering his voice as he took in the menacing glares all around him.

"I asked him to leave," Michael said.

Richard wandered up to stand behind me. The other men were on their feet, edging closer. Ray backed up. He caught sight of me and time seemed to stand still. A wave of dizziness swept over me. My sight wavered as though a powerful x-ray shot through me, so strong was his rage.

"Look, I don't want any trouble," Ray said, backing up a step.

"Then why don't you just go," Michael said.

"I'll call you later, Ray," Patty said.

"You promise?"

"Yes. Now please go!"

Ray glared at her for a long moment, an unreasonable fury seething from him. Then he turned and let the storm door bang behind him. He kicked aside the glass pitcher, which shattered on the concrete walk.

Michael stalked after him, and then stood at the bottom of the drive to make sure he left. Several cousins went out to pick up the mess. The others crowded around the windows to watch the show.

My head was ready to split. I took a breath and looked at Patty. "What was that all about?"

"Ray can't get it through his head that I'm not interested in him. I'm sorry you had to see that," she said, but she was looking at Richard, not me.

My overloaded brain felt like a saturated sponge. Nausea made me shaky and my knees gave way. Richard grabbed my arm, steadying me.

"We'd better go, too," he said.

"Too late. I gotta crash—now."

"Is something wrong?" Ruby asked, concerned.

"Can Jeff lie down for a few minutes?" Richard asked.

"Oh, Sweetie, I'm sorry you're not well. We all knew Chet's time was short, but it's still such a shock." Ruby moved closer, touched my face. The swell of compassion she transmitted was too much for my battered psyche.

I tried to push her hand away. "You don't understand—" I started, but Richard cut me off.

He shoved me forward. "Come on."

All eyes were on us as Ruby led us past the crowd in the living room to a bedroom off the side hall. Twin beds were heaped with coats and she and Richard cleared one for me. I shrugged out of my jacket and collapsed onto the chenille spread. Ruby lowered the shade at the window and discreetly left.

"Sorry I dragged you here, Rich. I thought I could make it—"

"We'll leave as soon you're able."

"You're the best."

He pulled the door closed and left me alone.

I lay there, breathing shallowly, desperate not to jostle my aching head, and trying not to listen to the muffled sounds of voices in the other room. My cheeks felt hot—humiliation at showing such weakness in front of all those strangers—my family.

I was really tired of that particular emotion.

I tried to blank my mind, but the image of Ray's hate-filled gaze was burned onto my brain cells.

What was it about Patty that inspired such passion in other men?

I MUST'VE SLEPT—UNDISTURBED by dreams of the dead man— for when I cracked open my eyes the shadows on the wall were long. The mound of coats on the other bed was gone and the house was still. My back and neck ached from the too-soft bed and flat pillow, but the pounding in my skull had diminished.

I found the bathroom and threw cold water on my face. I still felt like shit, but well enough to leave. I wondered about making an entrance and decided I was making too big a deal of my infirmities. After all, I never had to see these people again.

The late afternoon sky was washed with pink near the horizon and lamps blazed in the living room. How long had I slept?

Richard and Patty were together on the couch, huddled over a photo album, deep in conversation. Something about that irritated me. Jealousy? That didn't seem right. Richard's suit jacket was draped over the back of a chair. His loosened tie and rolled-up sleeves made him look more like a working class stiff than a wealthy physician.

I staggered closer. The book was open to a black-and-white photo of an elderly woman. Her face was familiar, as was that of the child on her lap.

They looked up. "Feeling better?" Richard asked.

"Yes."

"You've been asleep for almost three hours," Patty said. "But it's given Richard and me a chance to become friends." Her smile for him was sweet, or maybe beguiling.

"Sorry to be so much trouble." I couldn't keep the edge from my voice. Hadn't I made the same flip remark to Richard only days before?

"Oh, it's okay," Patty said, her attention totally focused on my brother. "Richard explained all about your problems. It sure is nice to have a doctor in the family." She beamed at him like a silly schoolgirl. But Richard wasn't a member of *her* family. And what precisely had he been telling her?

Richard obviously enjoyed the attention. And why not? She was almost half his age. I suppose she was attractive—in an incestuous kind of way.

I leaned against one of the upholstered chairs and looked at my watch. "We should get going. Brenda will be worried."

"I called her," Richard said. "Maggie's picking her up at the clinic."

Patty's hand snaked across Richard's arm—he seemed mesmerized. And his disregard for Brenda's safety bugged me.

I cleared my throat. "I can handle the car ride now."

Patty's short skirt was reduced to the size of a handkerchief, exposing a generous portion of her black-stockinged thigh. Was it my imagination, or did Richard's gaze seem permanently fixed?

"We need to get home to let Holly out," I said, reminding him of Maggie's dog locked in his house. "Unless you don't value your carpets."

He looked up at me. "Oh, yeah." He smiled at Patty, that stupid, sympathetic grin that had annoyed me earlier in the day.

I turned away and found my coat. Ruby emerged from the kitchen. The goodbyes seemed interminably long. Richard received hugs from the women like *he* was the long-lost relative. I stood back while my ire continued to rise, making my head pound.

Patty walked us to the door. She kissed Richard's cheek, pulled back, looked at him, a seductive gleam in her eye. "Thanks for making this day easier on me."

He patted her hand. "I was happy to help out."

My anger flared white hot. "Good-bye, Patty." I charged forward, and headed for the car.

Richard still had my keys—I had to wait for him to unlock the passenger side door. Patty stood behind the storm door and waved as the car pulled away from the curb.

Rush hour traffic choked Sheridan Drive. Every bump in the road conspired to jostle my battered brains.

"What the hell got into you back there?" Richard spat at last.

I eyed him coldly. "You. And *her*. The way she fawns over you. Can't you see what she is?"

"She's a nice person who's lost someone she loves. Why do you always think the worst of people?"

My head ached fiercely. I was in no shape for a battle with Richard. I stared out the window.

"Patty's not so bad," he continued. "You ought to give her a chance."

I squinted at him across the seat. "I don't plan to see her again."

His voice hardened. "She's your sister. As much as I'm your brother."

I didn't want to discuss it.

"What are you going to do about Hanukkah?" he pressed.

"I'm not Jewish. I don't celebrate it."

"Would it hurt you to go to Ruby's party?"

"I suppose Patty invited you?"

"Yes, she did."

"How about Brenda?"

"Of course she invited Brenda, too."

Was he so naive? Couldn't he see what she was up to? How could so intelligent a man—so educated a man—be taken in by a bimbo like Patty?

I took a breath, holding onto my temper. "Rich, I don't feel well. I don't want to talk about it."

"There you go, hiding behind your headaches to avoid any meaningful emotional contact."

"The reason I have headaches," I reminded him, "is because I have *too* much emotional contact. And what kind of doctor are you to lay this shit on me when I'm ready to puke my fucking guts up!"

"Go ahead, insult me. I'm immune to it."

He braked for a red light. I was tempted to get the hell out of the car and stalk off into the twilight. But I really was too sick to pull that kind of childish stunt.

The light went green. The car surged forward.

"Will you go to Ruby's party?" Richard pushed.

"Probably not."

"I think you're making a mistake. They're nice people. They care about you."

"Yes, they probably do." I left it at that, closed my eyes, and sank back in the seat.

Richard took the hint. We ignored each other for the rest of the ride home. But this wouldn't be the end of the discussion. And I had a feeling that ridding myself of Patty wouldn't be so easy, either.

14

I wasn't up to another lecture from Richard, so instead of going over to get Brenda the next morning, I took the coward's way out and called her. My car had been running for five minutes and the heat had finally kicked in by the time she came out of the house.

Brenda hopped in the passenger seat, and buckled up. "Jeffy, you still look like shit."

"I don't feel that great, either."

"Oh, hon, I can drive myself."

"It's not safe."

She shook her head and gave me a wry smile. "It looks like I'll be the one protecting you."

I put the car in gear and started down the drive.

"What's bothering you?" Brenda said. She's almost as adept at reading me as I am at reading her.

I called her bluff. "Who says anything's bothering me?"

"You phoned instead of coming over. That's not like you. You'd better tell me now—I know you don't like to be nagged, and you know I will."

Eyes focused on the road, I gripped the steering wheel. "It's Rich. He pissed me off yesterday."

"About Patty?"

I nodded.

"He did sing her praises for quite a while last night. But he still feels like he has to look out for you. It bothers him that you're such a loner. That apart from us, and Maggie, you have virtually no friends—no support system. It's okay, Jeffy," she hurriedly continued, "that's just the way you are. You have to do what feels right for you. And if that means staying away from Patty, then that's what you have to do."

I felt her eyes on me, but couldn't bear to look at her.

"Something about her repels me."

"Are you getting some kind of psychic message on her?"

I shook my head. "My father gave off strong impressions, but she's a blank, just like Rich."

Brenda was quiet for a moment. "Maggie thinks something bad happened when you were a child."

My hands tightened on the steering wheel. "She doesn't know what she's talking about."

"I think she does." Her voice was gentle, full of compassion.

"She's wrong. I don't remember much about those days, and I don't want to remember." That sounded like major denial, even to me.

"Did your father hit you when you were little?" Brenda pressed.

"No."

"You can tell me. I've been there, remember?"

I braked for slowing traffic. "There's nothing to tell."

She touched my shoulder, and looked like she wanted to say so much. Yet she knew me well enough not to push.

We drove the rest of the way in silence.

Half a block from the clinic I saw a familiar car parked along the curb. Pennsylvania license plates.

"Shit. Willie's here."

Brenda's eyes widened in panic. "Oh my God! How could he know where I work? Do you think he's been following me?"

"Let's not panic," I said, trying to calm her. "Maybe, maybe —" There really wasn't a good explanation. Had Detective Wilder let slip where Brenda worked when she'd questioned him? At least Willie wouldn't find Brenda alone.

"Maybe he just wants to meet you on neutral ground," I said.

"I don't want to see *or* talk to him!" she said, her voice teetering on hysteria.

"You don't have to." I found a parking space, and then looked up and down the street. There was no sign of Willie, but the protesters with their placards still marched on the sidewalk across the street. Maybe he was inside the building—or worse, lying in wait for Brenda.

I unbuckled my seat belt. "I'll go look for him. Stay in the car. Don't open the doors or windows. If he tries to get in, blow the horn and don't let up."

I locked my door and slammed it.

Willie came out the clinic as I approached. He saw me and picked up his pace to intercept. "Where's Brenda?" he demanded.

"She doesn't want to see you."

"Why'd she tell the cops to come after me?"

"It's their job to protect the public. Someone's harassing her. We had to tell them you're in town. If you aren't responsible, you've got nothing to worry about."

"The hell I don't! I just started a new job. My boss was pissed when a couple of cops showed up at the office yesterday. Where is she?"

The protesters had slowed in their circuit. Lou Holtzinger was among them, watching me with hawk-like interest.

"She doesn't want to see you," I repeated.

"No law says I can't talk to my ex-wife," Willie insisted, and stepped around me.

I darted into his path. "No, but there *are* anti-stalking laws."

"What are you talking about?"

"She's terrified of you."

"Why?"

"Think about it. How many times did you beat her senseless?"

Willie's eyes flashed in anger. "That was a long time ago."

"Yeah, well, Brenda hasn't forgotten. And what's the idea of sending her black roses?"

"What do you care—she's not *your* wife."

"And she's not *yours*, either."

"I've got a right to see her," he grated, moving forward.

I stepped in front, blocking him again. "No, you don't—"

Without warning, Willie's fist plowed into my face. I stumbled and he batted me aside like an annoying insect, knocking me to my knees.

Blood poured from my nose. My vision grayed and doubled. Blurry shapes danced around me. Someone helped me to my feet and dragged me onto the heath center's concrete steps, where I collapsed against the banister. I looked up, blinked at two Emily Farrells.

"Sit back." She pressed a wad of tissues into my hand, and held it against my bloody face.

"Brenda! Where is she?"

Heavy footsteps thundered. "Are you okay?" a deep voice said near my ear.

"That big black guy punched him out!" Emily said.

I blinked at the uniformed security guard standing over me.

"He's after Brenda Stanley. She's in a white Chevy Malibu down the block." I waved toward my car and the guard took off.

"Let's get you inside," Emily said, grabbing my arm, hauling me to my feet.

"No. I gotta help Brenda." I straightened and wobbled until I got my bearings. My eyesight wavered then cleared.

Brenda stood next to my car, shouting, waving her arms, and told the security guard to go after Willie. The Altima took off with a screech of tires, and flew past them.

I waved off Emily as Brenda caught sight of me, and ran to meet me on the sidewalk. She wrapped an arm around my shoulder. "My hero," she said. Her laugh sounded more like a sob.

"Some hero. Looks like I'm a pipsqueak after all." I wiped at my still dripping nose.

"Are you okay?"

"I don't think it's broken."

"Anything else?" she asked, serious.

"No."

"Let's get you checked out anyway," she said, already dragging me up the sidewalk.

"This is a *women's* health center—I'm a man!"

"Don't be so damned picky."

We left Emily behind as Brenda guided me up the steps. Within minutes I was being quizzed, poked, and prodded by one of the staff, a Dr. Newcomb. My skull fracture less than a year before made me a prime candidate for a concussion. I lucked out, although she warned me I'd probably have a nice black-and-blue mouse under my left eye if I didn't put some ice on it.

Brenda was waiting for me when I came out of the treatment room. "I'm taking you home."

"No, you're not. You're staying here. I'm going to the Amherst

Police Station and file a complaint. I'll try to talk with Detective Wilder, too."

"But—"

"No buts. I'll pick you up at four. Don't be late."

"Yes, sir." She walked me to the clinic doors. "Are you sure you're okay?"

"Yes. But I feel crummy. I let you down."

"You did not. You kept that horrible man from getting to me and I'm damned grateful. But what're we going to tell Richard?"

"The truth. But don't get crazy and call him. It can wait until he gets home from work to hear this news."

She nodded. "I love you, Jeffy." She kissed my cheek and threw her arms around me. "Thank you."

I wrapped my arms around her, buried my nose in her neck, held her tight, closed my eyes and thanked God she was safe.

She stiffened in my embrace.

I pulled back, stared into her deep brown eyes—fought the almost overwhelming urge to kiss her.

Her confusion swelled, fear trickling in.

Backing up a step, I laughed nervously. "Get to work, now."

She forced a smile and saluted me. "Aye, Captain," she said and turned.

I watched her slowly head down the corridor, wondering what had just happened between us. I turned to leave.

Pausing at the top step, I watched the protesters circle in front of the building. Emily hurried across the street to meet me on the sidewalk.

"Your jacket's ruined," she said, pointing to the bloodstains that marred my coat.

"It'll wash. Thanks for helping me."

Her eyes shone and she smiled. "What're friends for?"

It was my turn to force a smile. "I promised to take you for coffee. When's a good time?"

"My lunch break's about one."

"I'll see you then."

"I'm glad you're okay." She squeezed my arm, turned, and then looked both ways before crossing the road and rejoining her companions.

Lou Holtzinger glared at me.

Why did I feel like I'd been caught doing something wrong?

BONNIE WILDER FROWNED. "I would've sworn Willie Morgan was a reformed character."

I looked up from the paperwork before me. I'd gone straight to the Amherst Police Station and found the detective in. "Why?"

"He's been clean for eight years. Not even a parking ticket."

"Have you talked to the cops in Philly?"

She nodded.

"Tell me about the years when Willie wasn't 'clean.'"

She settled on a chair across the table from me. "Assault. He did thirty days in the county lock-up."

"Domestic abuse?"

She shook her head. "Against a co-worker."

"There's no record of him beating Brenda?"

She shrugged. "Apparently your sister-in-law never filed a complaint."

"She was probably too ashamed."

"I've heard that story too many times. I'm still digging."

I signed my name and handed her the form. "Will you follow-up on this?"

She nodded. "Mr. Morgan cooperated fully when I took samples from his computer printer the other day."

"And?"

"Same font, same type of paper. But they're almost universal. The State Crime Lab will run a comparison."

"How long will that take?"

"They're pretty backed up," she admitted. "A couple of weeks—maybe a month. Or more."

I pushed my chair back, stood. "What about Lou Holtzinger?"

"His past is well documented. Busted for joy riding at sixteen. It's a habit he hasn't quite kicked. He's been in and out of jail for the last twenty years."

"I heard he just got out."

"About six weeks ago."

"I suppose he found Jesus in jail?"

She laughed. "They usually do. The First Gospel Church's secretary said Holtzinger joined the flock through their Prisoner Outreach program. He's got a church sponsor, and he shows up every Sunday and Wednesday for services."

"That doesn't mean he's a model citizen."

"He hasn't stepped out of line so far."

"What about the damage to my car?"

"No one saw him do that."

"But we both know he did."

"Knowing it and proving it are two entirely different things." Her gaze was level, but her mouth hinted at an ironic smile.

Suddenly I realized why I liked Bonnie Wilder: she reminded me of Maggie. Sweet, smart, and practical.

And older than me. About the same age as my mother when she'd died.

Was I attracted to older women because my mother had been too preoccupied to show me any affection? Was I subconsciously searching for a mother substitute?

I didn't want to think about it. I didn't want to think about a lot of things lately. Denial, thy name is Resnick.

Detective Wilder walked me to the door. "Call me if anything else happens." She scribbled a number on the back of her business card. "If things escalate, call me at home."

"Thanks. I appreciate it."

I headed for my car, wondering just how one forty-something lady detective was going to protect Brenda—and me — from further harm.

I DROPPED my coat off at a dry cleaner, knowing the blood might never come out. But they had a better shot at it than me. At home, I grabbed my ski jacket and headed back to Williamsville to take Emily Farrell to lunch. We met at the diner around the corner from the clinic.

She took a sip of her coffee. "Your eye looks terrible."

"Thanks. You look swell."

She actually blushed. "I'm supposed to discourage you."

"Says who?"

"My friends. And Reverend Linden says you're just using me to get information on the group."

Caught, I didn't blink. "Is that what you think?"

"I don't know."

"You're an intelligent, attractive woman. I'd like to get to know you better." No lie there.

"You seem like a nice guy, too. But for all I know you could be a serial killer."

"Me?"

"Well, you do believe in abortion. Murder is murder."

Her words stung. I struggled to keep my face neutral. "Just because I walk my friend into the clinic every day doesn't mean I believe in abortion. Does anybody really believe in abortion? The issue is choice."

"There should be no choice."

She was so young and suddenly I felt old. How could I make her understand?

The waitress arrived with our soup and sandwiches. I waited for her to leave.

"My father died the day before yesterday."

Emily looked stricken. "Oh, I'm so sorry."

I waved off any further sympathy. "His doctor, my friend—" I didn't want to go into details on my relationship with Richard. "—approved a no resuscitation order."

"Is that what your father wanted?"

I nodded. "He'd been sick a long time. He was ready to die. It was his choice not to fight any more. But it bothered me."

"You wouldn't have made that choice?"

"I don't know," I answered honestly. "What about you?"

"I'd put my life in God's hands," she said without hesitation, "just like your father did. But it's not the same thing as abortion."

"Of course it is. It's choosing to end a life."

She shook her head. "There's a natural order to things. It's God's gift to us."

"God gives doctors the knowledge to prolong life—and sometimes suffering."

"It's the quality of life that counts," she countered.

"Could you compare a man with crippling emphysema to a severely retarded child with catastrophic birth defects?"

Her eyes blazed. "It's not the same thing."

"It is," I insisted.

"Look, I almost killed my baby. If I had my way, no one else would ever make that mistake."

"But it should be their decision. Not yours."

She shook her head, unwilling to listen.

I tried again. "Your baby was born healthy. What if she wasn't? What if you'd known before she was born that something went terribly wrong. That her life would be filled with misery."

"I would thank God every day for sending her to me. It would be my test," she said, her voice rising.

"Your test? For what?"

"This is a circular argument," Emily said, looking away. "You're not going to change your mind, and I'm not going to change mine."

I nodded tiredly. "I guess we're both stubborn."

Her answering smile looked strained. "Yes."

"Then let's drop the subject."

"I agree." She pushed her soup bowl away. "I'm sorry, Jeff, but I don't think we can ever really be friends."

"Why, because we disagree?"

She nodded.

"I'm sorry you feel that way." What's more, I really was.

Emily grabbed her coat and struggled into the sleeves. "Thanks for lunch." She hadn't eaten a bite. She picked up her hat and purse and was gone.

15

Lights were already on in the kitchen of the big house, and Richard's car was in the garage when Brenda and I arrived home. I parked my Chevy, and Brenda and I paused at the back door. She looked like a child about to be scolded.

"You better go in first," I said.

"He'll be upset."

I opened the storm door. "Don't anticipate."

Holly barked, prancing around as Brenda made a fuss of her. Richard sat at the kitchen table, reading the newspaper. He looked up as we entered the kitchen. "You're late," he said as she bent to kiss him.

"We had a little trouble today," she said.

"Trouble?" he asked.

I walked into the circle of light over the table. "Hey, Rich."

His eyes widened at the sight of my bruised, swollen face. He shoved the paper aside. "What in God's name happened to you?"

"Would you believe I walked into a door?"

"No. Who hit you?"

Brenda took off her jacket. "Willie."

"What the hell—?" he exploded.

"It was a sucker punch," I admitted.

He exhaled loudly. "Somebody better tell me what happened—"

"—Or there'll be hell to pay," Brenda finished.

"Is it too late to put ice on it?" I asked.

"'Fraid so," Brenda said.

"How's your head? Have you had any problems?" Richard asked as he sat me in a chair, tilted my head back to get a better look at my eye. I felt like a kid again, with him playing doctor.

"Yeah, but it feels more like a sinus headache. I took a couple of decongestants."

"When did this happen?"

"This morning," I answered.

"Why didn't you call me?"

"What for? So you could stew about it all day?"

He sat down again, glaring at both of us. Brenda folded her coat over her arm and headed for the closet to hang it.

"What did Willie want?" Richard asked.

"To talk to Brenda."

"About what?"

"We never got that far. I went to the cops. There's a warrant out for his arrest."

Brenda returned, her face pinched with worry. "I thought about it all day, Jeffy. I want you to drop the charges."

"Are you crazy?" Richard exploded.

"Believe me, I know what the man's capable of. And that could be a lot worse than letting him go free."

"Brenda, with Jeff's history of head injuries, that one punch could have killed him—that's murder."

"He'd only be charged with manslaughter," I countered. "That's five to seven years in Attica. And thanks for reminding me how close to death I am every day." I cleared my throat. "No, I won't drop the charges," I told Brenda.

"But, Jeffy—"

"Once Willie's in custody they'll get his fingerprints and compare them to anything they find on the letters you received. If it rules him out as a suspect, I can always drop the charges later."

"But what if it just makes him angrier?"

"An aggravated assault charge should make him think twice about bothering you again."

"He never paid for what he did to you," Richard added. "It's about time he did."

"That was years ago," she countered.

"But it still haunts you."

Brenda ignored him, opened the refrigerator and studied its contents like it was the most interesting part of her day. Moments later she closed the door. "I forgot to get something out to thaw."

"How about pasta?" I suggested. She nodded, and headed for the butler's pantry.

The silence in that kitchen was icy.

"So, how was *your* day?" I asked Richard.

He got up from his chair and headed for the liquor cabinet. "Bad." He took down a bottle of single malt scotch, found a glass, dumped in some ice from the freezer, then poured. "The only bright spot was a call from Patty."

Anger shot through me. "What did *she* want?"

"To thank me for going to the funeral yesterday."

Every muscle in my body tensed.

Richard frowned. "Jeff, will you stop judging her? She's not Shelley. You don't even know her. Hell, I've spent more time with her than you have. She's a funny, sweet, nice person. Give her a break."

I didn't want to give her a break. I wanted to hate her. And why? Because she'd said something stupid and thoughtless. Like I've never been guilty of the same. But not only that. I hated the way she fawned over Richard. That simpering expression on a face that looked too much like my dead wife. And there were too many other things about her that bugged me, but I couldn't put them into words.

I pushed back my chair, stood. "I gotta go."

Brenda came back with a box of penné pasta in her hand. "You're not staying?"

"I've got things to do," I said.

Richard leaned against the counter, sipped his scotch, and didn't say a thing. His condescending attitude was like a slap in the face—a side of him I'd never seen.

"I'll see you in the morning, Brenda."

"Tomorrow's my last day," she reminded me. "You can go back to sleeping in next week." She crossed to the cupboard, and took out a large pot. She obviously hadn't heard the last part of Richard's and my conversation. "What are you and Maggie doing for dinner on Saturday? Do you want to join us?" she asked.

"I'm working all weekend."

"Oh. Well, maybe we can do something during the week."

"Will you be here for the security guys tomorrow morning?" Richard asked, his tone defying me to say 'no.'

I met his steady gaze. "Yes."

Brenda turned, looked at us, puzzled. "You guys are suddenly cranky. Did I miss something?"

Richard straightened. "No. Everything's fine. Right, Jeff?"

I forced a smile. "Sure. I'll see you tomorrow." I headed for the door, glad to escape.

· · ·

I MUST'VE PACED my apartment for ten or fifteen minutes, risking the nap on my rug. Why were Richard and I sniping at each other like kids? After years of being estranged, we'd finally forged a friendship. In a matter of hours, Patty had ruined what had taken months to build.

God, I *hated* her.

But I wasn't the world's best judge of character. Richard had that sterling trait sewn up, too. Although he didn't know what Patty had said about Brenda. Or was I giving that slip of the tongue too much weight?

He and Maggie thought I should give my sister a break. Was I just being stupid—seeing things in her words and actions that simply weren't there?

My last boss at the insurance company had said I was a good worker, but not a team player. Minutes later, I was heading for the unemployment line. Was that the basis of all my life's problems?

And why was I torturing myself for Patty's faults?

Because I felt guilty. For using Emily, for not anticipating Willie's right hook. For all the problems in the world.

I never wanted to see Patty again. But she had information I wanted—no, needed.

I grasped the phone, punched in her number.

"Hello?"

"Patty, it's Jeff."

"Oh. Hi." She wasn't overjoyed. "I was going to call you. I'm going through some of Dad's things. I thought you might like to have something of his."

"Well, I—" Caught off-guard, I didn't know what to say. The old man didn't have anything of value. Did she mean his watch or something? "Sure. That would be nice."

"Can you come over now? We need to talk."

"Yes, we do."

Silence.

"See you in a while." She hung up.

The light outside Patty's front door blazed, illuminating the house numbers as I pulled up the drive. I got out of the car and pulled up the collar of my jacket. Stars shone weakly through the haze of city light. I knocked.

Moments later, Patty threw open the door. "You got here quick. I—oh my god, what happened to your face?"

I brushed past her into the house. "Nothing. Just a fight."

"Looks like you lost."

"I did."

She closed the door. "Did it happen at the bar?"

"No. Can we drop it?"

The corners of her mouth twisted with irritation.

"Are you okay?" I asked, more out of courtesy than a desire to know her emotional state.

"The place feels empty with Dad gone. I really can't stand being here alone."

She hadn't waited long to erase his presence, either. Stacks of cardboard cartons filled the living room. I followed her into my father's cleaned-out bedroom, which now resembled a cheap motel room. How many years had he slept there? The walls still vibrated with his aura, something she was totally unaware of.

"What'll you do with the house?"

"Sell it. I don't want to deal with the upkeep. I'll be lucky to get enough for a down payment on a condo."

The silence dragged as she sorted through a pile of clothes. I searched for more small talk.

"What happened with that guy who crashed Aunt Ruby's?"

"Ray? He's harmless. Everything's straightened out now," she said.

That was the end of that topic. I cleared my throat. "I was hoping you could answer some questions. You seem to know a lot about—" I still found it hard to say the word, "Dad's life before he met your mother."

"He didn't say much. But I know he was very bitter toward Richard's grandparents."

"So was my mother. She never told me why they broke up. Neither did Dad."

"It was the kidnap plot, of course," she said, folding a sweater and putting it into a carton.

Bingo!

"Kidnap plot?" I asked innocently, yet every muscle in my body had gone taut.

"Your mother wanted to grab Richard and go to Canada."

"My *mother*?" I blurted.

She nodded. "Dad said she had mental problems. Richard was a teenager, but she kept thinking of him as a baby. She wasn't rational."

Why did her words hold such a ring of truth?

"Dad couldn't leave the business," she continued conversationally. "He was just starting to make a go of it."

"So instead he left my mother?"

She nodded, calmly folding a shirt and putting it in the box. The story held no emotion for her—it was tearing me apart.

"Why didn't he take me with him?"

"I suppose because he loved her." Her eyes softened at my puzzled expression. "She'd already lost one child. He couldn't very well take you from her, too. But I know he regretted not having you come live with us when your mother died. He did it to spare my mother. I was glad, too. I liked being an only child."

I'll bet.

Patty opened a drawer and grabbed something. "Here." She

placed a gold ring in my palm. "It's Dad's wedding band from his first marriage. I figured you might want it."

I turned away, let my fingers close over the ring, waiting for a burst of emotion, but there was none. My father hadn't worn it in years. It meant nothing to him. My wedding band from Shelley also sat in a drawer, but every time I looked at it my anger still swelled.

"Richard sure is a sweetheart," Patty said. "Having him for a brother must be great."

"Yeah."

And having me for a brother wasn't.

"Doesn't Richard like white women?" she asked, keeping her tone neutral.

"What?" I asked, startled.

"Does he prefer black women?"

"I don't know," I answered truthfully. "I only met one of his other—" How should I put it? "—girlfriends. I don't think race has anything to do with it. He loves her. She's a helluva woman."

Patty seemed disappointed by my answer.

"Why are you so interested in Richard?"

"I'm just being friendly." She sounded defensive.

"Yeah, well, he and Brenda are very happy. I wouldn't want anything—or anybody—to try and come between them."

Her eyes were defiant. "Hey, I don't need to go after married men. I've got plenty of guys interested in me."

"I'm glad to hear it."

She glared at me, and then turned to clear out another dresser drawer, shoving socks and underwear into a large plastic trash bag.

The silence lengthened.

The cat lurked in the hallway and I broke the quiet. "What'll you do about Herschel?"

"Have him put to sleep." Her voice was icy.

"The old man wouldn't want that."

"He's a smelly fur-bag. Unless you want him, he's going to the pound. Probably tomorrow."

The cat rubbed against my ankles, looked at me hopefully with its golden eyes. "I guess I could try to find him a home. Is he current on his shots?"

"Who knows."

"How old is he?"

"I don't know—maybe three years old. Dad got him when I moved in with John. He's been fixed and declawed. That's all I know. You can take him tonight. I'll get the cat carrier."

She didn't give me a chance to protest. She disappeared into the basement, banging around for a few minutes, before she brought up a cardboard carrier. The cat saw the box and instantly disappeared—probably anticipating a trip to the vet. Patty spent the next five minutes chasing him around the place, slamming doors, and cursing a blue streak. The cat had a sly, mischievous glint in his amber eyes. She finally cornered him, picked up the flailing body, and stuffed him into the carrier, snapping the lid shut.

Then, she methodically gathered up toys, bowls, food, litter —shoved it all into a large trash bag and set it by the front door and stood there—waiting for me to leave.

"I better get going," I said, eyeing the box that held my new —albeit temporary—housemate. I picked up the carrier and she handed me the sack.

"Thanks for taking the cat," she grumbled, and looked away. "I'm sorry we—"

She didn't sound the least bit sorry.

"Yeah. I'm sorry, too," I said.

Patty opened the door. Overloaded with stuff, I shuffled through. It banged shut behind me. I opened the car door, tossed the plastic bag in back and put the carrier on the front passenger seat. The cat let out a piercing howl.

"Hey, I'm not thrilled about this either, pal," I said and started the engine.

My life was getting more complicated by the minute.

16

Brenda seemed preoccupied during the drive to the clinic the next morning. She wasn't particularly interested when I told her about Herschel and the adventure of our first night together. Maybe she didn't like cats, or was she just sick of hearing me gripe about Patty?

Or was it something else entirely?

Brenda gazed out the passenger window, distracted. It was the last day of a job she didn't want to quit. Her silence only increased my paranoia. Willie would *not* be hanging around, I kept telling myself. Not after what happened the day before. Still, I had a really bad feeling as I parked the car. We got out, and I kept looking over my shoulder, expecting Brenda's ex to charge out from a neighboring doorway.

The protesters were louder than usual that morning, promising hellfire and damnation to anyone who entered the clinic's den of death. Two security guards stood at the edge of the clinic's property. With no weapons, they were an impotent deterrent. Brenda trotted past them, oblivious to the zealots' taunts. I struggled to keep up with her.

Dr. Newcomb was ahead of us on the top stair in front of the clinic door. She juggled her purse, a grocery bag, and a couple of bakery boxes.

"Do you need a hand, Jean?" Brenda called.

"I sure do."

Brenda started up the steps, with me a few paces behind. The doctor dropped her purse, which tumbled down the steps. Brenda stooped to pick it up.

The clinic's plate glass door shattered.

Bakery boxes went flying.

A crimson stain blossomed across the front of the doctor's white ski jacket. She staggered, and fell back.

I caught Brenda's jacket collar, hauling her down the steps.

The crack of more gunfire split the air.

I lost my balance, dragging Brenda with me. We rolled onto dirt and dried leaves, into the cover of shrubbery.

Behind us the protesters screamed, scattering like frightened geese.

Another shot rang out.

Brick shards rained on our heads. The damp earth and sharp scent of broken yew branches stung my nose.

I shoved Brenda against the building, covering her body with my own, knowing bullets could tear through two sets of flesh and bone as easily as one.

"Jean!" Brenda screamed, struggling to pull free. "We've got to help her."

"No one can help her," I grated, holding her tight.

Footsteps thundered past us. The security guards flew up the steps, hauling the dying woman's blood-soaked, limp body through the destroyed door.

"Let me go!" Brenda cried.

The gunfire had stopped. The air was suddenly eerily quiet, with only the muffled sound of traffic over on Main Street.

"Let me help her!" Brenda begged.

"Not 'til I'm sure it's safe. I couldn't face Rich if I let anything happen to you."

Her lower lip trembled as her eyes filled with tears. She buried her face in my shoulder, and clung to me as great choking sobs shook her.

I rocked her, let her cry, trying to keep from shaking as adrenalin coursed through me. How close to dying had we been?

"Come on," I said at last, "Let's get you checked out."

"I'm okay."

"Then let's make sure junior's all right."

She nodded, and let me help her stand. My own knees were rubbery. We ended up steadying each other. Then a white-shirted security guard was pulling at us, yanking us up the steps and into the Women's Health Center.

Despite her years of medical experience, Brenda wasn't a trauma nurse. I didn't want her to see what I saw—her friend, torn apart, an exit wound the size of my fist in the center of her back. I turned her face away, wouldn't let her see the lifeless, blood-soaked form on the lobby floor as we were scuttled down a hallway.

I'D BEEN SITTING THERE, numb, staring at the wall for what seemed like hours. I knew every stray mark, had memorized the location of each grimy handprint made by the patients' children. Scuffmarks and dents marred the molding where a floor polisher had smacked into it countless times. Aged, wrinkled magazines with torn covers were haphazardly stacked on a chrome and glass table. Women's magazines, filled with diet recipes and sex surveys. It was all so pointless.

Bonnie Wilder was suddenly at my side. Like the rest of the cops on the scene, she wore a Kevlar vest over street clothes. Her face was taut with concern. She'd already questioned Brenda and me when she'd first arrived, only minutes after the shooting.

"Well?" I asked.

"I thought you might like an update." She took the seat opposite me. "We've got officers canvassing the neighborhood, looking for other witnesses."

"What're the odds of finding any?"

"Probably nil."

It figured.

"We've got some shell casings off the roof of a boutique on Main Street. It's a long shot, but we might lift a decent print."

"Do you have any suspects?"

She pursed her lips momentarily. "I'll find out if Willie Morgan has an alibi. We hauled a few of the protesters down to the station. They'll be questioned, but I'm not counting on getting anything."

"Was Reverend Linden out there today?"

"No."

"He's an expert marksman."

"I know." She pursed her lips. "Any minute now the FBI will descend and it'll be their ball game. We'll be out of the loop," she said bitterly.

Not surprising. Any incident involving an abortion clinic meant the feds were called in. But was Dr. Newcomb the target, or was Brenda?

Despite their protests to the contrary, would anyone in Reverend Linden's group be willing to help find a baby-killer's murderer?

"As soon as the FBI okays it, they'll remove the body. We'll have autopsy results by tomorrow."

"Why bother? She was shot. She's dead."

"We've gotta go by the book so we can nail the shooter."

"If you ever find him." God, I sounded cynical.

"It's a damn shame," she said, her eyes shadowed with compassion. "The victim was a single mom—three kids, all under twelve."

I hadn't known that. But I'd picked up a number of impressions from the somber-faced staff as they'd wandered through the lobby. Dr. Jean Newcomb was the one who'd checked me out the day before. I could see why she was so well-liked. She'd seemed to be the kind of person you could pour your heart out to. They mourned her, their faces radiating their shock, loss, and most of all their fear. They were reluctant to leave, afraid to return.

I looked over my shoulder. A knot of local press had gathered outside. Now that a newsworthy tragedy had occurred, was I assured a photographic sale to *The Buffalo News*? This wasn't the way I'd intended it to happen. I'd wanted to prevent this—draw attention to the danger . . . and nobody had wanted to listen. I'd warned Sam Nielsen, but this was one 'I told you so' I could keep to myself.

Detective Wilder craned her neck to see what I was looking at. "Vultures."

"Think how they'll tease this on the national news: 'Clinic doctor blown away in front of abortion protesters.'"

A work crew had arrived to install plywood in the shattered door frame. They were measuring the aperture when a maintenance man in white work clothes, carrying a galvanized pail filled with hot, sudsy water shuffled across the lobby and pushed through plastic draped where the door had been. He'd already swept the steps of glass. He dumped the soapy water onto the concrete steps. The blood had seeped into the porous concrete. How much soap and bleach would it take to erase all evidence of carnage?

I turned my attention back to the lady cop. "Now what happens?"

"The feds will try to find out who killed Dr. Newcomb."

"Jeff?"

Richard's voice.

Turning, I saw a haggard version of my brother behind me.

"What the hell happened?" he demanded.

"Rich, this is Detective Wilder."

"Detective," he said, giving her a cursory nod.

"I wasn't there for the security guys," I babbled guiltily. "I called them. They'll install the system tomorrow, but it'll cost you—"

"Where is she?" he demanded, ignoring me.

She. Brenda. His wife. The woman whose life he'd entrusted to me.

"Down the hall."

"Is she okay?"

"I think so. Just a little shook up." Talk about a stupid remark. "Make that a *lot* shook up. If Dr. Newcomb hadn't dropped her purse. If Brenda hadn't—"

Richard looked at me critically. "Are *you* okay?"

I hadn't given it any thought. "I guess I'm kind of shook up, too. It isn't every day you see—"

I couldn't finish. Richard wasn't listening anyway. His attention was fixed on the corridor behind me. He brushed past us. I turned to see Brenda with another white-clad nurse. She broke into a jog when she saw Richard, flying into his arms.

Something in my chest twisted.

"I'll keep you posted," Detective Wilder said, patted my arm, and continued down the corridor.

I took my time catching up to Richard and Brenda.

The nurse put her hand on Brenda's shoulder. "Talk to you later," she said, turned and walked away.

"Are you okay?" Richard asked, pulling back to inspect his wife's tear-streaked face.

"Aren't you going to say 'I told you so?'"

He exhaled, his eyes filling. "No."

"Can we go home?" she asked.

"There's a crowd of reporters out front," Richard said.

"Out back, too," I said.

"I don't want to talk to anybody," Brenda said.

"Bring the car around," I told Richard. "I'll get her through the mob. Then I'll meet you guys at home. Okay?"

They both nodded, and Richard headed for the door.

"I have to sit down," Brenda said. She sounded tired. Dead tired.

I steered her over to my former seat on the couch, and took the chair opposite her.

"What'll happen now?" Brenda asked.

"I don't know."

She bit her lip. "Were they after me?"

"I don't know."

"I'm afraid, Jeffy." Her eyes filled with tears. "My friend is dead and I'm afraid I'll be killed, too."

"Don't think like that."

"What if *I* was supposed to die, not her?"

"I'll make sure nothing happens to you. *Nothing*," I said and grasped her hand, yet as soon as I said it I knew it was a lie. I couldn't protect her. I didn't even own a gun anymore. But thanks to Richard's financial resources, I'd make sure every precaution was taken to protect her.

I rested my other hand on her shoulder and touched her fear. She looked at me with such trust.

I felt like a fraud.

Richard's Lincoln pulled up outside. I helped Brenda to her feet and hustled her out of the building. Dodging the press, I gave them the old "no comment." The Lincoln's tires spun and Richard took off. I headed down the street to my own car, ignoring the shouted questions that followed me. I got in, started the engine and took off in the opposite direction, relieved to escape.

THE LUNCH CROWD was long gone at The Whole Nine Yards. Silent runners sprinted across the large-screen TV, in time to an old Judds tune playing on the jukebox, while the few stragglers finished their Friday fish fries.

"What're you doing here?" my boss asked from behind the bar. "You're not on the schedule 'til tomorrow, you know."

I grabbed a stool. "Give me a beer, will you, Tom?"

He drew a Coors and set it in front of me.

"I'm gonna need some time off."

Tom picked up a paring knife and resumed cutting fruit for the happy hour garnishes. "You want to tell me what's wrong?"

"A woman got killed at the Women's Health Center a couple hours ago."

He paled. "Not Brenda."

"No." I took a sip. "But it happened right in front of us."

"Christ," he muttered.

"I want to hang around the house for a couple of days. Just 'til things settle down."

"Sure. Take as much time as you need. Dave and I can handle it here."

"Thanks." I swallowed another mouthful of beer, and stared at the bar's oak top. "She looked so surprised. I mean . . . she was alive, and then she wasn't. It happened so damned fast."

He nodded toward my glass. "You want a shot to go with that?"

I shook my head. "That makes two people who died right in front of me this week." I looked up into Tom's patient face and wondered if I adopted the same expression when people told me their troubles. I guess that's why I'd ended up here.

"Why don't you tell me all about it," Tom said.

When I arrived home an hour later, a strange car was in the driveway. I parked my crate and headed over to Richard's house.

Ken Tyler, the salesman from Amherst Security was seated at the kitchen table. "I heard about the shooting and came right over," he said.

"We were just going over various options." Richard looked back at Tyler. "How soon can the guard get here?"

"Within the hour."

Richard nodded.

"Where's Brenda?" I asked.

"Lying down. She said she didn't feel well."

"You'll need to take additional precautions," Tyler said. "First off, don't advertise yourselves. That means no open drapes at night. Don't go out alone. If you've got a set routine—change it. Anything to throw off whoever's stalking you."

"Standard protective measures," I said.

"A you familiar with them?"

I nodded.

The lines in Richard's face seemed deeper. "We'll do whatever you suggest."

Two grim-faced FBI agents from the Washington office showed up about the same time as the guard arrived, and as Tyler was leaving. Richard coaxed Brenda downstairs to be interviewed by the Washington hotshots. The case was apparently too big for the local boys to handle. They asked the same questions as the Amherst Police. Brenda's letters, already at the State Crime Lab, would now get top priority, they said.

Rehashing the day's events only upset Brenda more, and we were all relieved when the suits finally left.

I scrambled eggs and burned toast for a makeshift dinner. Conversation was at a minimum; none of us had an appetite and most of our dinner went down the garbage disposal. A vacant-eyed Brenda mumbled good night and shuffled off to bed early. I hoped her dreams wouldn't be haunted by grisly images of her dead friend.

Richard thanked me for my efforts and I headed for my own place. The uniformed guard, stationed in a cruiser at the end of the drive, gave me a thumbs up as I crossed the driveway for my apartment. He was supposed to do a circuit around the yard every fifteen minutes. Even so, his presence didn't make me feel much safer.

The phone was ringing when I let myself into my darkened apartment. Herschel assaulted me, winding around my legs like a boa constrictor. I turned on the lights and picked up the receiver.

"Jeff?"

Patty.

"Are you okay? I saw you on TV. How's Brenda?"

"She's fine." Then what she said registered. I crossed the room to close the blinds, with Herschel hot on my heels. "You saw me where?"

"On TV. They showed you helping someone into Richard's car. Did you know the woman who was killed?"

"She was Brenda's friend."

"Aw, too bad." The words were right, but they sounded insincere.

"Why are you calling?"

"I was worried about you, of course."

"You didn't sound worried last night when you gave me the brush off."

"I did no such thing. I—" She stopped in mid-denial and changed her tone. "I'm sorry you feel that way. You're my brother and I care about you. I always will."

Yeah. And pigs fly.

The silence dragged, only the cat's happy purring broke the quiet. I pulled off my coat, cradled the phone on my shoulder as I hung it in the closet.

"How is Richard taking all this?" Patty asked at last.

The real reason for her call.

"How do you think? His wife was nearly killed."

"Was someone really shooting at Brenda?"

Her phony concern irked me.

"She works at the clinic. It's a possibility."

"Do they know who did it?" she asked, anxiety in her voice.

"Not yet. Why?"

"No reason. I just— It's just terrible. There're too many guns out there." She launched into a spiel about gun control. I didn't listen to the words, more the tone. Anxiety bordering on fear. But not for me.

"Patty, what are you trying to say?"

"Nothing. I—" She broke off. "Just be careful. Please. And . . . look out for Richard, okay? I gotta go."

The line went dead.

I hung up the phone. Herschel looked up at me with pleading amber eyes then went to sit by the cabinet.

"You could at least pretend you see me as more than just a feeding machine."

Herschel let out a piteous howl and pawed the cabinet door.

I fed the cat and sat down with the phone, punching in Maggie's number. She'd briefly spoken with Brenda and had been waiting for my call. The silences between sentences hung heavily. I didn't want to talk any more. I rang off, promising to call her in the morning.

I poured a tall bourbon and tried to read, but I couldn't get interested in my book. Turning on the TV, I flipped channels for almost ten minutes until I came to the conclusion that I was too wired to concentrate. I kept reliving those terrible moments in front of the clinic. Jean Newcomb falling backwards as blood gushed across the front of her jacket. Brenda in the direct line of fire—me hauling her away just in time. Holding her in my arms . . . .

I finished my drink and hit the rack early, losing myself in heavy, dreamless sleep.

At first I wasn't sure I was really awake until I recognized the sound of the garage door opener grinding beneath the floor under my bed. The scarlet numbers on my bedside clock read four thirty six.

Adrenaline coursed through me and I was out of bed like a shot, heading for the window overlooking the drive. I pulled back the curtain to see Richard shuffling toward the house, his shoulders stooped. I grabbed the phone, punched in the numbers as he disappeared behind the door. It rang twice.

"Hello?" Weary resignation.

"Rich, what happened?"

Richard exhaled a shaky breath. "Brenda lost the baby."

A terrible silence fell between us. Dear God—everything I feared.

"Where is she?"

"At the hospital. Her OB met us at the ER a few hours ago. They had to do a D and C."

Holy shit.

"We asked for a post mortem, but it could be weeks before we know what happened. We—" His voice broke. "We got to hold him. He was tiny, but he looked . . . perfect."

"How's Brenda?" I somehow managed.

He cleared his throat. "She'll probably come home tomorrow afternoon."

"Oh, God, I'm sorry, Rich."

"Yeah, me, too. Listen, I'll call you in the morning."

"If you need anything—"

"Yeah—" he cut me off, and broke the connection.

The hardwood floor was cold beneath my bare feet. I wandered back to the comforting warmth of my bed, pulled the covers over me and lay there in the dark.

It was my fault. It had to be. When I'd saved Brenda from the assassin's bullet — I'd killed her baby—her son.

I pulled the covers tighter around me as shivers wracked me.

I'd killed my own nephew.

Herschel jumped onto the mattress and warily made his way across the down comforter. He looked at me expectantly in the dim light. Did he want to be petted or did I just need to pet him right then? My hand cupped the back of his head, skritched his ear. He hunkered down, and a steady, contented purr vibrated through his whole body.

I stared at the featureless ceiling.

Good-bye, baby boy—a life that wasn't meant to be. And another one of my premonitions come true. I'd tried to prepare myself—I hadn't wanted to believe it. But I *had* believed it. Didn't know I'd be the *cause* of it.

Maybe I should've said something to Richard. Maybe . . . .

But I also remembered what Sophie told me. Warning people about terrible events only made them resent—blame—you. Had she known I was responsible?

Herschel's deep, throaty purr filled that lonely room. I wished Maggie was with me, thought about and rejected the idea of calling her.

It could wait.

I kept scratching Herschel's neck. He hadn't judged me a murderer. Would Richard and Brenda?

"Thanks for being here, pal." The cat stretched his long black legs, rolled onto his back. In minutes he was asleep.

It took me a lot longer.

17

———————

Three blood-spattered corpses lay stretched out on the grass, their sightless gazes fixed on the relentless gray sky. Jean Newcomb, the dead man with the Roman features, and my ex-wife, Shelley, lay side-by-side like casualties in a war.

I circled the bodies, unable to tear my eyes away, looking for the elusive common denominator besides the most obvious: they all died from gunshots. Revulsion made me shudder at the sight of their mortal wounds.

I couldn't look at Shelley's face—at least not all at once. I zeroed in on the top of her head. It was gone, the surrounding tawny hair matted with dried blood. Her glassy, lifeless brown eyes haunted me. My gaze traveled down to her slightly parted lips, her mouth poised as though to tell me something, but no sound came forth. I tore my eyes away, and stared at her blood-stained, beige jacket with the silver snowflake pin on the lapel.

Dead. All dead.

Motion caught my attention. Brenda stood at the edge of a grassy field, waving to me. The lower portion of her long white gown was blood soaked, her eyes wild, haunted . . . but she lived.

For the moment, because the threat still loomed.

And was there any way I could save her?

IT WAS STILL DARK when I awoke feeling achy and miserable. I staggered to the bathroom, drank a glass of water, and headed back for bed.

Eyes closed, the images from the nightmare lingered in my mind. What did it all mean? What did Shelley have to do with these people? Why, after all this time, did she still haunt my dreams? Was my subconscious pulling in a thread from my past to make sense of the present? The dead man was a stranger to me. I hadn't witnessed Shelley's murder, but I had seen Jean Newcomb die. She was the link, but to what?

Three people who'd been murdered. Three unconnected deaths.

Shelley had been moldering in a grave in Jersey for over two years. I didn't know when the dead man was killed. But Jean Newcomb had been alive less than twenty-four hours ago.

It had to connect. Somehow it had to all make sense. But I couldn't see it. And I wouldn't figure it out by staring at a darkened ceiling.

A CAT's empty stomach makes a fine alarm clock. Not that I needed one that Saturday morning. I got up, fed the cat, then dressed, not knowing what to do with myself. But I needed to be doing something. I grabbed my coat, headed for the garage, and backed my car out.

The changing of the guard had already occurred, and I introduced myself to the stranger now manning the Amherst Security car at the end of the drive. He showed me his photo ID and gave me a brief report. There'd been no sign of intruders. All was calm.

Then why were my nerves stretched taut?

I drove to the grocery store, bought a basket of sweets and desserts—sinful chocolate cake, double mocha brownies, and a two pound box of assorted chocolates—all the stuff Brenda liked. I picked up a bouquet of carnations, too; pretty white ones streaked with red, like frilly candy stripers. By the time I got home it was after eight thirty—late enough to wake Maggie with the bad news.

I dialed her number, but voice mail caught it on the third ring. I hung up, frowned, and heard a car pull up the drive—Maggie's Hyundai. I grabbed the bag of groceries and made it down the steps in seconds, meeting her as she got out of the car.

"Richard called," she said in greeting, but there was none of the usual warmth in her voice. Her blue eyes were haunted. I saw an overnight bag on her passenger seat. "Brenda's sisters won't come," she said in explanation. "I'm going to stay with them for a few days."

I nodded, and put an arm around her shoulder as I walked her into the house.

Richard was waiting in the kitchen. Maggie went to him; embraced him. "I'm so sorry."

He nodded, but said nothing. He pulled away, leaned against the counter and cleared his throat, folding his arms across his chest. "Would you mind packing a case for her? Clean clothes—underwear. You know the kind of stuff she'll need."

Maggie nodded.

"There's an overnight bag in our closet, and—"

"I'll find it," she assured him, and headed out of the kitchen and toward the stairs and the master bedroom.

"How is Brenda?" I asked.

"She called. Thank goodness for cell phones, eh? She's pretty good. Considering." His gaze remained fixed on the floor, and his expression hardened. "I talked to both her sisters."

"Maggie said they wouldn't come."

"Brenda called Evelyn last night—before this happened—and asked her if she could stay with us for a few days. Evelyn's retired, but she said she couldn't come. Some flimsy excuse about it being too near the holidays. I called her this morning. She said she was sorry about the baby, but said it was probably for the best. Can you believe that?"

No, I couldn't.

He let out a shaky breath. "I called my supervisor at the clinic. I'm not going back. At least not until this situation is settled. Maybe not even then."

"What do you mean?"

He took a ragged breath, his brow puckering—and for one terrible moment I thought he might actually cry. "I can't do this anymore. I should've known. I couldn't hack it after my residency. Why do you think I took that job in California?"

"What are you talking about?" I asked, trying to keep my own panic in check.

Richard turned his tormented gaze away. "Patient care. I can't divorce myself from what they go through. I can't stay detached."

"It proves you care."

"Yeah. I care so much I can't keep my objectivity."

So that's what was eating him. But I sensed there was more going on. Helping a dying man had exposed my brother to HIV. So far the tests hadn't shown the deadly antibodies in his blood. The stress of waiting for them to show up had to be pressing on his mind. I know the stress had gotten to me. But I had to be encouraging. We'd come this far. I'd wished and even prayed to a God I wasn't sure I believed in to ensure Richard's good health. Maybe I should've prayed for his child, too.

"Look, now's not the time to make life-altering decisions," I said.

Richard's fists clenched. I'd never seen him so demoralized.

Not knowing how to deal with it, I turned my back on him, and started unloading the grocery bag.

"Did you know Brenda would lose this baby?" he demanded.

I couldn't look him in the eye. "Oh, come on. How—?"

He grabbed my shoulder and yanked me around to face him. "Because you know these things. You're psychic, remember!"

Holy Mary, mother of God.

"Yeah," I managed, my voice a whisper. "I knew."

He took a step closer and I tensed, expecting him to hit me. "Then why didn't you say something? Why didn't you warn us? We could've taken precautions. We could've—"

I stepped aside, needing to get out of his way. "What kind of precautions? It was me who shoved her to the ground. It was my fault. I didn't know that. I would've never done anything to hurt—"

He shook his head, wearily. "Don't do that to yourself. If you hadn't pulled Brenda out of the way, she would've been murdered—just like Jean Newcomb. Losing this baby is hard enough—I couldn't bear losing both of them."

Was he just being kind? Somehow I managed to meet his gaze. His eyes were bloodshot, but there was no anger in them. "I'm sorry." I couldn't say any more. Especially not what I feared —that Brenda would never have a child.

Not knowing what else to do, I unloaded the rest of the groceries, folded the heavy brown paper bag, and stowed it in the cabinet under the sink.

"I didn't get much sleep after I talked to you last night."

He turned an icy glare at me. My sleeping habits were the farthest thing from his mind.

"I had a lot of time to think about this whole situation."

His gaze shifted, betraying his interest.

"Until yesterday, and except for those letters, we didn't have any tangible evidence to link Brenda to whoever is behind all this. Now we do—the bullets that killed Jean Newcomb. And the casings they found across the street from the Women's Health Center."

His eyes flashed. "Do you think you could get something from them?"

"I'd sure as hell like to try. But it's likely the Feds took them." I thought about it for a moment. "Maybe Bonnie Wilder could pull some strings and get me in to see them."

He nodded, the barest hint of a smile quirking the corners of his mouth.

"I'll get right on it," I said, and turned for the phone. He said he held no grudge against me—for what I'd done. And I was determined to do all I could to keep Brenda safe.

Maybe then I'd be able to forgive myself.

RICHARD USED his cell phone to call the hospital to check on Brenda while I commandeered the landline to call the Amherst police station. As I'd hoped, Detective Wilder was already at her desk. I warned her that Richard and I were on our way. Maggie decided to head out for the hospital to be with Brenda until they released her—which wouldn't happen until at least eleven.

Three guys from Amherst Security showed up just as we were leaving, promising most of the system would be wired up before the end of the day.

At the station, a uniformed officer led us to a conference room.

"As you probably guessed," Wilder started, "the situation is now a federal case—and out of our jurisdiction. Despite what happened yesterday, we have no evidence to connect Dr. Newcomb's murder with the harassment your wife received."

"I realize that," Richard said. "But in case there's a chance—"

Wilder straightened the file folders in front of her. "I

tracked down Willie Morgan at his office yesterday afternoon. At the time of the shooting, he was in a meeting with five co-workers."

"What about Lou Holtzinger?" I asked.

"He wasn't on the protest line yesterday morning."

"Was he questioned?" I pressed.

"As far as I know, they haven't found him to talk to him yet. He's the most likely suspect. Witnesses say he's been one of the most vocal protesters."

"I can attest to that. And his truck has a gun rack," I reminded her.

She looked uncomfortable, but said nothing.

"What about Reverend Linden?" I asked.

"He's also wanted for questioning. According to his wife, he didn't return home last night. She doesn't know where he is."

"Interesting," I said.

"We have an unusual request," Richard said. "We'd like to see whatever evidence was collected at the scene."

"The bullets, if they're available, and the casings in particular," I added.

"What for?" Wilder asked.

I swallowed my pride. "I'm kind of . . . . "

"Psychic? Yeah, I heard," Wilder said, her voice, and her gaze, level. "I got a call from a Detective Hayden over at Orchard Park PD. He said if you touched them you might get some kind of intuition from them."

Carl Hayden had been the chief investigator on a murder that had occurred some seven months before. A murder I'd found myself connected to.

"H-how did he—?" I stammered.

"He saw you in the background on some news footage."

"I'm beginning to feel like a TV star. Well, what're the chances I can see this evidence?"

"I'll try calling a friend at the Bureau, but I can't make any promises."

Despite her pessimism, half an hour later we were on our way downtown.

Agent Dominic Segovia looked typically FBI. Short hair, wiry build, and completely humorless. Wilder hadn't told us what her connection to the agent was, but he treated the small-town cop with respect. However, he looked at me skeptically. That skepticism would turn to scorn if I came up with nothing. Segovia ushered us to an unused interrogation room and left us while he retrieved the evidence. Long, silent, minutes later he returned with a number of evidence bags. Using tweezers, he carefully emptied each of them, setting each item on the table before me.

I studied the spent casings. "Center fire, thirty ought six?"

Segovia looked impressed. "You got it. Semi-jacketed hollow points."

Richard looked at me in confusion.

"The ammo," I explained. I looked back at the agent. "Did they get any prints?"

He shook his head.

I turned my attention back to the shells. "Well, they're new. Can you still get these at any Wal-Mart?"

"All you need is a driver's license," he said.

"That narrows down the list of suspects," Richard remarked sarcastically.

The copper jacket had mushroomed on impact, ripping through Jean Newcomb's flesh, stealing her life. Surprise and disbelief had been plastered across her features. She was dead before she realized what happened.

"Can I touch them?" I asked Segovia.

"I'd prefer you to handle only one item."

Terrific. And if I chose the wrong one . . . .

I picked up a shell casing, wrapping my fingers around it.

"Are you getting anything?" Richard asked.

I concentrated. "I'm not sure."

Segovia waited for a better answer, his mouth a thin line.

I rolled the casing between my palms. I hadn't sensed anything from the letters, but the killer had held the bullets in his hand. He, definitely not she. He'd caressed them, relishing the thought of delivering death. Only he'd missed the target.

"This isn't what it seems," I said, still rubbing the metal between my fingers.

"What do you mean?" Richard asked.

"This isn't an issue-related shooting. It's . . . revenge. The man who loaded the gun meant to hurt—to kill—Brenda." I met my brother's worried gaze. He swallowed, but said nothing.

"Who'd want to hurt your wife?" Segovia asked Richard.

"Her ex-husband, for one. When they were married, he used her as his personal punching bag," Richard said.

"We've already ruled him out as a suspect," Wilder reminded him.

I continued to roll the metal between my palms. "I don't get a feeling of—" The words didn't want to come. "Connection."

"What do you mean?" Detective Wilder asked.

"The guy who loaded the gun doesn't even know Brenda."

"A for-hire hit?" Segovia asked, incredulous.

"Why not?" Richard said. "Willie could've hired someone to kill Brenda."

I kept palming the casing. "I don't know."

Segovia looked skeptical. "Sorry, Mr. Resnick, but we can't take your word on this. As far as the Bureau's concerned, this is an issue-related shooting. Unless we find evidence to the contrary, that's the route we're following."

I watched him replace the evidence into the numbered bags. He was wrong, but I wasn't about to push it.

Detective Wilder lagged behind as Richard and I left the office building. The cold December morning was bright; branches on the leafless trees swayed in the brisk wind.

Richard shoved his hands into his coat pockets. "Well, now what?"

"There's not much else we can do. You should be with Brenda."

He frowned. "Yeah."

We looked at each other for an uncomfortably long moment. Were our positions reversed, Richard would've asked me if I needed to talk. Spilling my guts was still a new concept. I'd done it with my boss only the day before. But experiencing the loss of a much-anticipated child—I still couldn't fathom that kind of loss. I was sure if Richard needed to talk about it, he would.

I waited.

The silence lengthened.

Finally, I nodded toward the car. "Let's go home."

18

As I pulled up the driveway, I noticed that Maggie's car was back, too. Had she already brought Brenda home? Richard had spent the ride across town staring out the passenger window, his expression guarded, playing strong and silent all the way home. I was glad to get back to the house where Holly greeted me with a wet tongue and a wagging tail.

"Maggie!" I called, and rubbed the dog's sleek ears.

"She can't be very far away," Richard said, peeling off his coat.

Approaching footsteps announced Maggie's arrival. "I hope you don't mind, but when I got to the hospital, Brenda was ready to leave. She's upstairs now."

Relief softened the lines in his face. "Thanks, Maggie."

Maggie's eyes filled. "It was kind of awkward. I didn't know what to say to her. I just gave her a big hug and we cried. I feel terrible. There's nothing I can do to make this situation better."

"Don't be so hard on yourself," Richard said gently. "You've been a good friend and she needs you more than ever right now."

"I'll never have a child. That's hard enough. But I never lost a baby," Maggie said.

"Neither had I. Until yesterday. So help me God, Maggie, I don't know what to say, either." Richard's voice cracked and his eyes were watery once again. She took his hand and squeezed it.

I shoved my hands into my pockets and looked away as guilt threatened to overwhelm me.

Richard cleared his throat. "I better go to her."

"Wait," Maggie said, wiping at her eyes. "The clinic called. One of your patients needs you. I told them you'd call as soon as you got in." She grabbed a note off the Post-It pad by the phone.

Richard straightened, regaining his composure. "I'll call them first."

"I'll hang up your coat," I said, and he handed it to me before heading for his study.

A dejected Maggie leaned against the counter. Holly settled at her feet, her tail thumping the floor, her dark eyes filled with hope, wanting only to please. Maggie reached down and patted the dog's head.

"I think I'll go see how Brenda's doing," I said.

"Okay. I was just going to make some lunch and a fresh pot of coffee for Brenda. Do you want a sandwich? There's ham in the fridge—or I can make you a grilled cheese."

"Surprise me," I said, and headed for the closet. I hung up the coats, then started up the main staircase. A veil of sadness clouded the long, empty corridor. The door to my former room —what was to be the nursery—was closed. The door to Richard's and Brenda's room was ajar.

I crept closer and poked my head inside. Original art decorated the pale blue walls; flowers . . . large watercolors of iris, pansies, and morning glories. Over the summer Maggie had helped Brenda redecorate the room. A loveseat by the large bay window overlooked the now-empty flower garden Brenda and I had worked on last spring.

I knocked on the doorjamb. "Anybody home?"

"Just me," came the low reply from a mound under the quilt on the bed.

"Can I come in?"

No answer.

"I hope you're decent—because I'm coming in."

Still no answer.

"Brenda?"

The mound was silent.

I stood there for a moment, not knowing what to do—or what to say. I tiptoed closer, and finally sat on the edge of the bed. "Hey, friend. Where are you?"

"In a hole. A deep, dark hole."

I swallowed, somehow managed to speak. "Can I crawl in with you—keep you company?"

At last Brenda raised her head and looked over her shoulder at me. "It's not a place you want to be." Her eyes were puffy and bloodshot from crying.

"I don't want you to be all alone." I kicked off my shoes, crawled across the large bed, lay beside her and put my arm around her. It felt so natural—so right. As her dark hand slid down to cover mine, all her sorrow and pain hit me like a sledgehammer. I winced, bit my lip and tried to breathe evenly. I deserved this. I'd *caused* this.

She noticed my reaction and pulled her hand back. "Go away. I'll drag you down—make you sick."

"If I share what you feel, maybe it'll be easier for you."

"You can't. Nobody can. Not you, not Maggie, not even Richard. This is *my* punishment."

"Punishment?"

She took a ragged breath. "When I was married to Willie . . .

." She paused, her voice catching, clearly pained to remember. "It was no time to bring a baby into the relationship. He never knew. I went to a clinic alone—killed my own child. Now God is punishing me."

Oh, dear Lord. "I don't believe in a vengeful God."

"Then why did He take my son?"

"I don't know," I whispered. I didn't know what else to say.

"As soon as I realized I was pregnant . . . I guess I knew all along something bad would happen. Somehow I knew . . . and so did you. Didn't you?"

I didn't answer.

"Jeffy? Didn't you know?"

God, how I wanted to say no. How I wanted to be anywhere else on Earth. But I was with her, in her pain, and I couldn't lie to her like I couldn't lie to Richard.

"I didn't know how or when . . . but, yeah, I knew. Richard blames me. *I* blame me. If I hadn't been so rough with you that day at the clinic—"

"You saved me that day. Richard knows that. We both do."

I shook my head. "He thinks if I told him about my premonition we could've kept you safe. That we—"

She wouldn't hear it. "No. This was preordained. It's my punishment."

"How do you know it's not mine?"

She looked at me, puzzled.

"I have to live knowing that if I'd said something, you might've quit your job earlier. You'd both have been safe." Dear God, had I just accused her of being responsible?

She shook her head—she still wasn't listening to me. "No, no, no. You can't take my punishment. It's my pain. I want it all to myself." She closed her eyes and rubbed at them, clearly exhausted. "That's not right, either. I'm a nurse—a rational person. And I believe in God. God sends us messages. Maybe this is just another one."

"What kind of cruel message?"

She pulled the quilt tighter. "Maybe . . . be grateful for what you've got. I don't know. I'm no philosopher. But I can't spend my days crying. I can't do this to me, to Richard, or to you."

"But you have to grieve. Brenda, you're *allowed* to feel bad about this."

She frowned. "Well, maybe for just a little while."

I wanted to smile at that flash of the old Brenda.

She was quiet for a long moment. When she finally spoke, her voice cracked. "Richard called my sisters. They wouldn't come."

Her sadness found new depths, dragging me with it.

"Maybe . . . they couldn't get away. Maybe—"

"I've been cut off," she said, her voice calm. "According to my mother, I did a terrible thing. I married a white man. So I'm punished again. But if loving Richard is punishment, I'll gladly take it. He's the best thing that ever happened to me."

My throat constricted. "And you're the best thing that ever happened to him."

A small smile crossed her lips. "Yeah. I am." She looked into my eyes, her own glistening.

Her sorrow eased, if ever so slightly. She let out a shuddering breath, reached for a tissue, and wiped her nose. Outside, snowflakes danced past the window. The branches of the oak tree in the back yard moved gracefully in the cold wind.

Brenda nestled against me and sighed. Eventually her breathing slowed as she drifted into sleep. Her sadness ebbed, leaving a hollow space inside me. I held her, stroked her hair, thinking about what she'd said.

Punishment. Blame. Death. Sadness. Guilt. We'd certainly had enough of them. Was happiness an illusion, a Disney dream that never happened in real life? It didn't often happen to me. Did the black cloud that followed me extend to those I cared about?

My father was gone, taking with him any chance of understanding why he'd abandoned my mother and me.

Suddenly the sadness I felt wasn't only Brenda's. I hadn't acknowledged my own loss. I didn't want to admit it *was* a loss. Until that moment, I hadn't realized just how much I'd wanted to care about the old man.

The bedroom door brushed across the deep pile carpet. I looked up as Richard stepped inside and stopped dead at the sight of me on his bed with his sleeping wife.

I motioned him closer. "Take off your shoes," I whispered.

He looked at me, confused.

"Take off your shoes," I repeated, and watched as he complied. Then slowly, I extricated myself from the bed, pulled back the quilt and gestured for him to take my place. His expression was a mix of embarrassment and irritation, but he complied, getting under the covers beside his wife. Brenda snuggled close to him. Even in sleep she knew the difference. Richard's angry expression melted as he gently placed an arm around her, resting his chin on the top of her head.

I grabbed my shoes, tiptoed across the room, and silently closed the door.

THE KITCHEN TABLE was set for three, with a lunch tray waiting on the counter. Maggie sipped her coffee, and looked up as I came into the kitchen. "Well?" she asked, unable to hide her concern.

"Rich is with her. She's sleeping."

Her gaze strayed to my ski jacket. "I thought you hung up your coat?"

"I did. I have to go out."

"Where?"

"There's someone I have to see."

She looked at the sandwich on the plate before her, and pushed it away. "I guess I wasn't hungry anyway. When will you be back?" Her voice was quiet, disappointed.

"An hour or so. It won't take long."

She nodded. I was glad she didn't ask me where I was going. I couldn't have explained.

The drive took fifteen minutes. The radio was background noise. Christmas songs had already joined the regular soft-rock rotation. I parked, headed for the door, and rang the bell. The storm door's thermal glass reflected the gray December sky—reflected my somber face. I pushed the bell again, and heard the thump of footsteps.

Aunt Ruby opened the door, a smile of delight greeting me. "Jeffrey, it's so good to see you. Come in, come in."

"Sorry to drop in without calling," I said, wiping my feet on the little throw rug.

"Why should family need to call? Would you like some tea? I was just going to make a pot."

"Sure. Thanks." I followed her to the kitchen and took a seat at the Formica table.

"Take off your coat, stay a while," she said and filled a kettle at the sink. She switched on the gas burner, and put it on the stove. "What brings you out this way?"

"I need to talk about my—"

"I'll be glad to tell you all about your father," she interrupted me, her smile widening with a blush of pride. "Oh, he was a wonderful man, and such a good brother. I wish you could've known him better."

"Me, too. But I really need to know about my mother."

Startled, she stared at me for a long moment, and then

glanced away, busying herself getting out china teacups and saucers. "That was a long time ago, Jeffrey," she said at last. "I didn't know her all that well."

Ruby wasn't a good liar.

"I made pound cake yesterday. Would you like a slice?"

"Aunt Ruby, you're probably the only one left alive who knew my mother. Please, I have to know."

She turned suddenly, her anger hitting me like napalm. "Why now? Why after all these years?"

"I'm remembering things that don't make sense. All I know is what my mother told me. I don't think she told me the whole truth."

Ruby pursed her lips, and came to a decision. "Jeffrey, I honestly don't know what to tell you. I never knew your mother before she married Chet. Of course, he'd known her for years. He always said she was a different person before she got sick."

He knew her for years? "I thought they met at the dry cleaning store?"

"Heavens, no! They worked at the Statler Hotel, across from City Hall. She was a waitress in the restaurant. Chet worked in the hotel laundry. That's where he got the experience to open his own shop."

My world wobbled. "They knew each other all those years ago?"

"Of course. He was sweet on Betty for ages. But Chet was Jewish and she was a good Catholic. And then she met that Alpert fellow. He was rich and a Catholic. You know the rest of the story."

"They got married and had Richard," I recounted.

Ruby nodded. "She loved that man and she loved his baby, poor thing. She fell apart when her husband died."

"Her nervous breakdown," I said.

"Chet said Betty's mother-in-law drove her crazy when the

old lady took her child." The kettle began to whistle. Ruby made the tea and sliced the pound cake. She put it on a dainty little platter and set it on the table before taking a seat across from me.

"Chet had a thing for your mother," she continued. "He was so in love he even converted for her. That didn't sit well with Papa. Mama was disappointed, but somehow she knew it wouldn't last."

"They married in the Catholic church?" I asked, astounded.

She nodded. "None of the relatives went. It just wasn't done in our family." She shook her head sadly. "And we knew something wasn't right. Chet was ashamed to come around. He told me most of this years later."

Ruby spoke in riddles. "Most of what?"

She frowned. "It started soon after they married. Betty was obsessed with getting her baby back. Chet thought they should start a family right away. So naturally when Betty became pregnant he thought she'd get over it. Of course, she never did. How could any mother get over the loss of her child?"

Her words cut me as I thought of Brenda. She poured the tea, and pushed the milk pitcher toward me.

"Then what happened?" I asked.

"After Papa died, Chet brought you and Betty around. You were such a cutie-pie, but oh, so solemn. We knew something wasn't right, but Chet wouldn't say—not at the time."

Her refusal to come right out and say what was on her mind was maddening.

"Patty told me about the kidnapping stuff."

Ruby stiffened in her chair. "Chet wouldn't go along with it. And Betty—she wouldn't accept that. Then she lost the baby—"

"Baby?" I interrupted her.

"Stillborn. You must have been . . . oh, nearly four. Poor Betty was irrational. She and Chet had some terrible arguments. Chet didn't know what to do. Betty wouldn't see the psychiatrist; she just kept going to church every day. Chet couldn't live with her anymore. We thought he was wrong to leave you. He said she needed you more."

"That wasn't the only reason he left. There's more, isn't there?"

Ruby took a sip of her tea, and then primly put the cup back on the saucer.

"Aunt Ruby," I pressed.

"It's not something a man could ever talk about."

"She hit him, didn't she?"

Ruby said nothing for a long moment. She wouldn't look at me. "Is that what you remember?"

"I remember screaming matches. Dishes breaking, yelling and . . . I wasn't sure if I remembered right."

"Betty was different after they took her child away from her. It changed her. She may have loved Chet, but I think she loved her little boy more than anything or anyone else on Earth."

"Me included?"

Ruby continued to stare into her teacup.

I let out a shaky breath. She didn't have to say it. I'd always known who came first in my mother's heart.

"Chet sent money, but all the envelopes came back marked refused. She didn't want anything to do with him. She thought he'd betrayed her." Ruby shook her head sadly.

"Patty said Joan didn't want me to live with them. That after my mother died—"

"Joan was a good woman, but that wasn't right. You were his son, his first born. He never even married her."

That was a discussion I didn't want to enter. But there were other things.

"After Dad's funeral, Patty and Richard were looking at a photo album. Tell me about Chet's mother—my grandmother."

She smiled, relieved to change the subject. "I wish you could remember her. She loved you so. You were her favorite. It broke her heart when Chet didn't bring you around any more."

"When did she die?"

"Oh, over twenty years ago." Her eyes darkened with repressed pain, like the loss was still an unhealed wound. "It was stupid. Mama did things her own way—you couldn't tell her anything. If she'd only listened. How many times did I move that hot plate? How many times did we all tell her? But no, she knew best."

"She was electrocuted, wasn't she?"

Her eyes widened. "Why, yes."

"She lived above a bakery, in Amherst, right?"

Ruby frowned. "No, Malczewski's on Walden Avenue. It's still there. Every time I go by there I think of her." Her eyes had a faraway, empty look. "You never really get over losing your mother."

I said nothing. Too many thoughts clogged my mind. My mother, Shelley—my father. So many emotional ties —shredded.

Somewhere a clock chimed three.

I thought about the old woman in the photograph. "My grandmother was special, wasn't she?"

Ruby's eyes narrowed with . . . fear?

"I don't know what you mean."

"She knew things—about people. About when things would happen. She knew."

Ruby got up from the table, and started wrapping the cake in plastic wrap. "Would you like to take some home?"

She'd give me no more answers.

"Yes. Thank you." I pushed back my chair, got up, and zippered my jacket.

She walked me to the door, and pressed a brown paper sack into my hand. "You'll come for Hanukkah, won't you?"

"I'll try."

Ruby kissed my cheek, and looked at me with such tenderness. Suddenly I realized who it was she reminded me of. But I'd have to wait until later to follow that lead.

19

———————

The cleaners were on my way home, so I stopped to pick up my jacket. The refrigerated glass case filled with pastries at the gourmet coffee shop next door reminded me of another stop I needed to make.

Emily Farrell answered the door after my second knock.

"Jeff? How'd you find me? I'm not in the phone book."

"City Directory. I looked up all the protesters for the newspaper article. Can we talk?"

Emily glanced over her shoulder. Her daughter played with Legos on the spotless kitchen floor.

I stood there, clutching a white bakery box of goodies, not unlike the one Jean Newcomb held the day before, moments before she'd been murdered.

"I brought a peace offering." I handed her the box.

Embarrassed, Emily opened the door to let me enter.

A pink valentine border lovingly stenciled near the ceiling, knickknacks and spice racks, gave Emily's small kitchen an air of warmth and security. Pages torn from coloring books and other examples of Hannah's artwork made a gallery of the refrigerator door. My single-parent home had had no such heartwarming touches. While immaculate, our apartment had been sterile by comparison.

"Would you like coffee or something?" Emily asked.

"No, thanks."

She gestured for me to take a seat at the kitchen table.

Hannah was on her feet, drawn to the box like a magnet. "What's in there?"

"Cut-out cookies. And a couple of chocolate chip ones for your Mom."

"Can I have one?" Hannah asked.

"May I have one," Emily corrected, "and it's not polite to ask."

Hannah hung her head, pouting.

"Sure you can have one," I said. "If your Mom says it won't spoil your dinner."

Eyes shining, the little girl pressed close to her mother. "Please, mommy?"

"Just one," Emily said, and opened the box. She placed a yellow-iced reindeer cookie on a paper napkin and set it on the table. Hannah climbed on the chair. She broke off the head, and nibbled on an antler.

Emily took a seat beside her. An open Bible lay on the table. She marked her place, and closed it.

"Looking for guidance?" I asked.

"The whole city thinks our group is responsible for what happened to that doctor."

"I don't."

Relief played across her features. "Tonight we're holding a prayer vigil for Dr. Newcomb. We took up a collection for her children."

"That's very kind of you."

She stared at the Bible's black leather cover for a long moment, her expression filled with indecision. "Were you really using me just to get information on our group?"

She looked up at me, her eyes troubled. Hadn't Maggie asked me the same thing when I was investigating Matt Sumner's death?

"I was worried about Brenda," I answered truthfully. "I had to keep her safe. Getting information was part of the process."

"Then all the things you told me were lies."

"I never lied to you."

Her gaze held mine. "You said that nurse was just a friend."

"She is my friend, but she's also my sister-in-law."

Her eyes widened. Was she a bigot, as well as a religious zealot?

"I have to find out who killed her friend and caused Brenda to lose her baby."

Emily's sympathetic gasp was genuine. "Oh, Lord, she was pregnant?"

"They don't only do abortions at that health center, they help women have healthy babies, too. She can't have any more."

"Oh, poor thing," she murmured. She glanced at her own child, who was systematically reducing the cookie to mere crumbs.

"The theory is Lou Holtzinger pulled the trigger," I said.

"I'll admit he's kind of a scary man, but I don't think he'd stoop to—" Emily looked at her daughter, mouthed the word, "murder."

"I don't know about that, but I don't think he's responsible, either."

"Then who—?"

"I don't know." I studied her face and sensed that she wanted to help me. "Did you see anything out of the ordinary that day? Was there anyone you didn't recognize hanging around?"

Emily shook her head. "Just the regular clinic employees, the people who work in the next building, and members of our church group."

I frowned. I hadn't really expected more from her.

She glanced back at her daughter. "I won't take Hannah to another protest. In fact, I don't think I can go back again. Not after what I saw yesterday." She looked up at me, and her eyes filled with tears. "You were right. It's too dangerous. There're too many crazy people with guns."

I reached for her hand and experienced what she felt: a swell of fear and disappointment.

"That doesn't mean you have to give up what you believe. There're other ways you can work for the cause."

She looked at me in surprise. "But, I thought you—"

"We may disagree, but that doesn't mean I don't respect you for holding onto your convictions."

She offered me a small, shy smile. Her hand tightened on mine and the feeling I got was different this time. Attraction —to me.

Gently, I disentangled my hand and sat back, flashing an embarrassed smile in return.

Hannah was humming. She wet her finger, dipped it into the pile of crumbs, then sucked on it, taking delight in each sweet morsel. She looked up at me and a weird feeling of déjà vu passed through me. But it was another blue-eyed child who stared back at me in my mind's eye. Dressed in a red polka-dot dress with a white pinafore, the little girl smiled, and lifted her chubby brown arms to me.

"Is something wrong? You look like you've just seen a ghost," Emily said.

"Maybe I did," I murmured. "Maybe I did."

· · ·

PLOWING **back** into the glut of negative emotions that charged Richard's house drained me. Maggie took her role as Brenda's stand-in sister seriously, making sure Brenda's time was occupied with projects and conversation that had nothing to do with babies or children. Brenda sat at the kitchen table working on needlepoint, while Maggie pulled together a gourmet dinner worthy of Julia Child.

The depth of Maggie's maternal feelings startled me. Her presence seemed to have pushed Richard aside. I had to practically drag him from the solitude of his study to join us in the dining room.

Starched linens, antique silver, their best china, and tall, white candles in ornate holders graced the table. Maggie held court, roping me into polite, innocuous conversations on good books, holiday plans, and fabric choices for reupholstering the living room furniture.

Brenda's gaze moved from Maggie to Richard, her attention divided between the ongoing conversation and her puzzlement at her husband's unusually quiet demeanor. Richard and I are on different wavelengths, but I could tell he was annoyed about something. He barely touched his beef burgundy, but kept refilling his wine glass. Was withdrawal his survival technique for handling grief?

After dinner Richard retired to his study while Maggie and I hand-washed the tableware and Brenda looked on. Then, armed with a box of chocolate and a bottle of zinfandel, Maggie and Brenda headed for the master bedroom for a marathon Monopoly match. Never one for board games, I declined the invitation to join them. I'd already reached my emotional saturation point. Instead, I sat at the kitchen table and studied the new security system's manual for the better part of an hour.

Rubbing my tired eyes, I noticed how eerily quiet the house

was. I tossed the instruction book on the counter and went in search of Richard.

He was on the phone and didn't bother to hide his irritation at being interrupted. "I have to go," he said, and rang off.

"Who was that?" I asked.

Richard hesitated, looked away, and picked up a file folder on his desk. "Take a look at this," he said and handed me a sheet of paper.

I read the e-mail's subject line: Willie M. Morgan.

"What's this?"

"It's from Tomkins Investigations in Philadelphia. The firm my lawyer hooked me up with."

I skimmed the terse paragraphs. Willie Mayes Morgan, husband of five years to a Vanessa Block, father of four-year-old Jason—he hadn't mentioned those facts to Brenda. He had a good credit record, including a mortgage and car payments. He'd been an active member of Society Hill Baptist Church. The family home was up for sale, meaning his wife and son intended to join him in Buffalo. The report included character references from his former boss, the pastor of his church, and several family members. But none of it explained why he was so intent on seeing the ex-wife he'd abused more than a decade before? Did he want to apologize? Why hadn't he done it the day he'd visited? Or had my presence disrupted his plans?

I handed the paper back. "What do you think?"

"They say a leopard doesn't change his spots, but if you believe this report, and the fact he has an iron-clad alibi, Willie has," Richard said.

No wonder he was depressed. The man he wanted to blame for all his problems was undoubtedly innocent.

"You didn't answer my question," I reminded him. "Who was on the phone."

He looked away again, face coloring. "Patty."

Just the mention of her name triggered my temper.

"She wants to see me," he continued. "She said she had something important to tell me."

My gut tightened. I tried to keep my voice level. "Such as?"

"I don't know."

"You're not going, are you?"

Richard looked guilty. "Well, I—"

My anger swelled. I was about to say something we'd both regret when he spoke first.

"Brenda's not jealous of her. Why the hell are you?"

I ground my teeth. Would he even believe me?

He looked away, and rubbed his forehead. "Maybe I've had too much to drink. I'm not thinking clearly. I can't leave Brenda here alone."

"No. You can't."

He looked up. "Would you go for me?"

No, I wanted to shout, but then I thought better of it.

"Yeah. I'll go."

And I'd tell her off once and for all.

NEWLY REMODELED, the Commotion Diner on Transit Road still managed to look shabby. Cardboard Santas decorated the cheap paneling while limp, crepe paper streamers hung from faux Tiffany lamps over each table. The vinyl seats were the hard, uncomfortable kind that make your ass cheeks fall asleep one at a time. The place reeked of stale grease and vile coffee. I'd just stepped into the joint and already I wanted to wash my hands.

Patty sat in a corner booth away from the plate glass windows, as though hiding. The beige jacket draped over her shoulders barely concealed an open-necked red blouse. Her short, dark skirt showed off her legs. She saw me and her features twisted into an angry scowl.

"What are *you* doing here?"

I slid into the hard seat across from her. The coffee cup in front of her was half empty—the contents looked cold.

A fiftyish, overweight waitress waddled over to the table. "Coffee, sir?" Even her voice was weary.

"Sure."

She nodded and shuffled to the urns on a narrow table against the wall.

"Where's Richard?" Patty asked.

"With his wife. Where he belongs. You can tell me whatever you wanted to tell him."

The waitress was back with a cup. She placed it before me and took out several vials of non-dairy creamer from her apron pocket. "Get you anything else?" I shook my head. She frowned and walked away.

"Well?" I demanded.

Patty gathered her jacket and purse. "I don't want to talk to *you*."

"Well you're going to have to." I grabbed her arm before she could escape.

"Let go. You're hurting me!"

"Leave Richard and Brenda alone," I grated, still holding her forearm.

"Why? You want him all to yourself? Are you afraid I'm going to replace you or something?"

I let go as though burned. If she only knew how close to the truth she'd come.

"Sit down!" Incredibly she obeyed. "Talk."

For the first time since I'd met her, Patty looked unsure of herself. "I know something. Something that might help Richard."

"Tell me."

Despite the no smoking law, she shook out a cigarette from

her pack, and lit it. "What's it worth to you?"

I knew she'd eventually try to shake him down for money. "What're you asking?"

"Are you in a position to negotiate?"

"Tell me!"

She tapped the ash on the table. "I don't want money. I want to be his friend."

"How close a friend?"

She took a deep drag, held it, then exhaled fully. "That's up to him."

I hoped my expression alone was enough to convey the depth of my contempt. "So tell me."

She looked past me to the parking lot. "Ray's been asking a lot of questions about you two. Being a real pest."

Talk about something coming from out of left field. "The guy at Aunt Ruby's?"

She nodded. "When he first came to work, he asked me if I had a brother named Jeffrey."

"When was this?"

"A few weeks back—before I even met you."

"The way Aunt Ruby spoke, I assumed—"

She shook her head. "He showed up at her house during Thanksgiving dinner. I must've mentioned I was going there. I never told him where she lived. I think he followed me there. Aunt Ruby was real nice, she invited him to stay. He behaved himself that night, but he asked a lot of questions. The night of the party, he wanted to leave before I was ready and we argued. Michael asked him to go. I told him I'd meet him at a bar later."

"Did you?"

"Yeah. He was drunk when I got there. He kept asking about you and about Richard."

"Why?"

She shrugged. "He said you'd captured a murderer last

winter. That Richard got shot. I didn't know what he was talking about."

"It was in the paper and on the news last Easter."

"I was in Mexico with a friend," she said, and this time tipped her ash into her cold coffee.

"Didn't dad tell you?"

"I wasn't living at home back then. I thought Ray was crazy—that he was making it up. But he had a newspaper clipping."

"Why didn't you ask me about it?"

"I asked Richard, the day of the funeral."

They'd covered a lot of conversational ground that day. "Why's Ray so interested in us? Do you think he might be behind the shooting at the Women's Health Center?"

Her eyes widened. "I didn't say that. I just thought he was overly interested in Richard."

"You called him away from his wife at a time like this to tell him that?"

"What's the big deal? She wasn't the one who was killed."

"She lost their baby," I blurted.

My announcement wasn't met with surprise—Richard had probably already told her. Patty's face held no hint of sympathy. If anything, her mouth curved up, her eyes taking on a sly glint.

God, I hated the bitch.

"What's Ray's last name?" I asked.

She was still thinking, plotting. "What—?"

"Ray's last name," I repeated.

"Sampson."

"Is he from around here?"

"Yeah. But he was living downstate for a long time."

"Doing what?"

"How should I know?"

"Then why did you want to tell Richard this?"

Her eyes blazed. "I was looking for an excuse to see him, okay?"

I glanced around the place. "In a dump like this? Honey, Rich has a lot more class. And if you haven't figured that out yet—"

"Why don't you just shut up," she said and got up. "Ask Richard about Dr. Concillio. Just ask him!" She grabbed her purse, jumped out of her seat, and stalked off.

The waitress got up from her vigil on a stool at the counter, and handed me the check. "Looks like she stiffed you."

I reached for my wallet, and took out a five. "Keep the change."

Patty's Mustang was gone by the time I got to the parking lot. I was so angry I wanted to punch something—or someone. Why the hell was Ray Sampson so interested in Richard and me?

But that wasn't why I was angry. It had been gnawing at me ever since Richard put down the phone. Patty couldn't have called him—she didn't have his newly unlisted telephone number. That could mean only one thing.

He'd called her.

I sat behind the wheel of my car, quietly fuming.

Family.

It was time to get some answers.

20

The old woman's face lit up as she saw me standing in front of the bakery's plate glass door. She shuffled forward on stiff legs and let me into the shop. Her delighted smile faded, however, when she caught sight of my hooded expression.

"You're early tonight. You didn't have to work, eh?" Sophie Levin asked.

"No."

"Come in, sit down. You want some coffee? How about cocoa?"

"No, thanks." Hands stuffed into my pockets, I followed her into the back room.

She took a chair behind the wobbly card table. A well-thumbed deck of cards was laid out in the classic solitaire pattern. She picked up the pack, turned over the first card.

"Tell me about your family," I said.

Sophie studied the layout, avoiding my gaze. She put the four of hearts on the five of clubs. "You don't want to hear about them. I've bored you so many times already."

"How many children do you have?"

She didn't look up. "Three. Two girls and a boy." Her laugh was more a snort. "They haven't been children for a long time now."

"How many grandchildren do you have?" I asked.

She turned over the next card, the Queen of diamonds, and set it on the discard pile. "Five. Four girls, one boy."

"You talk about your grandson like he's a small boy. How old is he?"

"Not so small any more," she admitted.

"How about your youngest granddaughter?"

"Pretty grown up by now," she admitted.

"Younger than your grandson?" I pushed.

She shrugged. "A little."

"Ten years younger?"

Her eyes darkened, as though with loss. "It seems like only yesterday they were all babies."

"Where's your family now?" I pressed on, relentless. "Why do they let you live here all alone? Why don't they visit you?"

She got up from the small table. "I'd like some tea. How about you?"

"No, thanks. Where's your son?"

She hung her head, her face hidden in the shadows.

"He died, didn't he?"

Her head bobbed ever so slightly. "Not long ago."

"Your son was my father, wasn't he?"

She turned, her face filled with anguish. "Why would you ask that?"

"I saw your picture in an old photo album the day of his funeral. You with a little boy on your lap. That boy was me."

She wouldn't look at me. "There are some questions you shouldn't ask. Things you won't want—or need—to know."

I was on my feet. "Why didn't you tell me you're my grandmother?"

Sophie shrugged, turned to face me, tears filling her brown eyes. "I am here for you. I am *only* here for you."

"Why?"

"Because you need me. To accept these things that happen to you. Not so much the how or the why—just to accept them."

A shiver of panic went through me. My grandmother had died decades ago. Yet, impossibly, Sophie was here, now.

She was right. I didn't want to know the why of it.

I looked away, my voice shaky. "I . . . never knew my father, and now it's too late."

"I didn't want it that way. He didn't, either," she said, her voice filled with sadness. "Things sometimes don't work out the way we want. Only sometimes, if we work hard enough, if we believe, we can reach out—beyond our usual senses—beyond all disbelief. If you want to, you can find a way to touch those you love. I know. I've done it."

I didn't know what to say—or to believe.

"You could try," she said. "Please, just try."

Shame flooded through me. I'd been too afraid to reach out —to touch—my father in his last moments. Was it too late? I looked into the old woman's eyes and wanted to believe. But how? How could I connect with a dead man?

Through his daughter said a tiny voice in the back of my mind. I wanted to reject the thought—reject Patty.

Sophie shook her head, as though reading my mind. Maybe she did. She loved Patty, too.

"Please try," she again pleaded.

"I will," I said, unsure if I could. Suddenly I was unsure of everything.

Sophie pulled out a wadded tissue from her sweater sleeve and dabbed at her eyes. "It's time for you to go. They need you at home."

We walked toward the exit. "Please be careful," she said.

"There's still danger. Keep a sharp eye out these next few days. Watch out for Brenda."

"I will."

"And take care of Patty. If only for me, eh?"

I let out a weary breath. "I'll try."

Her expression brightened. "Come and see me Tuesday night. I'll make macaroons."

"I'll plan on it."

She unlocked the door. I paused, looked into her deep brown eyes. "I need you, Sophie Levin. I think I always will."

Her smile was beatific. "And I will be here for as long as you do. I promise."

I hugged her, felt the warmth of her body, the depth of her limitless love, and reveled in it.

It was almost eleven by the time I got back to Richard's house. I'd driven home, pondering exactly what I should tell him and wondering why I even considered not telling him everything Patty had said or intimated. I didn't intend to mention my visit with Sophie. I didn't understand it—and I wouldn't know how to explain it.

I opened the door and Holly loped into the dimly lit kitchen to greet me, with Maggie following close behind. She was silhouetted in the doorway, dressed in a filmy nightgown and robe, looking like something out of a wet dream.

"What did Patty want?" she asked.

"Richard—as a sugar daddy."

"I hope you put her straight."

"Maybe."

The dog nosed my hand and danced around me in a circle. "Does she need to go out?"

"Yeah."

I let Holly out, and closed the door behind her.

"Where are they?" I asked, unzipping my jacket.

Maggie moved into the light cast by the lamp on the stove hood. "They went to bed early. Brenda was worn out. I've been watching TV and waiting for you."

"Are you staying here or at my place?"

"Here." She stepped close, trailing a finger down my throat, toying with my shirt collar. "Will you stay with me?"

I couldn't see her eyes in the weak light, but I caught the scent of her perfume, and felt her need for company. I put my arms around her, letting my hands slide down the silky softness of her thin robe. "Sure."

I pulled her close, kissed her as my hands trailed down her hips. Her warm lips brushed across my neck, nibbled my ear. I was so tired, so ready to fall straight into bed with her, reaffirm our connection, but I was also practical.

"I have to feed the cat."

She pulled back, her smile seductive.

"I'll, uh, grab some stuff and be back in a few minutes," I said.

Her lips pressed against mine. "Okay," she murmured, and gave me another long, sensuous kiss.

"You're making it very hard for me to go—so I can hurry back to you."

She slid from my embrace. "Then don't be long."

The wind was brisk as I crossed the drive. Holly was nowhere in sight. Probably on the trail of another squirrel.

I trudged up the stairs, opened the door, and found Herschel waiting for me. Yowling, he wound round my feet as I shook some dry food into a bowl. I needed to hit the grocery store for litter and more canned cat food. I hadn't stocked my own cupboard in over a week. I gave him fresh water and left the cat to his dinner.

Grabbing my shaving gear, I tossed some clean clothes into a duffel and left the apartment, not overjoyed at the prospect of spending the night in a strange bed. But sleeping with Maggie was worth it, no matter where.

"Holly? C'mere, girl."

No dog. Maggie must've already let her in.

I entered the house and flipped the deadbolt behind me. Then I armed the security system and turned off the stove light.

Only the hall sconces blazed. I headed up the stairs, and switched them off when I reached the landing. Light from the open guest room door spilled into the hall. Maggie was curled in bed, reading.

Nudging the door shut with my foot, I dropped my duffel, yanked off my jacket, and tossed it onto a chair.

Maggie looked up over the top of her book. "Where's Holly?"

"Didn't you let her in?"

"No. I came right up after you went out."

"I called her, but she didn't come." I grabbed my jacket. "Damn that dog."

"Don't yell at her. You'll wake the neighbors."

The backyard was filled with shadows. The security firm hadn't yet installed all the new motion-sensor lights.

"Holly! Holly!" She usually came when I called.

I walked into the darkened yard and called again. Still no dog. I hoped to God she hadn't jumped the fence. I wanted to go to bed, not search the neighborhood for her.

The sky was heavy with clouds—no moon. The street lamps in the next road cast scant light. I ventured deeper into the yard. "Holly!"

A low growl came from the bushes to my right. I squinted in the darkness. "Holly?"

She sprang, but not at me. Someone—a man—roared as she

tore at his clothing. Her growling turned to angry barking, then she yelped.

I dove at the figure, grappling with him. He was shorter than me, skinny, with a wad of hair at the back of his neck.

Lou Holtzinger kicked and bucked, his arms flailing, but he wasn't much of a fighter. His sour breath assaulted me. Drunk, too. I pinned him in seconds.

"What the hell are you doing here?"

"I came to talk to the doctor," he panted. "I got some information—about the shooting at the health center."

"Why didn't you come to the door?"

"The cops are all around. I don't wanna go back to the joint."

I yanked his arm behind him, made him howl. "You can tell me!"

"No. Only the doctor. He's got money—doctors always got money."

"He won't pay you a dime. You're going to spill your guts to the cops. Come on!"

He started to struggle and I slugged him, a blow that sent him reeling. "That's for breaking my headlight the other night!"

I hauled him to his feet, shoved him forward and marched him toward the house and down the driveway. The startled rent-a-cop got out of his cruiser. "What the hell—?"

"Have you got handcuffs?"

He grabbed at his belt, unhooked the cuffs. I took them, clamped them around Holtzinger's wrists, then yanked open the cruiser's passenger side door, shoved Pony-tail in.

"The Amherst police have a warrant out for his arrest. Call 'em—then get this piece a shit outta here."

Winded, I started back for the house, only then realizing that Holly hadn't followed us down the drive.

"Holly!"

No dog.

I headed for the backyard again. My gut tightened as I saw a light-colored mound near the bushes where I'd fought with Holtzinger. I broke into a jog, skidded to a halt, and found Maggie's Golden Retriever lying on her side.

Crouching, I placed a hand on her chest, felt the damp stickiness.

Holly whimpered.

At least she was still alive.

The knife lay in the grass, inches from her, glinting dully in the scant light.

I lifted her—all sixty-plus pounds. She let out a tortured wail as I staggered across the grass toward the back door.

I must've been gone five or six minutes—where the hell was Maggie?

I found the door locked, and didn't remember doing it. I leaned on the bell and yelled to the guard at the end of the driveway, who seemed to have gone deaf.

I waited and waited. Holly was panting, her head lolling. She weighed a ton. Maybe I should just put her in the back seat of my car. Only I didn't have my keys.

"Hang on, girl."

I sat down on the step, my newly cleaned jacket stained scarlet again. I reached up and kept my bloodied hand on the bell.

The pantry light flashed on. Dressed in a dark velour bathrobe, a sleepy-eyed Richard opened the door. "What the hell—?"

"Lou Holtzinger stabbed the dog!"

I struggled to my feet. He held the door open and I crashed into the house, stamped through the butler's pantry and into the kitchen, where I dumped Holly's limp body on the kitchen table. "Do something!" I yelled.

"I'm not a vet."

"Then stop the bleeding 'til we can get her to one!"

Richard grabbed clean dishtowels from a drawer. "It's not an artery, or it would be spurting." He wadded the cloth, pawed through Holly's long hair searching for the wound. He tossed me one of the towels. "There're two wounds. Her chest and her leg. Grab the phone book. Find an Emergency Vet."

I wiped my shaking hands, and then flipped through the yellow pages. "The guard's calling the cops. We got Holtzinger handcuffed in the back seat of the cruiser."

"Jeff?" Maggie called. She entered the room and stopped short at the sight of her bloodied dog stretched out on the table. "Ohmigod!"

"Help me, Maggie," Richard said, the epitome of professional calm. "Get more dishcloths from the drawer."

A voice came on the line. "Animal Emergency Care."

"My dog's been stabbed. Can I bring her right over?"

Maggie held the dishcloth, tears already streaming down her pale cheeks.

"We're making a pressure bandage," Richard told her, his voice calm. "It'll slow the bleeding until we can get her to a vet."

The voice on the phone asked more questions, which I answered numbly before hanging up. "They'll be waiting for us."

"Maggie, go get your coat," Richard said.

She nodded, and disappeared into the hall.

"Will she make it to the vet?" I asked.

"I don't know," Richard said, and Holly whimpered softly. "I really don't know."

21

———

The sun was barely over the horizon, but the crisp, clear morning was bright when I left the warm comfort of Richard's house and headed for the spot where I'd found Holly the night before.

Dark patches of dried blood stained the short-cropped grass. Holtzinger's knife was gone, probably in police custody.

I couldn't shake the memories from hours before. Of driving through darkened streets while a sobbing Maggie sat in the back seat of my car, holding a near-lifeless Holly. The vet techs were waiting for us, and whisked the dog into surgery.

I'm so in tune with Maggie I don't even need to touch her to be sucked into what she feels. 'Shattered' seemed an apt description. She wanted to be held during the hours we waited at the animal hospital. It was impossible to appear strong and supportive when I was sentenced to experience every emotion right along with her. God knows what the staff thought. Prolonged exposure to such raw emotion sets my head pounding, an added complication.

Afterwards, I pulled out my Visa card, authorizing the more

than six hundred dollars the emergency surgery had cost. I would've paid a million to save Maggie's dog.

Richard had waited up for us. He hugged Maggie, and kept apologizing to her. He wanted to know all the details about Holly's surgery and her expected recovery. After that, he told us that the Amherst cops had taken Holtzinger into custody. He felt better knowing the creep was in jail.

I didn't.

I laid in the dark, thinking about Brenda while holding Maggie as she cried herself to sleep. What was it I felt for Brenda? Gratitude. Friendship. But most of all guilt. For not mentioning my premonition about the baby. For knowing she'd be hurt and being unable to prevent it.

What did I feel for Maggie? Tenderness, for sure. Love? I still wasn't sure about that, but I felt a strong sexual attraction to her. I didn't feel that way about Brenda. I couldn't allow myself to ever feel that for my brother's wife. And that's all she would ever —could ever—be to me. There was no way I'd ever betray Richard's trust.

Eventually I dozed off, but too soon I was awake again— feeling like I'd gotten no rest at all.

I brushed my fingers over the leaves that still clung to the shrubs. Holtzinger had waited, hidden there. An empty pint bottle of whiskey was still caught in the branches. He'd caressed it, almost sensually, while formulating his plan. I picked up anger and avarice—but nothing like the impressions I'd received from the rifle casings. There was no doubt in my mind: Holtzinger had not killed Dr. Newcomb.

Sophie had been right about danger still being close at hand. I could feel it, but couldn't identify its source.

I straightened, and headed for the garage and the trashcans, where I tossed the empty bottle. That's when I remembered the cat upstairs. I wasn't used to pulling pet duty and reconsidered keeping my father's pet. Herschel was used to a full-time companion. I'd hardly been home since he came to stay with me. But I liked the little guy. He was a bundle of happiness, needing little more than a scratch behind the ear to trigger a burst of kitty joy. It felt good to have him around. And I didn't like to think of his chances of finding a new home if I dumped him at the local humane society.

Herschel was waiting behind the door, purring like a buzz saw, reinforcing my guilt. I gave him some food and noticed the light blinking on my answering machine. I hit the play button.

"Jeffrey, it's Patty."

Was she being theatrical or did she really sound frightened?

"It's eight o'clock. You've got to come to the house. Now. You and Richard. It's a matter of life and death!" The call ended.

"Yeah, right," I muttered, and rewound the tape.

An emergency, huh? Then why did she only call once? Hadn't she ever heard of crying wolf? She just wanted to get at Richard. In his wallet, if not his pants.

Still . . . .

I dialed the number and let it ring eight times before hanging up. Whatever the emergency was, she must've handled it. Probably just a spider in the bathroom.

A red-eyed Maggie was making coffee when I got back to Richard's place. "Are you okay?" I asked.

She shook her head, but her expression wasn't hopeless. "I called the vet. They told me Holly's sitting up in her cage, waiting to be fed."

I put my arm around her shoulder, gave her a smile. "See, she'll be just fine."

Richard's pressure bandage had saved the dog's life, the young vet on duty had told us. Because of ligament damage, Holly would probably always limp, but he was pretty sure she'd make a full recovery.

Maggie kept staring at Holly's empty food bowl on the floor. "It wasn't real to me. Brenda's friend was killed—but it wasn't real to me until—"

"Until some creep hurt you, too."

Maggie sniffled. "I'm scared."

"You don't have to stay," I told her. "I'm sure Brenda and Rich would—"

"What kind of a friend would I be if I just abandoned them?"

"A safe friend," Brenda said from the doorway. Dressed in robe and slippers, she looked just as exhausted as Maggie. "I'm so sorry this happened, Maggie. We wanted Holly here for our own safety. It never occurred to us someone might hurt her." Her voice broke. "Can you ever forgive us?"

Maggie hurried to Brenda and hugged her. "There's nothing to forgive. She's going to be fine." She looked at me over her shoulder, forcing a brave smile. "Right, Jeff?"

"That's right."

The tension was electric. Time to defuse it. "Anybody hungry? I've decided to make my world-famous waffles."

"Oh, no," Brenda groaned in mock despair, giving us all a much-needed laugh.

The phone rang and I grabbed it. "Mr. Resnick? This is Bonnie Wilder. We're going to be talking to Lou Holtzinger this morning. Are you interested in listening in?"

"You better believe it. When?"

WE TOOK RICHARD'S CAR, and his cell phone, not wanting to be out of touch. Maggie and Brenda assured us they felt safe enough with a guard planted at the end of the drive. Brenda even joked that she didn't expect the house to be attacked in broad daylight. Still, I would've felt better if Holly was there. She'd been a better—more alert—guard than the one we'd hired. And it hadn't escaped my thoughts that she'd probably saved me from Lou Holtzinger's knife the night before.

Bonnie Wilder met us in the station's reception area. Her eyes were bloodshot—probably from lack of sleep. She clutched a cup of coffee in one hand, with file folders in the other.

"Us being here isn't standard operating procedure," I said.

"This *is* an unusual situation," she admitted.

"Did Reverend Linden ever surface?" I asked, as we headed down the empty corridor.

"About noon, yesterday. He'd been counseling his secretary. She swore on a stack of Bibles that he was with her at the time of the shooting."

"Had he been there all night?" Richard asked.

"Yes. Apparently she leads a very sinful life," Wilder said straight-faced.

She showed us to a small, stark, gray room. Two-way glass let us watch as Agent Segovia conducted the interrogation. The two Washington stiffs stood against the wall, nearly hidden in the shadows.

"Let's go over it again, Lou," Segovia said

"Don't you guys ever give up?" Holtzinger asked, stubbing out a cigarette. He lit another and leaned back in his chair. "I left the car in the alley a couple blocks from the health center because that bitch of a hairdresser at the strip mall threatened to have me towed the last time I parked there. I was just getting out of my truck when I heard the shots."

"How did you know they were gunshots?"

Holtzinger scowled. "I watch a lot of TV."

"What did you see?"

"At first, nothing. I started walking down the alley, then I seen this guy running away, carrying a rifle."

"Give me a description."

Holtzinger sighed, bored. "White guy, six foot—more or less. He had on a hooded sweatshirt."

"The color?"

"Black, navy—I don't know."

"Did he see you?"

He shook his head. "I ducked in a doorway."

"Then what?"

"He jumped into a silver pick-up."

"License?"

Holtzinger shook his head again. "No plates."

"The make?"

"Do I look like a fucking brochure? How the hell do I know?"

"And?" Segovia prompted.

"He took off—headed east, turned onto Main Street."

"Why didn't you stick around? Why didn't you tell the officers on the scene what you saw?"

"Get real. I'm on parole. I wasn't about to talk to the cops. Besides, you already thought I shot the baby butcher."

Segovia glared at the slimy little bastard. "Did it ever occur to you they might've believed you?"

Holtzinger stared right back. "No."

"What were you doing at Dr. Alpert's house last night?"

"I figured he could pay me for what I seen."

"Why him?"

"His wife works at the health center. She just missed getting shot."

"How did you know that?"

"I saw it on TV."

"How did you know where she lived?"

"The church has addresses on all the clinic's employees. They were gonna picket some of the doctors."

"Why didn't they?"

He shrugged. "I don't know. Ask Reverend Linden."

"Why did you stab the dog?"

"You think I'da been hiding in the yard if I know'd they had a dog? That damn thing was vicious. It went for my throat."

Bonnie Wilder looked at me and raised an eyebrow.

I shook my head. "Holly's a Golden Retriever—she's practically a lap dog. She's never bitten anyone."

"Let's go over it again," Segovia said, and we turned away from the glass.

"So far he's stuck to his story," Detective Wilder said. "How is the dog?"

"She'll live."

"Do you want to press charges? We can get him on cruelty to animals and trespassing. Otherwise he's going to walk."

I looked at Richard, who'd been silent, his expression grim.

He met Bonnie Wilder's solemn gaze. "Nail the sonuvabitch."

WE WATCHED as Segovia took Holtzinger through it again, and again, but Pony-tail never changed his story. Bonnie Wilder took us back to her office, and Richard filled out the complaint form.

Afterwards, Richard sat behind the wheel of his car, his gaze fixed on the dashboard. The silence between us dragged.

"Are you okay?" I asked.

He looked at me. "No, dammit. I'm sick and tired of being taken advantage of. Of being hounded. If Holtzinger isn't the one who's been harassing Brenda and didn't shoot Jean Newcomb, and if Willie or Reverend Linden didn't do it, then who the hell did?"

I didn't answer. I didn't know.

I rubbed my eyes. "God, I'm tired. I'm working on about three hours sleep."

"I didn't get much more," Richard groused.

The silence lengthened. His hands kept clenching the steering wheel.

"What is it?" I finally asked. "You've been a bastard since yesterday."

"Don't you think I've got the right?"

"Yeah, but there's more to it. Why don't you just say what's on your mind?"

Richard's knuckles were white. He turned, glared at me. "Have you got feelings for my wife?"

His icy tone rattled me.

"Of course I do. I love her."

Then I realized just what I'd said—and what he'd meant. He hadn't forgotten the sight me and Brenda in his bed the day before.

"Wait a minute. No. Nothing like that."

"Because if you do . . . . " His voice broke and he looked away.

"Rich, you know I'm with Maggie. I care about Brenda as my friend. I care about her because you love her. I care because some dick-ass is making her life hell and she doesn't deserve it. You guys are my *family*," I said. God, this was hard. "I've been thinking about that word a lot lately. Brenda means more to me than Patty ever can. I never wanted or needed family until you guys took me in, until you . . . ."

I was blathering. Didn't that just sound like classic denial?

As quickly as it had surfaced, his anger faded. He patted my shoulder. "Thanks, kid. I'm sorry, but I had to ask."

I took a shaky breath. "Now I've got a question for you. Why did you call Patty last night?"

His face colored.

"Why?" I demanded.

"Because . . . I had too much to drink. I wasn't thinking straight. I didn't understand what was happening with you and Brenda. I needed someone to talk to. A sympathetic ear."

"You couldn't just ask me?"

His voice was hard. "You don't make it easy."

Ouch. But I wasn't going to let him off the hook. "Then why didn't you talk to Maggie--or even the damn dog? Why in God's name did you call Patty?"

"I don't know." He was quiet for a moment. "What did she tell you last night?"

"Not much. Her friend Ray's been asking a lot of questions about you—and me. He read about the Sumner murder in the paper." I thought about it for a moment. "She said Ray just came back to Buffalo after being away for a long time. If that's true, how did he know about our involvement in the case? That was eight months ago."

He shrugged. "Did she say anything else?"

"Yeah, but I didn't understand it. Something about a Dr. Concillio."

Richard's back stiffened, his eyes going wide. "What?"

"She said to ask you about Dr. Concillio."

He took a ragged breath. "I told you a colleague of mine was killed recently."

"The guy downstate."

He nodded. "Marty Concillio."

"What's he got to do with Patty?"

Richard's eyes darkened with worry. "I don't know."

"Who was he?"

"A friend. At least before our malpractice suit."

I blinked, disbelieving. "Malpractice. You?"

He nodded. "I was an intern. Marty was in his last year of residency. We were the only doctors on duty in the ER during a blizzard. A pregnant woman in her late forties came in and she was in trouble. We were short staffed. The OB on call was in surgery. We were on our own."

"To do what?"

"An emergency C-section."

"Did you have any surgical training?"

"Not at the time. The ER was my first tour."

"What happened?"

He swallowed down remembered pain. "We had two deaths that night."

His words chilled me. "God."

"That was the first time I questioned my career choice."

"What was the woman's name?"

"Dorothy Pfister," he answered without hesitation—the memory was deep and as painful as a fresh wound. "The lawyers said it was gross incompetence."

"Was it?"

"Hell, no. She'd had no prenatal care and was a diabetic with toxemia—no one could've saved her or her baby."

"What happened?"

"The hospital settled out of court. I forget the amount, but I remember thinking they'd settled cheap. Especially since the husband was so vocal."

"Did the woman have other kids?"

"I don't remember. It was a long time ago."

"How would Patty know about Marty Concillio?"

"Why don't we ask her?"

"I tried calling her this morning. I got no answer. She left a melodramatic message on my answering machine last night. Said she needed to see us both. That it was a life and death situation."

I grabbed the cell phone, dialed her number. It rang and rang. I hung up.

Richard turned the key and the engine purred. "Let's go to her house. It's on the way."

"I'll call Maggie and let her know why we're delayed," I said and started dialing as Richard pulled into traffic.

We were halfway to Patty's place when I spoke again. "How come you never mentioned this lawsuit stuff to me?"

"It wasn't the highlight of my career. Besides, you were just a kid. I didn't want to worry you."

A plausible explanation—and another example of his lack of candor? Still, we'd come a long way since those days.

"Tell me more about Marty Concillio," I said. "What did he look like?"

"I hadn't seen him in years."

I took a good guess. "Is he tall, with olive skin—kind of ethnic? Thin nose, thin lips, a heavy beard. Thick hair?"

"Yeah, why?"

I let out a shaky breath. "That's the man in my recurring nightmare. You said he was killed in a hunting accident. Was he gut shot?"

"Yes."

My insides twisted. "Didn't you say his son died?"

"A hit and run motorcycle accident. His wife was murdered earlier this year. The sicko mailed him a videotape. Last I heard, the case was unsolved."

I thought about that unreasonable anger Ray Sampson had transmitted the day of Chet's funeral, and realized it hadn't been directed at Patty or me, but at Richard. I told him so.

"First Concillio's son, then his wife. Now he's dead, too. Do you think that's just coincidence?" I asked.

"What're you thinking?"

"I think I'm jumping to conclusions with no evidence."

Richard stole a glance at me, his eyes troubled.

We were only a couple of blocks from Patty's house.

The latest version of the dream flashed through my mind. The three faces. The dead man, Jean Newcomb and—

I hadn't wanted to look at her face. If I had, I would've seen it was—

"Oh my god, it was Patty, not Shelley."

"What?" Richard asked.

"In my dream. I thought it was Shelley I saw dead—they look so much alike—but it was Patty."

We exchanged worried glances.

Richard pulled up the driveway. Patty's Mustang wasn't parked there. "It looks like there's a note on the door," he said.

I opened the car door, jogged up the steps, snatched the note taped to the glass, and hurried back to the car. "It says, 'Richard and Jeff—meet me at Medsco.'"

"What's Medsco?"

"Where she works, in Lockport."

"Is that her handwriting?" Richard asked.

"I don't know."

He studied the note. "Did you get anything from it?"

"Patty doesn't leave a psychic signature I can read."

"We ought to call Bonnie Wilder," Richard said.

"We don't have any proof. All we have is a note. For all we know, she's pulling some kind of scam."

"Maybe," he said thoughtfully. "In your dream—are you sure Patty was dead?"

I nodded. "The top of her head was blown off."

"These dreams always come true, don't they?"

"So far."

His hands tightened on the steering wheel. "What're the odds that I've been the target all along?"

"How so?"

"What better way to get back at me than through the people I care about."

"Including Patty?"

He nodded.

"That's a stretch, isn't it?"

"Maybe. But say this guy thinks Marty and I took something

—someone—from him. What would you be willing to do in his place?" His voice was calm, but I knew Richard too well. He was scared shitless.

"This doesn't make sense. Why wait decades to come after the two of you?"

"Why does anyone kill?"

Another good question.

"What do you want to do?" I asked.

"Let's go to Lockport."

"We could be walking right into a trap."

"This is all supposition anyway. With everything that's happened, we could just be paranoid. If it looks like a set-up we'll back off and call the cops."

His plan sounded all right. Why didn't it feel all right?

22

———

We crossed the Niagara County line and headed for Medsco. Its vast parking lot was empty, save for Patty's Mustang sitting alone at a rear entrance. Being a Sunday, the entire industrial park was deserted.

No potential witnesses.

The perfect place for a murder.

"I don't like this," I told Richard, as we pulled alongside the vacant car.

He turned off the Lincoln's engine and pocketed the keys. "We'll just have a look. If it doesn't seem safe, we'll leave."

"Are you on some kind of macho ego trip? This guy wants to *kill* you."

I glanced at the factory's white-painted, concrete exterior, devoid of windows, except for narrow panels of safety glass in the double steel doors. I didn't see anyone behind them.

"Come on," he said and opened his door.

My senses screamed "get the hell out of here!" but I got out of the car and followed him anyway.

The Mustang looked innocent enough. Richard circled it

and looked through the passenger side window. A brown stain marred the pristine gray carpet.

"Go on, touch it. See if you get anything," he said.

Suddenly sweating, I had to force myself to reach for the driver's door handle. An image of Patty flashed through my mind from another's point of view: she was tied, gagged, and terrified. The door opened and a blast of pure rage assaulted me, tearing the breath from me. Ray had driven the car—Patty was curled on the passenger side floor, her cheek bruised, mouth bleeding from where he'd kicked her.

I slammed the door, whirled, heading for Richard's car.

"What did you see?" he demanded.

"He's got Patty! We've got to get out of here and call for help."

"Hold it right there!"

I whirled. Ray stood at the building's open doorway, the barrel of a rifle leveled at us. It was probably the same rifle that had killed Jean Newcomb.

"You were supposed to be here last night! Where the *hell* have you been?" Ray shouted.

We had two choices: stand there and both of us die, or make a break and maybe only one of us would get killed. But there was nowhere to go—Richard had the car keys.

Ray pushed clear of the doors. "Hands where I can see 'em!"

He charged toward us. It was déjà vu—only this time I was the victim—seeing what Marty Concillio had seen in the last seconds of his life.

"You've inconvenienced me. Shortened my playtime," Ray said as he approached us.

"What're you talking about?" Richard bluffed.

Ray marched up to him, raised the rifle and smashed the butt against his temple.

Richard went down.

I lunged for him, but Ray spun around, shoving the barrel inches from my nose.

"Make a move," he challenged.

I stared into his cold, gray eyes.

Richard groaned, faltered to his knees.

Ray backed up a step, planted a foot on Richard's shoulder, and shoved him down again.

"Stay there. You—" He reached into his shirt's breast pocket, tossed me a cable tie—a thin, heavy-duty plastic strip, not unlike what cops use in lieu of handcuffs. "Bind his hands behind his back."

I couldn't take my eyes off the gun—and fumbled to obey.

"Stand back," Ray ordered.

He tested my handiwork and decided it would do.

"Now flat on your stomach, hands behind you."

I lay prostrate on the cold asphalt, closed my eyes, and waited for a bullet to be fired into the back of my skull. Instead, he knelt beside me and bound my hands tightly.

Fear coursed through me. What had he meant by playtime?

Ray yanked on my arm. "On your feet."

I struggled to stand, stared down at a groggy Richard still on the ground.

"Get up," Ray ordered, kicking him in the ribs.

Richard rolled onto his knees, stumbled to his feet and fell against me, nearly toppling us both. Ray stood behind us and yanked my coat, wrenching the sleeves back to further bind me. He did the same to Richard.

"Now, over by the door." We stood by numbly while he opened it. He motioned Richard in—I filed in after him.

High ceilings with exposed pipes towered above us. Safety lights cut shafts of yellow, leaving the rest of the place bathed in gloom. We followed a painted pathway on the concrete floor, past rows of ceiling-height shelves and stacked pallets. The place was deadly quiet, with no hum of machinery or the bustle of workers—just our hollow footfalls echoing through the cavernous room.

Ray called out directions, left, right, right, left. I tried to memorize the way so I'd know how to get out—*if* we ever got out. Maggie knew we'd come here, but how long would it be before our absence made her suspicious?

More lights loomed ahead. A fork lift was parked near scores of shelves enclosed by a chain link fence. "Stop," Ray called out. We halted in front of a tool crib. Close by, Patty hugged a support beam, her wrists tied by the same plastic strips. She heard us approach, lifting her swollen, tear-stained face. Blotched mascara gave her raccoon eyes. A puddle of urine encircled her bare feet. How long had she been there?

I recognized her torn, rumpled beige jacket. A silver snowflake pin gleamed on the lapel.

Just like in my nightmare.

"I'm sorry," Patty sobbed. "I didn't know what he was. How could I know?"

"Shut up," Ray growled.

A video camera on a tripod stood ten feet from Patty. Marty Concillio had received a video of his wife's murder.

"Stop," Ray commanded. He shoved the rifle barrel into my back. "On your knees."

I did as I was told, stayed put as he marched a still-punchy Richard over to the tool crib, looped another plastic strip through the bindings and fastened it to the crib's chain link door. Then he looped a strand around Richard's ankles, attaching it to the fence.

"On your feet," he ordered me.

I hauled myself up. He grabbed me by my coat sleeve, shoved me to the crib's door then bound me to the other side so Richard and I were back to back.

I avoided Ray's gaze, unwilling to challenge him. He backed off, leaving us.

I glanced over my shoulder at Richard. A rivulet of drying blood marred the side of his face where Ray had hit him.

"Are you all right?" I whispered.

He didn't answer. His breathing was too fast. Humiliation or shock?

Ray set the rifle on the bench in front of the crib. He grabbed an open beer and took a gulp. His flush of victory bombarded my senses. Thankfully, I couldn't read Richard or Patty because my own escalating fear spiraled into panic.

"What're you going to do with us?" Richard asked.

"What do you think?" A self-satisfied smirk twisted Ray's features. "You don't even know why, do you?"

"Dorothy Pfister," Richard said.

"She was my mother."

Richard let out a sharp breath. "We tried to save her."

Ray's laugh was mirthless. "Yeah, right."

"How old were you when it happened, Ray?" I asked. "Six, seven?"

"Eight."

"Then you only had a kid's perspective—you really don't know what happened."

"I know enough. My mother died. It took ten years for my stepfather to drink himself to death. He beat the shit out of me nearly every day. You haven't got a clue."

Oh, yes I did.

"You can't trust what a drunk tells you," I said. "They'll say anything—believe the worst."

"When my mother went to the hospital, she was fine. Then she died, and I lost a brother."

"Your mother wasn't fine," Richard said.

Ray ignored him, tipped the can back, and drained it. He

crushed it in his fist and tossed it into a trash barrel. His smile was chilling.

"Until his wife died, Dr. James Martin Concillio was a dedicated employee of New York State," Ray said. "I recognized the name immediately. I'd heard it every fucking day for ten years. We finally met my first day as a guest of the state. I knew him—but he didn't know me. Three years in a stinking cell in Sonyea. Three years, I planned. I took my time. Why be in a hurry?"

"You killed his son and his wife," Richard said.

"And let six months pass between each one." Ray's malevolent smile tightened. "The cops never put it all together. All three—different modus operandi. Yeah. Real different. I made sure to drive Concillio crazy. It was nothing less than he deserved. Then there was just you," he said, his gaze nailing Richard.

Richard said nothing.

"Once I got back to Buffalo, everything just kind of fell together. I spent a lot of time at City Hall and the library finding out about you two. Even dabbled in a little genealogy. That's how I knew Patty was *his* sister," he nodded toward me. "I staked out your wife and found that Medsco was a supplier for the Williamsville Women's Health Center. Getting a job here was a piece of cake. I just took out one of the drivers."

"You killed him?" Richard asked, aghast.

"Nah—just broke his legs. I'm a firm believer in networking, and prison introduced me to people from all walks of life. Course, I was pissed when Patty told me she'd never even met her brother. Lucky for me your old man was sick and died," he said, and laughed. "Otherwise, I might not have had as much fun. The letters, the calls. I had you going there, didn't I? And you jerks thought it was her ex-husband—or those stupid church fucks." His smile widened.

Just what had Patty told him? I strained to look at her over my shoulder.

"Everything was right on schedule 'til last night when you didn't show," Ray continued. "I lost patience and started the fun without you," he said, and stepped close to Patty, lifting her chin. She wouldn't look him in the eye. "Now I want *Dr.* Alpert," he announced the title with revulsion, "to suffer. Like my family. Like my mother."

"I tried to save her," Richard said.

Ray stroked Patty's face, trailed his fingers down her neck, continued over her chest, and squeezed her left breast. She recoiled, clamping her eyes shut, a squeal of anguish escaping her lips.

"Leave her alone," Richard said.

Ray withdrew his hand and glared at my brother, a lascivious grin covered his features. "Are you fond of the bitch?"

Richard kept silent.

Ray's grin widened. He reached for Patty's bound hands, took hold of the little finger on her left hand and yanked, the crack of bone and her agonized scream reverberated through the factory's silence.

"Stop!" Richard commanded.

Ray's laughter cascaded through the room, shock waves of his triumph echoing through me. This show was for Richard's benefit.

"What about you, big brother," he said to me. "You want me to break another finger?"

"Why should I care?" I bluffed. "I only met her two weeks ago."

Richard glared at me over his shoulder.

Suddenly Ray was in front of me and leaned close, snorted sour beer breath in my face. "That's the problem with *your* family. You don't give a shit about anyone," he grated. "That's why my mother died."

He turned, reached under the bench, and brought out a wrapped bundle. Unfastening it, he spread out a gray flannel cloth, arranging four bone-handled knives of various sizes, their blades glinting dully under the fluorescent light. Then he unwrapped a sharpening stone.

Ray looked up at me before selecting a knife. "Concillio never knew 'til the day I gut-shot him that I'd whacked his kid. His wife was even more fun. The papers said it was a ritual slaying, because her re-pro-ductive organs were missing."

He laughed. The sound of steel rubbing the wet stone grated on my nerves.

"I read the anatomy books in the prison library, so I knew what I was doing . . . but it was a sloppy job. Kind of like what *you* did." He glared at Richard for long seconds before going back to sharpening the blades.

"I watched that tape I made when I did Concillio's wife over and over. Next time, I'll do better."

"Next time?" I asked.

Ray didn't answer.

Time.

I glanced at the opposite wall. A plastic-faced clock with a sweep hand kept vigil. How long had we been here? Five minutes?

Ray concentrated on his work. "Lucky the way it all fell together. No, it was more than luck—it was fate. I even got to scope out your house the day I drove Patty there. I know where the phone lines are. Where the electrical comes in. That new security system should be easy enough to disable."

"I suppose you learned that in prison, too?" I said.

"It's the State's goal to rehabilitate every inmate. We have to make a living on the outside, you know." He tested the knife's sharpness, found it lacking, and started in again.

"I heard your old lady lost your kid, *Doctor* Alpert." Ray

continued. "Ain't that too bad. Maybe now you know how it feels. But that's only the half of it. Next you're gonna lose your woman. But before I do her, I'm gonna have me a piece of brown sugar."

Richard sagged, yanking me backward. "No, please."

Ray laughed. "Then I'll come back for *her*," he pointed at Patty, "then *you*—" Me. His shark-eyes bored into Richard. "I'm saving *you* for last."

"You—you can't, Ray," Patty cried. "You said you'd let me go. You said if I called them you'd—"

"I've had just about enough of you, bitch. If you don't shut your goddamned mouth . . . . "

Patty's hiccoughing sobs started anew.

"You'll never get away with this," Richard said.

"You got away with butchering my mother."

"She came in too late. Her condition—the weather—"

"She died because you screwed up!"

"The Medical Board said—"

"Doctors stick up for their own. Besides, the hospital paid. They wouldn't have if *you* weren't at fault."

Richard sighed, as though realizing the futility of arguing.

Something clicked inside my head. The money. Was that the focus of Ray's anger?

"What happened to the money?" I asked.

Ray looked away.

"I take it you didn't get your share?" I tried again.

"Keep quiet."

It all made sense, now. A sociopath and probably a career punk, he'd fucked up, landed in jail, and had three years to think about the cause of all his troubles, figuring his life had soured the day his mother died.

"Was there a trust?" I asked. "Or did your old man drink it all away?"

"Shut. Up."

"Sure. Why else would you kill? You tried to squeeze Concillio for money. He refused to pay."

"I told you to shut up!" he said, eyes widening, his anger rising.

"You never gave a shit about your mother," I said, knowing I should keep silent, but I was on a roll. "All you cared about was the money you thought you'd get. And when you found there wasn't any, and the only person to blame was dead, you decided to go after the people who actually tried to save Dorothy Pfister's life. You poor sick bastard," I said, contempt coloring my words.

Ray rushed me, knocking me and the hinged gate back, slamming Richard against the chain link wall. Ray's hands gripped my throat, throttling me.

"Stop, Ray—stop! Please," Patty begged.

"Shut up, bitch."

Richard pulled against his restraints, yanking the cage door and me backward. "Stop! Sweet Jesus, stop it!"

Ray hung on, his thumbs pressing harder against my windpipe. His murderous eyes drilled mine.

I couldn't escape, couldn't breathe. My heart pounded, and my vision dappled.

"Ray, you spineless sonuvabitch," Patty screamed. "You can kill him, but you can't kill the truth!"

Ray let go and whirled on her. "I said shut up!"

Chest heaving, sweet air filled my tortured lungs as my knees buckled, pulling the chain link door forward, yanking Richard off-balance.

Grabbing one of the knives, Ray stalked over to the post, cut the plastic binding Patty's wrists. He grabbed her by the hair, threw her to the floor.

"Not again," Patty whined like a frightened child.

Muscles trembling, I strained to look past my shoulder, but

they were out of view. Richard yanked at his bindings, rattling the chain link.

Fabric ripped.

Patty's wail echoed off the vaulted ceiling, searing my soul.

"Stop it, you sonuvabitch. Stop!" Richard shouted.

"Don't," I rasped. "He wants us to react. It makes him feel more powerful."

"For God's sake, he's raping her."

"Don't you think I know that?"

Ray's hands muffled Patty's anguished cries.

I looked around, searching, searching the tool crib for some way out, some weapon. I had to keep my mind off what was happening. What was going to happen.

I'd promised Sophie I'd keep Patty safe.

I'd failed.

And we were all going to die.

I scanned the rows of drawers, boxes, in the tool crib. A pegboard wall held hammers, tin snips, pliers, and screw drivers. A fire extinguisher hung by the door. CO_2 could freeze the plastic at our wrists, make it shatter—but the result would be useless hands from chemical burns.

Ray yelped. "You little bitch!"

A slap.

Patty cried out.

A dull thunk—flesh and bone slammed onto concrete. The sounds of struggle subsided. Only Richard's haggard breathing broke the terrible quiet.

Shuffling noises. Ray's zipper. Booted feet on concrete scuffed past Richard. Ray. Sweaty. Sated. Blood welling along a deep scratch across his cheek.

He took the video camera off the tripod, rewound the tape. He pressed play, shoved the previewer under Richard's nose. "That's what I'm gonna do to your woman—before I off her."

Richard swung his head aside, but Ray grabbed a hank of his hair.

"You sonuvabitch. You goddamn sonuvabitch." Richard's voice was a harsh whisper.

Ray laughed. "I haven't even started yet."

Richard sagged, pulling the door—and me—off balance.

Ray went into the tool crib, grabbed more cable ties, went back to Patty's still form, bound her hands behind her back, then her feet.

I looked away—impotent rage like acid on my soul—and noticed the phone. Hope surged. If he planned to leave us—to go after Brenda—somehow I'd get to it. Somehow I'd—

He stepped back into my line of vision, noticed what I was staring at. He pivoted, yanked the phone wire from the wall. "Does that spoil your plans, big brother?"

I ground my teeth to keep from answering, and Ray laughed at my stifled fury.

"I got a lot to do before the day is done," he said.

Before the supply house workers came back the next morning, I thought. Had he thought through how he'd dispose of three bodies? Or didn't it matter?

Ray went back to the bench, carefully rewrapping all but one of his knives. He grabbed his jacket from a nail in a support stud, and donned it, shoved the deadly bundle into the right pocket. He walked around me and stood in front of Richard. Metal chinked. I craned my neck. Ray pocketed Richard's keys. Knife poised at face level, he leaned close to my brother.

"When I come back, I'll bring you a souvenir. How about yer old lady's heart?"

"If you hurt her, I swear I'll kill you," Richard grated. I'd never heard such murderous fury.

Ray's laughter echoed in the cavernous room. He raised the knife, slashed Richard's face. My brother fell back with a yelp, pushing me into the crib, the door clanging on its metal frame. I stumbled back, regaining my balance.

"That's just a taste," Ray said, wiping the bloodied knife on the back of his thigh, staining his jeans. He grabbed the rifle and the camcorder from the bench and strode off into the darkness, his footfalls echoing hollowly before fading.

"Did he cut you?" I asked.

Richard was shaking. "My chin."

"Bad?"

"Bad enough," he said, head thrashing to his left, apparently trying to staunch the flow of blood on his shoulder.

I glanced at the clock—one thirteen—and yanked at the bindings on my wrists.

There was no way out. No way.

Unless . . . .

"Patty? Patty can you hear me?" I called. "Patty!"

Somewhere behind me I heard movement and quiet sniffling.

"Patty. Get up. Now! You've got to help us. Do you hear me?" I said, venom in my voice.

"Don't be so goddamned hard on her," Richard growled.

"If you wanna save Brenda, Patty's our only hope. Patty!" I tried again.

She wormed her way to her knees. "What?"

"Get over here. Now!"

"He hurt me. God—he hurt me."

"I know," I said more kindly, trying to level my voice. "Patty, Ray's going to kill Brenda and Maggie if we don't stop him. Please, please help us get out of here."

She sidled to the support beam, shimmied her bound hands past her backside, pulled her legs through, then pushed herself onto unsteady feet. "Wha—wha'd you want me to do?"

"Get the tin snips. Here, in the tool crib."

Pale and shaky, she had to hop to the workbench, then slumped against it to catch her breath. The muscles in my neck went into spasms, but I couldn't tear my gaze from her. Pushing off again, she hobbled forward, crashed into Richard, burying her head against his shoulder.

"Patty, don't," he whispered.

I strained to see behind me. She straightened, raised her hands to gently caress his face, and looked him in the eye. "I'd do anything for you, Richard. Anything."

"Please, get the tin snips," he said.

She gazed into his eyes, a tear sliding down her cheek. Then she leaned forward, kissing him on the mouth.

And he let her.

"Patty, please!" I begged.

She pulled away, her lips trembling, a smear of Richard's blood on her chin. Then she shouldered past me, and awkwardly hopped into the crib. "Where?" she asked, voice hard.

"Above you," I said. "Hanging from the pegboard."

Patty pulled uselessly at the bindings on her wrists.

"How can I—?"

"Pull out a drawer, stand on it!"

She flexed her hands, wincing at the pain from her broken finger, and tried to yank open a drawer, became wedged between it and the narrow bench behind her. "I can't," she whimpered.

"Yes, you can," Richard said.

She drew in a ragged breath, moved aside, grasped the metal pull. The drawer jerked forward, toppled under its own weight, its contents clattering on the concrete floor.

The sweep hand on the clock finished another circuit.

Four minutes.

Patty climbed onto the overturned drawer, wood splintering

under her bare feet. She raised her elbows to chest level, cried out in pain. She'd been tied up too long.

"Use the yard stick—to your right. You can knock it down with the yard stick," I told her.

She groped for the long slender ruler. Her short skirt didn't hide the bruises on her blood-streaked thighs. I looked away. If I hadn't goaded Ray, if she hadn't called him off me—

Biting her lip, Patty scraped the ruler across the pegboard, hitting the hanging tools.

"To your left. Higher," I told her.

She batted at the wall. "This'll never work! I can't do it. I can't!"

"You can, Patty. I know you can," Richard said.

Another minute. Five down.

Tools rained onto the floor, clunking dully. The heavy tin snips tumbled forward, smacking her shoulder. She caught them, dropping the stick.

"You've got it! Fantastic!" I cheered. "Come on, Patty. Hurry!"

Grasping them clumsily, Patty shuffle-hopped closer to us. Now if she could just use them without slicing off our fingers.

She pressed close to the chain link door, fumbling for a better hold on the snips. "What if I cut you?"

"You won't," Richard said.

"Just go slow," I warned.

I couldn't see her hands as she maneuvered the snips into place. Her cold skin touched mine.

"Ready?" she said.

"Go for it," I said, and balled my fists.

She drew the pincers shut, wincing with effort, tried again, hacking at the chain link. Her breath caught as her broken finger brushed mine. Chink went the snipped metal.

"Keep going," I encouraged her.

She was shaking with effort, quietly sobbing, I realized, pain, misery and fear taking its toll. Another chink and I pitched forward from the sudden release—but I was only free of the chain link. My hands and feet were still bound, although now I could at least twist around.

"Hold it. Open them up, don't close them 'til I tell you." I fumbled the electrical tie into position. "Okay, cut."

She closed the snips.

Metal sliced skin.

I jumped.

"Jesus!"

Patty backed off. "Ohmigod! Did I hurt you?"

I bit my lip to keep from swearing.

"Jeff?" Richard asked, anxious.

"Again," I told her.

"No," she cried.

"Patty we're wasting time. Do it!"

She pressed closer, jabbing my back with the snip's sharp tips, let me maneuver the tie on my wrist into position. "Do it."

She lopped away, and my hands came loose. I flexed them and yanked the snips from her and freed my feet, then I cut her hands loose. "You did great, baby sister," I said, brushed a kiss on her cheek, then went for Richard's bindings.

It had been ten minutes since Ray left.

Richard rubbed the circulation back into his hands. Blood still oozed down his chin. "Let's get the hell out of here," he said.

"Show us the way," I told Patty, grabbing her arm and hauling her along the painted walkway.

Richard caught up, and we dragged Patty between us, running for the exit.

23

———

We burst through the building's unlocked double doors into cold fresh air and found Richard's Lincoln gone. Panting, he and I stared at one another.

"Where's the nearest phone?" I asked Patty.

"I don't know," she cried.

"We could break into one of the offices," Richard said.

"It won't do any good," Patty said. "Ray messed with the system last night. No outgoing calls. He said it was insurance."

"Christ, everything in the area's closed. We're at least half a mile from anywhere. There're no houses—nothing!" Richard said.

"Why can't we just take my car?" Patty asked.

"Have you got keys?" I asked.

"Ray took them. But there's an extra ignition key in the front left wheel well. Daddy made me put it there 'cause I kept locking myself out."

I sprinted to the car, knelt on the tarmac, pawing behind the tire, and found a little plastic box attached to the firewall.

"Thank you, Chet. Get in!" I called.

Richard helped Patty into the back seat. I jumped in the driver's side, started the car, tires squealing as I hit the gas.

"Stop at the first pay phone," Richard said. "We gotta let the cops know what's happening."

"He's got a ten-minute head start, but they could still get to the house in plenty of time," I said.

Did I believe it?

I had no intuitive assurances. Nothing but fear.

We roared onto Transit Road, scanning for a pay phone.

"There." Richard pointed at a strip mall up the next block.

The car jumped the curb. I stomped on the brakes. The seat belts locked, and stopped Richard from sailing through the windshield, but sent Patty slamming into the back of my seat. She howled as Richard jerked open the door and spilled from the car.

Patty pulled herself up, her face only inches from mine. "He really loves Brenda, doesn't he?" she asked, gazing after Richard.

Of course he does! I wanted to yell, but seeing her swollen face, smeared make-up and torn clothes—a testament to what she'd endured—made me soften my voice.

"Yeah, he does."

"Maybe," she said, her voice childlike, "maybe one day somebody will love me like that."

Guilt washed over me. She was my sister, and I hadn't protected her. Yet she'd saved me from Ray's lethal hands—and at a terrible cost.

I tore my gaze away and honked the horn. We were losing precious time.

Richard hung up, jumped back in the car, slammed the door and punched the dash. "Go!"

Shoving the car in gear, I wheeled back into traffic, just missing a pick up, and was rewarded with a one-finger salute.

"Are they gonna meet us?" I asked.

"I didn't hang around to find out. I gave them the address—told them we were on our way. Then I called the house. There was no answer."

Patty patted Richard's shoulder. "It'll be okay."

I glanced over to see his worried gaze meet hers—and couldn't identify the mingled emotions in his expression. He reached back to squeeze her hand.

I turned my attention back to the road.

Thank God traffic was light. I drove like a maniac, running red lights, careening around other vehicles, and not once did I see a cop lying in wait for speeders.

"Where the hell are the cops when you need them?" Richard grated, echoing my thoughts.

"It's Sunday—they're all watching the Bills on TV."

The dashboard's digital clock read one thirty three. It had been twenty minutes since Ray left us.

The cops will get there in time, I told myself. Maggie and Brenda will be safe. And they're not alone. There's a guard at the end of the driveway, goddamn it. There was no way Ray could get through those kinds of defenses.

Yeah, a guard. A pro . . . who probably made a buck or two over minimum wage. What the hell were we thinking leaving Brenda and Maggie alone?

One thirty eight p.m.

Twenty-five minutes down.

Folded into the Mustang's cramped interior, Richard had little room to fidget, yet he couldn't seem to keep still, his right hand absently pounded the dash. A horn blasted as I turned onto Main Street. I cut off a Lexus and zipped between a Jeep Cherokee and a Stratus, looking for my next break.

"Come on," Richard urged.

"I'm doing the best I can."

"I know. It's just—"

"Don't torture yourself," I said, taking in his grim expression. "You're not responsible for freaks who—"

"But I am. My God, Jean Newcomb's dead. Ray tried to kill you, he raped Patty, and now—"

"We'll get there." I wanted to say more, to reassure him, but how could I, when I couldn't reassure myself?

Fists clenching the steering wheel, I ran the red light at LeBrun, took the corner and gunned the engine.

I broke into a cold sweat when I saw no swarm of cop cars surrounding Richard's house—just the Amherst Security cruiser stationed at the end of the driveway, the guard still behind the wheel. Richard's silver Lincoln was parked half on the grass, half on the sidewalk—with the driver's door open.

Where the *hell* were the cops?

I jammed on the brakes, slammed the car in park, left it running in the street and bolted for the rent-a-cop. I yanked open the car door, ready to ream him a new asshole, and saw the flood of scarlet staining his uniform, his throat a jagged mess, the microphone still clutched in his hand, its cord dangling.

I hitched a breath, backed up a step. "He's dead," I yelled.

"Stay here," Richard told Patty.

We ran for the house. Richard paused at the locked front door. I raced for the back door. Hunks of glass still clung to the window frame; the woodwork around the door was splintered where Ray must have kicked it in.

I yanked open the door, and barreled through the kitchen to the main entry.

"Maggie! Brenda!"

Smeared, bloody handprints marred the walls.

Bolting through the hallway, I made for the stairs.

Where the hell was Maggie?

I rounded the corner, a blue mound blocked my way.

It moved.

"Maggie!"

She raised a bloodied hand, reaching for the banister. I crouched beside her, noticed a welling cut along her scalp.

Enraged male screams from above shattered the quiet.

"He hit me with a camcorder—went after Brenda. He's up there now," Maggie cried. "Go!"

"Find a phone—call the cops!" I stepped over her and took the stairs two at a time.

Topping the landing, I skidded past the master bedroom, nearly tripping on the discarded video recorder—saw only the empty rumpled bed in the room.

Sounds crashed above me: Ray's frustrated yelling, splintering wood, and breaking glass.

The attic!

I sprinted for the back stairs at the end of the hall. Flinging open the door, I dashed up the narrow steps, stopped at the top, taking in the pack rat's paradise of stacked boxes and discarded furniture.

I saw no one.

A gale blew through the open door to the room on the left. Had Brenda gotten out—scrambled to safety on the sunroom's roof below?

I sprang into the doorway. Ray had climbed out the gaping hole where the window had been—one leg in, one leg out. Chunks of shattered glass still stuck to the frame.

"Goddamn you, bitch," he screamed, oblivious to me. He drew back to throw a knife—the others, still wrapped in flannel, were clenched in his other hand.

I plowed through the junk, the noise distracting him. The knives fell with a dull thunk as I knocked him off balance, sending him through the opening. But he caught my jacket sleeve, jerking me with him. I crashed into the wall. My right knee jammed against the sill and stopped me from tumbling after him.

Richard hollered somewhere below.

Panicked, Ray scrabbled for purchase against the house's brick exterior. He clutched the sill and hauled himself up. Our eyes locked as my jacket ripped.

"Let go!" I yelled, yanking my arm back.

Thrown further off balance, Ray shrieked and we slammed —my shoulder, his wrist—against the jagged glass. A spray of crimson wet my face.

"Patty!" he snarled, grinding the last of the glass into my bicep.

He teetered and I pushed myself from the window frame. My knees smashed into the studs. Ray's flailing hand found my collar, his fingers clawing my throat.

"Kill him, Patty, kill him!" he shouted.

I looked back, and saw Patty's silhouette filling the doorway. Ray held on, his feet still slipping.

"He stole your father's love—he cut you out of the will!" Ray hollered.

"Liar!" I managed.

I slid to my knees, pulling him back into the attic. Had Brenda gotten away?

Ray toppled onto me, his elbow smashing the mangled flesh on my chest. Blinding pain choked me. Ray righted himself, pinned my right shoulder with his left hand, his right methodically smashing my sternum.

"Do him—do him—do him!" Ray chanted with every punch.

"Patty!" I grated, through clenched teeth.

"Do him—do him!"

Patty charged forward and scooped up a knife from the floor. I opened my eyes and saw the shiny blade arc—shut them, and sensed rather than saw the knife come crashing down.

Ray screamed, letting go as another gush of scarlet spattered my cheek.

The heel of Patty's palm slammed against my throat.

"Leave. My. Brother. Alone!"

I squirmed away. The knife plunged into Ray—again and again. His screams changed to a sickening gurgle.

Patty's mad screeching cut the air.

His arms and chest sodden with blood, Ray pitched back—disappearing out the shattered window.

Even with her prey gone, Patty's arm came down like a pile driver, the wooden sill splintering under her gouging thrusts.

"Patty, stop!"

I threw myself at her—and caught her arm in mid-swing. Her stricken face crumpled and her legs wobbled. She buckled and I eased her to the floor. Prying the bloodied knife from her fingers, I tossed it aside. She curled into a fetal ball, weeping like an abandoned child.

Taking a couple of ragged breaths, I pulled myself over the gory sill. Amid the remains of a broken chair and chunks of glass, a blood-soaked Ray lay in a heap on the winter-faded grass, his neck twisted at an impossible angle, sightless eyes staring at the gray cloudy sky.

Just like Marty Concillio.

Something fluttered at the edge of my vision. Brenda's bloodied nightgown. She hung from the gutter, feet dangling.

Richard hovered beneath her. "I've got you! It's okay, I'll catch you," he coaxed.

She lost her grip.

He caught her, momentum sending them into a tangle of arms and legs. Then she was in his arms, whimpering, her face buried against his chest.

Maggie rounded the corner, Richard's cell phone from the

Lincoln clutched to her ear. "My God! My God!" she cried, taking in the carnage.

I slid down, turning so I faced into the room. Wetness—more blood—soaked into my jeans. It was everywhere. The place looked and reeked like a slaughterhouse.

I sat there, trembling from adrenaline in the god-awful quiet. Not silence, thanks to Patty's sniffles. What had been a killing machine only a minute earlier was now a huddled, child-like form on the floor. I reached for her, brushed the hair from her face, smearing Ray's blood on her forehead.

Patty's haunted, watery eyes met mine. "Oh Lord," she breathed. "What have I done?"

"You saved Brenda. And me." I gathered her in a tentative embrace. Her whole body quivered as the tears started once again. I patted her heaving back. "It's over, Patty. It's all over."

In the background, sirens wailed.

The cavalry—at last.

24

The icy wind burned my cheeks. The gray sky, thick with clouds, waited, as though for some mystical signal to tell it to let down another crystalline blanket of snow. But the bleak day hadn't kept me from accomplishing something I'd been meaning to do for weeks.

This was my second graveyard stop of the day, a repeat of only weeks before. Only now I was at a different section in Mt. Calvary Cemetery. It wasn't exactly how I'd planned to spend Christmas Eve afternoon.

The dual headstone was polished pink marble.

ALPERT

JOHN AND ELIZABETH

JOINED IN MARRIAGE

SEPARATED BY DEATH

UNITED FOR ETERNITY

Underneath were the dates of their births, marriage, and deaths. Richard had chosen the words. I never knew he was such a romantic.

I didn't protest when he'd asked my permission to move our mother's casket to another grave site. I didn't even care that the name on the tombstone was his, not mine. I was certain our mother would have approved.

I set up the metal easel, attached the bow-bedecked wreath of evergreen boughs and stood back. The seasonal colors gave the grave a festive air. Well, as festive as a grave can get. Maybe I'd come back in the spring, plant some begonias. My mother had liked the variety named after liquor: gin, brandy, whiskey and vodka—apropos for an alcoholic, I suppose.

Nice thoughts, I chided myself. If only things had been different.

If only John Alpert hadn't died in a car crash.

If only my mother had been more mentally stable.

If only Chet had loved her—and me—just a little more.

If only . . . .

The wind gusted, bringing with it a scattering of dry leaves. I thought about the sister I really didn't know. She'd saved my life —twice. It was a debt I didn't know how to repay. But I had to try, if only for our father's sake.

I'd seen her a couple of times since that awful day. Hollow-eyed and silent, she'd retreated into her own private hell, looking small and fragile. Forever changed by what she'd seen— and done.

She'd gone to stay with Ruby for a while, pending the grand jury's decision. No charges, of course. I didn't think there would be.

My gaze wandered to the left of the grave. I bent down to brush the snow from the flat buff-colored granite embedded in the ground. Only the year and a name were etched on the stone: Charles John Albert. Richard's and Brenda's son. They hadn't asked Maggie or me to attend the burial. It was something they'd wanted to do for themselves, and we'd respected their wishes.

I straightened, staring at the tiny grave. "I'm sorry, baby Charles. I'm so sorry."

A silver Lincoln pulled up behind me. The engine died and Richard stepped out. "Looks like we had the same idea."

I had to clear my throat before I could speak. "You know what they say about great minds."

He opened the trunk, took out another wreath and easel. I moved mine to one side, making room for his.

He nodded toward the stone. "What do you think? I had it done at the same time as . . ." His gaze moved to the other granite stone. He didn't elaborate.

"It's a pretty place. It would've made her happy."

"We should've done this years ago," he said quietly. Somber-faced, he stared at the monument.

I wondered what else he was thinking. I was thinking how damned grateful I was he hadn't joined his parents in eternity. He and Brenda. As it was, they'd lost a child.

I thought back to three weeks before, when I'd sat with Brenda for a while at the hospital. Bruised and bandaged, we were okay, but we had to bully Richard to go get his chin stitched.

The ever-unflattering fluorescent light made Brenda look haggard and traumatized. Could she ever go back to that house? What she needed was a shot of hope. Only I didn't know how to approach the subject of the blue-eyed, dark-skinned child who'd stayed in the back of my thoughts since I'd visited Emily Farrell the day before.

So I reached for and took Brenda's hand. She looked up at

me, puzzled, and something tugged at my soul. Regret, I think. She would always be, after all, Richard's wife.

Clearing my mind, I closed my eyes and thought about the little girl. Concentrated first on the red polka-dot dress, working up to the mop of unruly curls and finishing with the mesmerizing blue eyes, like those I'd come to know so well.

Brenda gasped, her hand convulsing around mine.

I opened my eyes. She stared at me with what looked like distress.

"Did you see?"

"Yes," she whispered. "But . . . how?"

I shrugged. "I don't know."

Her grateful smile was full of hope and promise for the future. She threw her arms around me, and I held on, savoring the rush of affection she felt for me. It would be enough. And I knew then she'd be okay, that she wouldn't let this whole, terrible nightmare rule her life.

I don't know if she told Richard. It wasn't something I could talk to him about. And Brenda and I haven't spoken of it since. But every now and then, she gives me a knowing smile.

"I know you've been torturing yourself over this, Jeff," Richard began, "but it wasn't physical trauma that caused Brenda to lose our son. There were chromosomal aberrations."

I frowned, unsure what he'd just said.

"There was something wrong with the baby. Something Brenda and I caused." He let out a shuddering breath. "He would have died anyway."

I wasn't sure how to react. Was he just trying to spare my feelings?

I studied his face. There was acceptance in his expression.

"Sometimes," he continued, "these things just happen."

Richard cleared his throat and shrugged deeper into his topcoat. "Damn cold," he said.

"Cold as the grave?" I asked.

His smile was pained. "I got the results of my last blood test this morning."

I held my breath.

"Negative. Looks like I can get on with my life."

Relief flooded through me. It was the best Christmas gift I'd ever received. Now we could all get on with our lives. Well, mostly. "Congratulations, " I managed.

He smiled and glanced at his watch. "I'd better get going. I still have a few more errands to run and gifts to wrap."

"Me, too." I said, thinking of the five little red, polka-dot dresses with white pinafores that Maggie and I had bought, ranging from newborn to size six. But first I had to deliver belated Hanukkah gifts—the last photos of my father —to Patty and Ruby.

Richard slapped me on the back. "See you at home, kid."

Yeah. Home.

I watched the Town Car head down the narrow ribbon of asphalt. Huddled in my jacket, I turned back to the grave.

"Merry Christmas, Ma."

THE NEXT ADVENTURE...

Don't miss the next exciting Jeff Resnick Mystery: Bound By Suggestion

In exchange for helping her unlock the emotions of a disturbed young woman, psychiatrist Dr. Krista Marsh promises to cure Jeff Resnick's recurring headaches via hypnotism. Things start out rocky and quickly get worse when both the young girl and the Doctor begin to manipulate Jeff. Soon he's experiencing the young woman's emotions and can't tell where hers leave off and his begin, and Krista has other reasons for ingratiating herself into Jeff's life. Meanwhile, Jeff's brother Richard is vying for a chairman seat on the hospital's fundraising board. Two seemingly unrelated events that suddenly converge with deadly results.

"There were hints of murder and mayhem on the horizon, but this time Jeff's psychic gifts just might not be enough to save his own life, let alone anyone else's!

"This fast paced paranormal thriller will keep everyone wanting to see a LOT more of Jeff Resnick."

--Feathered Quill Book Reviews

Get it here!

ABOUT THE AUTHOR

The immensely popular Booktown Mystery series is what first put L.L. Bartlett's pen name Lorna Barrett on the New York Times Bestseller list, but it's her talent -- whether writing as Lorna, or L.L. Bartlett, or Lorraine Bartlett -- that keeps her there. This multi-published, Agatha-nominated author pens the exciting Jeff Resnick Mysteries as well as the acclaimed Victoria Square Mystery series and has many short stories and novellas to her name(s).

Visit her website at: http://www.LLBartlett.com

If you enjoyed *Cheated By Death*, please consider reviewing it on your favorite online review site. Thank you!

Connect with L.L. Bartlett on social media
www.llbartlett.com

ALSO BY L.L. BARTLETT

THE LOTUS BAY MYSTERIES

Panty Raid (A Tori Cannon-Kathy Grant mini mystery)

With Baited Breath

Christmas At Swans Nest

A Reel Catch

After The Tempest

The Best From Swans Nest (A Lotus Bay Cookbook)

THE VICTORIA SQUARE MYSTERIES

A Crafty Killing

The Walled Flower

One Hot Murder

Dead, Bath and Beyond (with Laurie Cass)

Yule Be Dead (with Gayle Leeson)

Murder Ink (with Gayle Leeson)

A Murderous Misconception (with Gayle Lesson)

Dead Man's Hand (with Gayle Leeson)

A Lethal Lake Effect

LIFE ON VICTORIA SQUARE

Carving Out A Path

A Basket Full of Bargains

The Broken Teacup

It's Tutu Much

The Reluctant Bride

Tea'd Off

Life On Victoria Square Vol. 1

A Look Back

Tea For You (free download in most countries)

Davenport Designs

A Ruff Week

Recipes To Die For: A Victoria Square Cookbook

Tales From Blythe Cove Manor

A Dream Weekend

A Final Gift

An Unexpected Visitor

Grape Expectations

Foul Weather Friends

Mystical Blythe Cove Manor

Blythe Cove Seasons (free download in most countries)

Tales of Telenia

(adventure-fantasy)

STRANDED

JOURNEY

TREACHERY (2025)

Short Women's Fiction

Love & Murder: A Bargain-Priced Collection of Short Stories

Happy Holidays? (A Collection of Christmas Stories)

An Unconditional Love

Love Heals

Blue Christmas

Prisoner of Love

We're So Sorry, Uncle Albert

Sabina Reigns (a novel)

Writing as Lorna Barrett

THE BOOKTOWN MYSTERIES

Murder Is Binding

Bookmarked For Death

Bookplate Special

Chapter & Hearse

Sentenced To Death

Murder On The Half Shelf

Not The Killing Type

Book Clubbed

A Fatal Chapter

Title Wave

Poisoned Pages

A Killer Edition

Handbook For Homicide

A Deadly Deletion

Clause of Death

A Questionable Character

A Controversial Cover

A Perilous Plot

A Critical Conjunction